THE DRAGON
FINDS FOREVER
NOCTURNE FALLS, BOOK SEVEN

KRISTEN PAINTER

THE DRAGON FINDS FOREVER:
Nocturne Falls, Book Seven

Copyright © 2017 Kristen Painter

ISBN: 978-1-941695-27-2
Published in the United States of America.

Welcome to Nocturne Falls, the town that celebrates Halloween 365 days a year. The tourists think it's all a show: the vampires, the werewolves, the witches, the occasional gargoyle flying through the sky. But the supernaturals populating the town know better.

Living in Nocturne Falls means being yourself. Fangs, fur, and all.

Monalisa Devlin is a Will O' The Wisp, a rare and potentially dangerous creature. Unfortunately, her greedy father makes sure she lives up to that potential. Monalisa is magically compelled to obey her father's evil commands—until he finally agrees to free her in exchange for one, last mission: Travel to Nocturne Falls and use her powers to force Ivan Tsvetkov back into the ring.

Once a champion on the supernatural MMA circuit, Ivan 'The Hammer' Tsvetkov retired after a devastating injury that left him unable to shift into his dragon form. Wounded and embittered, Ivan wants nothing more than to be left alone. Until an infuriating, stubborn, delicately beautiful stranger shows up on his doorstep and demands that he rebuild his life.

Posing as a rehab therapist seemed like the easiest way to get close to the smoldering recluse, but Monalisa quickly realizes that nothing about this mission is going to be easy. To gain his trust, she shares more of herself than she ever has before, and as their connection deepens, so does the weight of her secrets. She thought she was willing to do whatever it took to win her independence...but when her deception blows up in her face, will Monalisa discover that the loss of Ivan's heart is too high a price to pay? Or will their love rise from the ashes to burn stronger than ever?

Dedicated to everyone who ever wished dragons were real.

A single gold coin.

It should be hers. It was her birthright. Her freedom.

Her prison.

Monalisa Devlin watched the shiny coin dance through her father's fingers like a toy. It was one of the countless many that Padraig Devlin owned but, this one he spun over and under his long, nimble digits, like it was a game. Which it kind of was. A game about reminding her. About taunting her. About keeping her hungry.

She could practically feel the weight of the gold against her palm. Not that she'd ever touched it, because he'd never given it to her like he was supposed to when she turned eighteen. Just one more disappointment on her ever-growing list.

And to think, she'd even done her pedicure in a gold glitter polish because she'd been so excited that she was finally going to get *her* coin.

What a waste.

Leprechauns were strange creatures. Crafty. Greedy. Mean. Ambitious. And the one before her wasn't just her father, he was also the king.

She forced herself to tear her gaze away from the gleaming object and meet his eyes. "I did what you asked. I want the coin."

He smiled and shook his head. "And I told you this loose end still needs to be resolved. Take care of it and the coin is yours."

It should have been hers on her eighteenth birthday. Twelve years later and she was still waiting. She closed her eyes for a moment and gave herself briefly over to her emotions. Anger. Frustration. Irritation. Helplessness. And a little fear. All of those swirled inside her as she stood before her parents. But she shoved them down and opened her eyes. "You can't make me do this. I won't."

"I can, Monalisa." Her father's stern look was something she'd seen so often, it held little sway. His toothy grin was still unpleasant to look at, though. "And I will."

He absolutely could, and he absolutely would. That was the story of her life. "I don't *want* to do this."

Her mother, Tavia, sighed and rolled her beautiful, pixie eyes. "You should have thought about that before you stepped into the arena. What's done is done. Now you must finish it."

"I didn't step into the arena by my own will either, in case you forgot."

2

Padraig waved a lazy hand. "I am your father and your king. You have no choice."

Monalisa ground her teeth together to keep from saying the things dancing on the tip of her tongue. She let a long second pass, gathering her control. "If I do this, I get the gold. I get my freedom. I have to. You cannot go back on your word again."

Her father jumped to his feet, anger turning his face uglier. He was nearly half a foot shorter than she was, but then, most leprechauns were short-statured. Even the king. "I did not go back on my word. You didn't finish the job you agreed to."

She'd seen him angry before. It didn't frighten her. "I did exactly what you asked me to do. How was I to know he'd end up injured and refuse to honor his contract with the League?"

Padraig shook his head. "It doesn't matter what happened. You have to finish the job. Get him to agree to the fight, and I'll give you your piece of gold." He snorted in obvious disgust. "And you call me greedy."

"Greed has nothing to do with it." Anger overtook the other emotions. "That coin should have been mine years ago, but you've held it over me because you know the second I have it, I'll leave." She would too. Being gifted one of her father's precious coins would release her from his power. She would finally be able to do whatever she wanted. And heaven knew, her life had been on hold long enough.

Her mother clucked her tongue. "Such an ungrateful child."

"Because I want my freedom? Because I want to be free from both of you?" The hurtful words left Monalisa's mouth before she could stop them, but her parents knew how she felt.

Her father was a bully. King of the leprechauns and as mean-tempered and greedy as any who'd reigned before him. And her mother, the beautiful pixie, had been married to him in an arrangement meant to bring peace between the leprechauns and the pixies. The marriage had accomplished that, but Tavia had been swept up in the power and glamor of the royal life, becoming just as manipulative as her husband.

Together, the pair was given a healthy respect in Nevada's supernatural community and was known worldwide because of her father's casino, the Shamrock, and the supernatural fights held in its secret arena. It wasn't like the Titan Fight League could hold its MMA bouts just anywhere.

Having mythological creatures like dragons and griffins and centaurs going round after round for an equally supernatural audience really limited the available venues.

Her father provided one of only fifty arenas in the world where the TFL could hold bouts, and his was one of the largest. Throw in the private gaming and party rooms in the casino reserved for supernaturals, and Padraig Devlin wasn't just the king of the leprechauns, he was also the unofficial leader of Las Vegas's supernatural Mafia.

Monalisa had had enough. She lifted her chin. "I

want to live my own life. I don't want to be a princess anymore, I don't want to live in Vegas, I don't want to be part of this fast-paced, corrupt life." She just needed that coin. Then her father's sway would finally be broken.

"This life you hate so much," her mother said, "has kept you from wanting for a single thing."

"Except for my freedom!" She groaned. "And I don't need or want the rest of what this life provides. The cost is too high. Don't you see that?"

Tavia sighed as if her daughter's opinion was ridiculous. "And what will you do? How will you support yourself in this new life? You have no real skills. Life requires money. And you have no way of earning any."

Because her parents had made acquiring those skills nearly impossible. They'd kept her reliant on them and, except for the errands her father sent her on, separate from the world. "I'll find something to do. I'll survive."

Padraig barked out a laugh. "You're good at two things, Monalisa. Being pretty and leading men astray. That's what Will-o'-the-Wisps do. Having the kind of gifts best used for darker ends is nothing to shy from. Not when they can be so valuable."

She sneered. "Sure, to a man like you." She'd had enough of that.

"That's right." He smiled. "You might not like me, Monalisa, but would you really rather end up doing another man's dirty work?"

She glared down at him. "My powers aren't my

5

only usable skills, and besides that, I won't use them for evil purposes ever again. You can go after that fighter yourself."

He grabbed her arm. "You brat. The only way I'm going to let you go is if you get him to abide by his contract. I need that rematch to take place. Once it does, I'll give you your piece of gold and you'll be free. But not before. And not ever if he doesn't step foot into that ring."

She yanked her arm out of her father's grasp. "This is the last thing I'm ever going to do for you. The last."

"Don't be so dramatic." He snorted. "It'll be over before you know it."

She stared at him. "You don't even care, do you? You're sending your only daughter into the den of a dangerous—"

"The danger is in lingering," he snapped. "Get in, use your power on him, and get out. Over and done. Once he's under your thrall, he won't be able to say no."

Just like she couldn't say no to her father. But using her gifts against another person was wrong. She didn't want to be the kind of supernatural who took advantage of people, employing her inherent abilities to bend them to her will or make them do things they had no desire to do.

That was what her father did. And she didn't want to be anything like him.

The muscles in her jaw ached from clenching her teeth so tightly. She managed to get out a few words. Enough to appease the man in front of her. "I know what to do."

"I hope so. Now prove it. Bring me that dragon."

Van Tsvetkov studied the roomful of dogs on the other side of the glass. He liked dogs. Liked that this was a no-kill rescue center. Liked the idea that he was giving another creature a chance for a better life. Even if it was with a washed-up MMA fighter like himself.

One of the dogs was sleeping. Two of them were playing tug-of-war with a knotted rope. Another was chewing on his own foot like it was a delicious snack. But one was staring back at him, eyes filled with the kind of hope that Van couldn't refuse.

He nodded. "That one. With the brown and the black and the pointed ears."

Pandora Williams, Van's good friend and a woman he trusted very much, gave him a stern look. "I'm pretty sure that's a Rottweiler or something equally big. And I don't think it's full-grown yet. Look at the size of its paws. It could be a monster when it gets older."

"I don't care. I want that one." How many times in his life had he been called the same thing? *Monster* might as well have been his middle name growing up. The people in his village in Russia had not been kind. And after they'd found out what he and his family were, they'd turned violent out of fear. That was when his family had left. Escaped, actually. "He looks like a good dog."

"I'm sure he's a great dog. But how about that little white one over there? I bet that one's awesome too. And you could put him in a carrier. Or a backpack."

"No. No yippy dogs that fit in bags." Van poked the glass with his finger, directing it at the gangly animal that continued to watch him. "I want that one."

"Van, how exactly are you going to walk a dog that's the size of a deer? You're on crutches."

"I will not be on crutches forever." Van's eyes narrowed as he looked at her. He knew she was only watching out for his best interests. It's what Pandora had always done for him, starting years ago with overseeing the building of his house in the hills of Nocturne Falls. But he wouldn't be traveling anymore. From now on, this was where he'd be. And a dog was a big step in settling down. "I will hire a dog walker until I'm healed."

"Oh good. So you're going to get a dog and then let it bond with someone else? That sounds like a fabulous plan." She crossed her arms as she faced him. She was one of the few people he could count on to always be honest with him, and he liked that. Pandora didn't care who he was and wasn't intimidated by his dragon side either.

She kept going. "And who's going to watch this dog while you're off at a fight? Or training somewhere? Or doing a promotional tour? Or—"

"I told you, I am retired. Done." The muscles in his jaw tensed, and he forced himself to relax. "I am settling down now. Here. Nocturne Falls is where I live."

Her expression was full of skepticism. Then it shifted to one of concern. "You really think you can give all that up and be happy?"

Happiness wasn't something he was worried about at the moment. "Already done. I'm content to read books and work on my English. And play with my new dog."

She shrugged. "Okay. But you've gotten rid of enough of your accent already. Chicks dig that, you know." She winked at him.

"*Kotyonok*, I have no interest in chicks. This dog is all the companionship I need right now." And he did not want Pandora trying to set him up. He wasn't in the right head space to even think about a relationship.

"If you say so." She waved at one of the rescue workers. "Can we go into a room with the big tan and black one?"

A few minutes later, Van maneuvered himself into one of the chairs in the visitation room, careful of the brace that kept his right knee from bending. He set the crutches against the wall as Pandora took the chair beside him.

The worker, a young man named Tim, came in with the dog. "Okay, this is Pup. Pup is a three-month-old Doberman. He's a great dog."

"Doberman. Huh." Pandora nudged Van. "Told you. Big dog."

Big was good, Van thought. He studied the dog,

who seemed to be studying him right back. "Pup is no name for this dog."

"Well, whoever adopts him can change that." Tim shrugged. "People change the names all the time."

"Sure," Pandora said. "How did Pup end up here?"

"He's from a litter rescued from an animal hoarder. He's the only one that hasn't been adopted yet. Probably because he's a little on the timid side, and most people want dogs like this for protection."

Van held out his hand to the dog. The animal stretched his neck and sniffed Van's fingers, then tentatively licked them and gave a nervous wag of his tail.

Eager, but fearful.

It was enough to make up Van's mind. "I will call him Grom."

"Gum?" Pandora asked.

"Grom," Van corrected.

"Grom?" Pandora looked at him. "You mean Gromit, like in Wallace and Gromit?"

Van scratched the dog's head. Grom closed his eyes. "Grom means thunder in Russian."

Tim laughed softly. "That's a lot of name for this dog."

"Good dog," Van whispered as he patted Grom gently on the head. "He will grow into it."

Tim nodded. "Does that mean I should get the paperwork together?"

"*Da*," Van said, then he corrected himself. "Yes." He smiled. "Grom is a Tsvetkov now."

"Great," Tim said. "I'll be right back."

"You're sure?" Pandora asked after he'd left. "An animal is a commitment, you know. It's like marriage. For better or worse, sickness and health and all that."

"I know. And I am sure," Van answered. It was also the only commitment he wanted, because if he was going to hole up and pretend the world didn't exist, he didn't really want to do it completely alone. But he also didn't have the time or the patience for female companionship.

A woman wouldn't like how he was right now. Sour. Unhappy. Mopey. Cranky. Purposeless. The list went on.

Pandora tolerated him, but she also knew him well enough to let him be.

He imagined someday his mood would change. But that day was not today. And it was not tomorrow either.

The flight to Georgia had been long, but it had given Monalisa a chance to skim the e-books she'd bought on physical therapy and life coaching. If rehab therapist was going to be her cover story, she had to know enough to fake her way through however long it took to convince Ivan "The Hammer" Tsvetkov to honor the contract he'd signed.

A dragon shifter. Such was her luck. Which was nonexistent. There was some irony in that, considering her father owned a casino called the Shamrock and was a leprechaun, supposedly one of the luckiest creatures alive.

So much for any of that getting passed down to her.

Finding the dragon's house had been tricky. The Ryde driver had gone past the driveway twice. It was easy to see why. The place sat up in the hills, surrounded by trees, and set back at the end of a long, winding drive. There was no indication from the road that there was even a house at the end of the dirt road.

Well, it wasn't truly a dirt road. As soon as it made the bend, the road was paved smooth. Almost like the visible part had deliberately been left to look abandoned.

Which was how she was feeling right now. Abandoned. She would have much rather rented a car and driven herself, but her father thought that would make it too easy for Ivan to turn her away. That she'd have a better chance of getting into the house if Ivan thought she had nowhere else to go. Maybe, but she couldn't help but watch longingly as the Ryde driver disappeared into the trees.

Her easy out gone, she turned her attention to the house. It was nice. Really nice. And bigger than she'd expected. More like the fancy chalets at high-end ski resorts than a cabin in the hills. But then, a dragon shifter would want room.

She carried her rolling bag up the steps to stand on the front porch. Her heart in her throat, she lifted her hand and rapped on the door.

Barking erupted on the other side.

She jerked back. His file hadn't said anything about a dog. And this one sounded large. She wasn't super happy about that. She'd never had any kind of pet growing up, and the thought of a big dog scared her. *Please don't let it be trained to attack.* But then, what other kind of dog would an MMA fighter have than something big and mean and looking to gnaw on her?

She glanced toward the road again, but the Ryde

driver was long gone. *Great.* She pulled her jacket closer against the cold.

"Grom, *sidet.*" The deep, Russian-accented voice and the sound of the door opening brought her head around. Ivan the Hammer stood before her. He was a heavily muscled, stone-faced man with a shaved head, a few visible tattoos, and a bent nose. He had the same kind of thin-tempered look all the fighters did. Like he could strike at any moment, and you'd never see it coming.

It was unnerving and one of the many reasons she wanted nothing to do with that part of her father's business. (Her father didn't exactly like her being around men, which had something else to do with it.) Also, besides having tempers, most of these guys were rarely going to be the next Jeopardy! contestant.

She swallowed. If she could survive her father, she could get through this.

Ivan leaned on a single crutch. A large, black and brown dog sat at his side. Staring at her. Ivan's right leg was encased thigh to calf in a steel brace. "Can I help you?"

For a second, her cover story went right out of her head. Then she managed to pull herself together. "I'm Lisa Devers. The organization sent me. I'm your rehabilitation therapist."

He gave her a once-over. "I don't need rehabilitation."

His accent wasn't as thick as she'd expected, but it was definitely present. "The TFL sends a therapist to work with all its injured fighters. It's part of your contract."

He shook his head. "My contract is done. Sorry for your trouble." He started to shut the door.

"Wait. Don't you want your final check?"

He hesitated. "I got last check."

She hated to give her father credit, but this part of the story was all his doing. "If you complete the therapy sessions, they send you a bonus. It's the same as whatever you earned on your last fight."

His brows lifted slightly. "That is a large sum. How many sessions?"

She thought fast. "I won't know until I can assess you."

He stared at her. "*Nyet*. I don't need the money."

She thought faster. "Please. They'll fire me if you send me away. And I really need this job." More than he knew.

His eyes narrowed. It wasn't a secret how capricious the League could be. "What was your name?"

"Lisa. Lisa Devers." She stuck her hand out and put on a brave face. "Nice to meet you, Mr. Tsvetkov."

He wrapped her hand in his big one. He was incredibly warm, but then, dragons were. All that fire inside. "Call me Van."

"Van, then." She nodded, not sure what else to say. "Does that mean you're good with the therapy?"

He looked at her bag, not really giving her an answer. "You are staying here?"

She took that to mean the job was hers. She

glanced down. "Oh, yes. It's part of the therapy. With the morning sessions and evening sessions, it's just easier. Plus, there are the daily assessments." She was just making it up as she went along now, pulling from different parts of the books she'd looked through.

He frowned.

She persisted. "You do have a guest room, don't you?"

"*Da*." He backed up with some difficulty, the dog moving with him. "Follow me."

Van had no interest in any kind of therapy, but he didn't want to be responsible for this woman getting fired. The League was strict and full of rules. That much he knew.

As Lisa stepped into his house, he took her bag in his free hand.

"Oh, uh, thanks." She smiled at him tentatively, like she hadn't expected him to help.

"You're welcome." He wasn't a Neanderthal. Chivalry wasn't dead. But he didn't smile back. He didn't want her to think he was happy about the organization intruding like this.

He'd probably donate the money to the rescue Grom had come from. They could use it, and he didn't need it. At all. He was a dragon. And dragons had hoards. But again, he didn't want her to lose her job because of him. Whatever kind of supernatural she was, she obviously wasn't the kind that was good with money if this job was that important.

She stepped toward him. "Thank you for not sending me away."

He nodded and took a breath.

She smelled fresh and earthy, in a good way. Like the deepest forest after a rain. On her, it was a powerful, feminine scent. Like Mother Earth had just walked into his house. It was intoxicating.

But then, this was the closest he'd been to a woman who wasn't Pandora in a long time.

He shook his head and leaned back, weight on his crutch. "This way." He called to Grom. "*Ko mne.*"

The dog jumped up to follow.

Lisa was a little slower.

Van kept limping forward, putting more space between them. Space was good. Space would keep her from getting any ideas.

"Wow, you have a lot of books."

He glanced back.

She was looking at the shelves that lined his living room. "Your house is amazing."

He thought so too. He stopped at the stairs that led to the second floor. "Take the bedroom upstairs." It was his, but he'd moved to the guest room on this level since his injury. Steps and crutches were pointless. The second guest room was his office and trophy room. So she either slept up there or took the couch.

"You can't do the stairs right now, can you?" She reached for her bag.

He put the rolling suitcase on the bottom step and

hobbled to the side. "Not yet. Soon. Maybe we work on that." If he had to do this therapy, he should at least get something out of it.

"What? Oh, yes. Definitely." She smiled quickly.

"Good. Get settled, and then we start."

"Right now? Today?"

"Is there reason to wait?" He wanted this over as soon as possible.

"No, I suppose not." Her smile thinned a little. "I just thought we could start fresh tomorrow. Bright and early and all that."

He realized she might be tired from traveling. Not everyone had the constitution of a mythological being. "Tomorrow morning is fine."

"You're sure?"

His leg was aching anyway. "Tomorrow."

"Okay. Thank you." She hesitated. "I realize you weren't expecting me, so I'm happy to pay for takeout for dinner."

He almost laughed. "No takeout. I'm making steaks. There is enough."

"You're sure? I know I'm here because the League sent me, but it's not really fair that you have to put me up and feed me too." Her mouth scrunched to one side. "Although I guess the check you're going to get will more than cover whatever costs you incur because of me."

"*Da*. I mean, yes. Is no problem." He sighed and corrected himself. "It is *not* a problem."

She smiled. "Thank you. What time should I be down?"

"Whenever you like. Dinner is at seven."

"Okay. See you then." She went up the steps.

He stood there, admiring the view until he realized what he was doing. Then he frowned and turned toward the kitchen to get the steaks out. She was pretty. And she smelled nice. But she was a temporary distraction.

Nothing about her being here changed the fact that his perfect record had been broken. That for the first time in his entire MMA career, he'd been injured by an opponent so severely it had cost him the fight. No amount of therapy was going to erase that black mark.

Not from his record. And not from his soul.

Monalisa dropped her bag on the enormous bed and looked around as she unzipped her jacket. The room was large enough to have a sitting area, which was a massive leather chair and ottoman in front of French doors that led to a small balcony. The grouping had a plush throw and a reading lamp, making it a very cozy little spot. The bedroom also had its own fireplace. On a chilly winter day like today, she couldn't imagine a better place to be.

The overwhelming effect was all very masculine, but considering that it was Van's house, that was understandable. The view through the windows was incredible. The sun was starting to set, streaking the sky with orange and pink over the Georgian hills.

She draped her jacket over the bed's footboard, then gazed at the colorful sky for a few moments before going back to unpacking. Her toiletry kit was on top. She took it into the connected bath and flipped on the light.

The space was a study in granite and wood. A real man's bathroom with double sinks, an enormous soaking tub, and a walk-in shower that probably could have held several people.

Or one dragon shifter.

She frowned as a thought came to her. Acting on impulse, she walked to the medicine cabinet and opened it.

Shaving supplies, a couple bottles of men's cologne, and a black leather grooming kit.

This wasn't a guest room, this was Van's room. He'd already admitted the stairs were a no-go.

He must be using the guest room. Which was probably on the first floor.

Okay, this was a little weird. She was going to be sleeping in his bed. And showering in his shower.

It gave her a strange sense of intimacy that she hadn't counted on. Granted, it wasn't like he was sharing the space with her, but still. This was his room. His sanctuary. His private space. It made her feel worse about everything she was here to do.

Which was saying something, since she already felt pretty bad.

She put her bag on the vanity and stared at herself in the mirror. She didn't look like a fake. Or did she? She peered closer. What did he see when he looked at her? Did he buy that she was a rehab therapist?

Or did he see what she really was? A woman kept under her father's thumb for so long that all she knew was how well her gifts could be used for nefarious purposes. A woman without any real skills. A woman

21

who was so desperate to be free that she'd ruined Van's life once already. And now she was here to ruin it again.

She closed her eyes and dropped her head. If Van knew who she really was, he hadn't let on. There'd been no spark of recognition in his eyes when he'd opened the door, so he either had no idea or he was really good at hiding his reactions.

And if he did know who she was and hadn't said anything, was he plotting some kind of retaliation? Had he let her into his house only to give himself time to plan his revenge?

She opened her eyes and stared at herself again. If so, she'd have no choice but to use her powers against him.

There'd be no happy ending for either of them. Just for her father, who would once again get what he wanted.

They were both his pawns. Both deadly, dangerous creatures unable to use their gifts to save themselves.

She snorted softly. In that way, she and Van were a perfect match. A new image filled her head. One where she and Van stood side by side in front of her father. Like a team. Like friends. Like people who cared what happened to each other.

Wait. She shook her head. That wasn't what she'd meant about them being a match. Not in a romantic sort of sense. Not in any kind of friendly way, really.

She was just here to finish what she'd started. That was it. That was all. Because, if he ever found out who she really was...she shivered. Facing the wrath of a dragon wasn't something she ever hoped to have to endure.

But if he refused her gentle suggestions to return to the arena…what then?

She would be forced to use her powers on him. Because there was no point in trying to outrun her father. She'd tried that when he'd failed to give her a coin again on her twenty-first birthday. She'd made it to Argentina. And then he'd summoned her back. She'd lasted a week before the pain in her head got to be too much.

That was what happened if she refused him. A headache of unimaginable proportions. It started as a dull throb around day two. By day three, it was a constant ache. By day four, it was splitting. On day five, a medically induced coma seemed like a reasonable idea.

On day seven, she'd been bent over with pain, unable to speak, unable to think, unable to see. She'd managed enough words to call the head of her father's security team, Sean, and tell him where she was so he could send someone to pick her up and bring her home.

It wasn't something she thought she could bear again. And she'd searched for years to find another way to break his hold on her. But every answer was the same.

The coin.

So if Van refused, she'd be left with no choice but to force him to comply or suffer the consequences of refusing her father.

She went back to her bag and finished unpacking as the sadness of that thought crept over her. She didn't have much. Some casual clothes, plus some rehab-therapist-appropriate work clothes and a dress. All mix and match and enough for a week and a half. Longer than that and she might have to go shopping.

Her father could pick up the tab for those clothes. That idea cleared some of her blue mood.

In fact, he could pay for a few more things. Like some dinners in town. She'd tell Van it was part of his therapy and that the League was paying. He wouldn't turn that down. And then she could be out in public with him. That would be more comfortable than being stuck in the house with him and his dog for ten days.

Although, she hoped it wouldn't take that long.

She stared into her bag. There was something unfamiliar in the bottom. Something dark wrapped in the same tissue that her mother's favorite boutique used.

Monalisa pulled the item out and unwrapped it. A sleek little black dress so unlike anything she would have picked out for herself, but not nearly as risqué as what her mother favored. It was somewhere in between. Her mother's idea of a compromise.

Undoubtedly a very expensive compromise, knowing her mother's taste and the boutique's prices.

She'd return it to her mother when she got back to Vegas. It was silly, really. Where did her mother think she was going to wear a thing like that here?

The dress and the rest of her things went into what hanging space there was in the closet, but there were no empty drawers, so she couldn't really unpack everything. Which was fine with her. Tucking her unmentionables next to Van's boxers wasn't a place she wanted to go.

She was a little unsettled that she'd even opened that drawer. The man liked colorful underwear. She wasn't sure what to do with that, but it felt like information she shouldn't have. But she hadn't been snooping. He'd told her this was the guest room.

She should have guessed otherwise by the scent of smoke. It was all throughout the house—she'd picked it up as soon as she'd stepped foot inside. Of course, it was February and the smell of wood smoke was everywhere. It was just stronger in this space.

Because it was his. His space, his scent.

It wasn't an unpleasant smell at all. It was sort of homey and comforting, even though it wasn't a smell she was that familiar with. A lot of the fireplaces in Vegas were gas. At least, they were in her part of town.

The smoke, which she knew was a mark of him being a dragon shifter, was also a very manly scent. One she hoped she'd soon grow used to so that it would just disappear.

But for now, she'd have to deal with it. With that in mind, she headed downstairs to begin the charade she hoped would set her free.

Leaning on his crutch, Van stood in front of the

refrigerator, door open. The grill was fired up. All that was left was the cooking. He stared at the platter of steaks he'd planned on having for dinner. Two for him. One for Grom.

Van would still have his, but Grom wouldn't. Not tonight. Yes, he spoiled his dog. And anyone who thought that was a waste of steak could get scorched.

Grom sat at his side, whuffing and whimpering softly. His nails clicked on the tile as he shifted in place.

"Sorry, Grom." Van took the platter out with one hand, slid it onto the island counter, then used his crutch to reach back and shut the door. "No steak for you tonight. This has to be for our visitor."

Grom whuffed unhappily.

Van limped to the spices and got to work seasoning the steaks. Garlic, salt, pepper. "Don't worry, pup. She won't be here long."

Three days, tops. That was how long he figured it would take to satisfy whatever requirements the League had for this rehabilitation business. Then the League would be happy, Lisa could keep her job, and the animal rescue would get a nice fat check as his thanks for bringing Grom into his life.

He smiled down at the dog, who seemed to understand that he wasn't getting a steak for dinner. "I'll make it up to you. You'll see."

"You'll make what up to him?"

Van twisted to see Lisa leaning against the wide breakfast bar that separated the cooking space from the great room. "Not getting steak for dinner."

"Why not?"

He suppressed a smile. "Because you're eating it."

She made an odd face.

He waited for the lecture on how she thought he should be raising his dog, or how he was wasting food, or whatever.

But instead, she laughed. "So you're feeding me dog food?"

Her comment caught him off guard, and he barked out a laugh as well, but turned quickly to hide his amusement. "I suppose I am."

He hadn't expected the sense of humor from her at all. He liked it. Liked that she could joke. It was one of the many reasons he and Pandora had hit it off. People thought he was such a serious guy because of his profession, but he liked having fun as much as the next person. Maybe more. But a lot of people never found that out about him because they were too scared to even try to get to know him.

"What kind of dog is Grom?"

"Doberman." Van slanted his gaze in her direction. She'd moved a few steps closer, putting her in his field of vision, but her attention was focused on Grom.

"He's, uh, very handsome. And seems pretty well behaved."

"Grom is a good dog." He slathered the steaks with good olive oil and gave them a little massage, working the seasonings into them.

"He must have been expensive."

"He was a rescue." He kept watching her. She seemed hesitant to come any nearer.

"Really? Wow."

Van hobbled to the sink, washed his hands, then grabbed a towel to dry them and turned to face her. "He's very well trained, but still young."

She nodded. "Does he bite?"

"Not unless I tell him to."

She paled a little, and Van realized that had been the wrong answer.

He tossed the towel onto the counter. "He won't hurt you. Are you afraid of dogs?"

"I don't know if afraid is the right word. I never had any pets growing up. And he's so big. I just don't know what to expect, I guess."

Van leaned his crutch against the counter, then, with great effort, crouched next to Grom. It required him to keep his injured leg out straight and support his body weight on the other, but it was doable. Once down, he scratched Grom's head. "He won't hurt you. I promise."

Almost on cue, Grom flopped down and rolled over to show off his belly, legs in the air.

Lisa let out a small laugh. "He is kind of cute."

Van patted Grom's taut belly. "Come. Pet him. You'll see."

With hesitant steps, she walked over and squatted beside Van, then reached out to stroke Grom's stomach. "He's softer than I thought he'd be."

Grom bent his head to see her, his pink tongue lolling out of his mouth. There was a look of sheer pleasure on his doggy face.

She smiled. "He does seem nice."

Van just nodded. Her perfume was filling his head, making it hard for him to think. Or maybe it was the half inch of space between her thigh and his that was causing his brain to short-circuit. Or all that flame-red hair.

It was too much. She was too close.

With a burst of energy, he pushed himself upright. "I must get these steaks on the grill."

The move caused Grom to scrabble to his feet, startling Lisa, who fell onto her backside with a small yelp.

Van's gut response was to help. Without thinking, he reached a hand down to her, bending. His strength was no match for the brace.

Pain shot up through his leg and into his gut like he'd been run through with the blade of a giant knife. He stiffened and growled in pain, freezing in place.

Lisa crawled backward, fear in her eyes. They flashed with green fire, an indicator of whatever kind of supernatural she was.

That look of fear was something he knew well. Just as he knew how to bring himself under control. He ignored the pain, breathing deeply. "Don't be afraid. My leg. I forget."

She nodded and got to her feet, still a good distance away from him. "You bent it."

"*Da*." And that was all the discussion of his injury he planned on having. Grimacing, he reached for his crutch. He settled it under him, then picked up the plate of steaks. "Grom, *ko mne*."

Grom did as he was told, staying at Van's side as

he made his way toward the deck where he kept the grill.

"Can I help?"

"*Nyet.*" Van didn't want help. Didn't need help. Just like he didn't need Lisa here. It was bad enough she was making him forget his English. Without another word, he got the door open and went outside.

Monalisa stared after him. Well, that hadn't gone as planned. Not even remotely. And her heart was still thumping in her chest. Her father's brand of scary was nothing compared to Van Tsvetkov in pain.

The smell of smoke had intensified as the man's eyes had gone as red as hot coals. Shimmers of heat had burst off him like he was on the verge of combustion. She'd half expected flames to shoot out of his mouth. But maybe he could only do that in dragon form.

She didn't want to find out.

And yet, she might, because she was stuck here. At least for a little while longer.

The idea of using her powers and getting this over quickly was tempting, but not tempting enough for her to turn down the dark path her parents were so willing for her to walk. No, she'd befriend him (that had to be possible) and then convince him that honoring his contract was the right thing to do.

And pray to the saints that she didn't get turned into a human s'more in the process.

So first, the befriending part. She swallowed. She'd started to think he wasn't so bad, then he'd hurt his leg (trying to help her, so points for that) and turned into exactly what she'd expected him to be before meeting him.

His storming out afterward had only solidified that image.

But this was her job. Correction, this was what she had to do if she ever wanted to be free. And frankly, that was the depth and breadth of her heart's desire.

She brushed herself off, got her pulse under control, and walked out onto the deck. His back was to her, and the grill was open, steaks sizzling away on the jumping flames. "Are you okay?"

He turned a skeptical gaze her way. "Why? You think this will prolong my therapy?"

She shrugged. "I was just concerned is all. You hurt yourself because of me. That hardly seems like something I should ignore."

He glared a moment longer, then his expression softened and he turned back to the steaks. "It is not your fault."

"It kind of was. You were bending to help me. And you wouldn't have done that if I hadn't been here, so…"

He didn't respond. Grom stared up at her, tongue out, his expression kind of making her feel like he was happy to see her. Which seemed odd, because why would he like her? He'd just met her. But then, what did she know about dogs?

She knew Van liked them. That was clear. And maybe it was also her way in. "I like Grom. He's really nice. And I never knew I'd feel that way about a big dog."

Van grunted. "He will get bigger."

"Really? How big?"

"I do not know. But larger, for sure. One hundred pounds, maybe."

"Wow." She looked at Grom with new eyes. "But he seems like the right kind of dog for a guy like you."

"Is that so?" Van glanced at her again, his eyes unreadable. "How?"

She was walking a fine line here, and she knew that, but Van's decision earlier to help her gave her some confidence. "Tough exterior with a gooey nougat center."

His eyes narrowed.

"Okay, wait. Maybe not a gooey center. But you know what I mean, right? Grom looks tough, and he is. But he also likes to have his belly scratched."

Van frowned and picked up a long fork with two sharp tines. "I do not like to have my belly scratched."

"Wouldn't dream of attempting it, I promise." The very idea made her smile, and she was glad he wasn't looking at her in that moment.

"Good." He flipped the steaks and, thankfully, put the fork down. "How do you want your steak?"

"Medium well." That earned her another look. She

gave it right back. Dragons might be okay with bloody food, but she wasn't. "Can I help with anything? Fix the side dishes maybe?"

His brow furrowed. "Side dishes?"

"You know, salad, green beans, baked potatoes, that kind of thing."

He shook his head. "No side dish."

Her mouth came open in surprise. "You're just eating steak for dinner?"

"*Da.*" He growled softly. "I mean, yes."

Okay, that might be fine for a dragon, but that wasn't going to fly for her. No pun intended. "That must be a dragon thing."

He glanced at her. "What are you?"

She knew what he was asking. She couldn't tell him the truth. Will-o'-the-Wisps were rare, and revealing that much would give everything away. She'd prepped for this, though. "I'm a dryad, but only on my mother's side, and unfortunately, that bloodline's gotten pretty thin." She shrugged. "It's enough to qualify me as supernatural, but I'm one of those with no real supernatural skills. Sadly."

His eyes tapered for a second, then he went back to the steaks. "Dryads like trees. So you want vegetables, don't you?"

"They are part of my diet, yes."

He grunted. "There might be something in the freezer."

"You mind if I look?"

"Help yourself."

She left him on the deck and went back to the

kitchen. His fridge had steaks, pork chops, a rotisserie chicken, a couple six-packs, and some condiments. His freezer looked about the same, minus the condiments and six-packs, but under a butcher-paper-wrapped pack of grouper filets, she found a solitary box of frozen broccoli growing a couple of substantial ice crystals.

She took it out, shut the freezer, then started rummaging for a microwavable bowl. Maybe she could find a way to get to the grocery store tomorrow. If she had to call another Ryde and charge it to her dad, she would. She couldn't eat like her carnivorous companion for a week. Her body would rebel.

The doorbell rang just as she found a plastic bowl that would work. Grom barked, but Van quieted him with another Russian command Monalisa didn't understand. She set the bowl and the box of broccoli on the counter, then shouted in his direction, "I'll get it."

Van didn't respond, so she headed to the door. She opened it and found a pretty, petite redhead on the other side. "Hello."

"Oh, hi." The woman gave her an odd look. "You're not Van."

"No, I'm not. I'm Lisa Devers. I'm his rehab therapist."

"Huh. He didn't say anything about hiring one."

"He didn't exactly. The League sent me." Who was this woman that Van might tell such things to? His girlfriend? Monalisa didn't need any complications, but the woman might be useful as an ally. "Can I tell him who's here?"

"Oh, sorry." She smiled and stuck her hand out. "Pandora Williams. I'm a good friend of Van's. Helped him build this house."

That sounded like a really good friend. Monalisa shook Pandora's hand. "Nice to meet you. Van's cooking steaks on the deck."

Pandora nodded. "I can smell them. My mouth is watering. No, don't bother him. I was going to see if he needed anything, but I'm guessing you've got that covered. Just tell him Cole and I are expecting him for the housewarming tomorrow night. At the Victorian, not my old place. Obviously. Well, to Van anyway. He knows. Oh, and you too, of course. If you're going to be here."

Monalisa nodded. "I'll probably be here for at least a week."

"Great. We'll see you both. Nice to meet you." She headed down the steps with a little wave.

"See you then." Hopefully, they'd have vegetables. Monalisa closed the door and went back to the kitchen.

Van was just coming in with the platter of steaks, Grom at his side. He used his crutch to shut the door. "Was that Pandora?"

"Yes, good ears."

"What did she want?"

"We're supposed to be at the Victorian for a housewarming tomorrow night. She said you'd know."

He put the platter on the counter next to the sad box of broccoli. "We?"

Monalisa shrugged. "She was nice enough to invite me too."

He got plates out of a cabinet and silverware from a drawer. Steak knives came out of a wooden block near the coffeemaker. "That was the polite thing to do. Pandora is very polite."

"She's also very pretty."

"And very involved." He leaned on his crutch. "With Cole."

"I assume that's her boyfriend since she mentioned him."

Van went silent for a moment, his gaze far away, like he was thinking. "She knows I cannot drive." He looked at her. "She knew you were here somehow. Witch's instinct."

That was interesting. "She's a witch?"

"A very good one." He forked the steaks onto the plates.

She stared at the plate with the two steaks. That had to be for him. "Dragons must have big appetites."

"Yes. Also, the protein helps me heal."

She nodded. That made sense. "I can't imagine how painful the bite of that manticore must have—"

"I do not wish to discuss it." He picked up his plate and his utensils and limped off to the living room. Grom followed. Van settled into a large recliner and turned on the television, a massive thing that rivaled the screen in her father's home theater. A basketball game roared to life.

With a sigh, she threw the broccoli back into the freezer, then grabbed her utensils and plate and sat at the breakfast bar to eat. Van might not want to talk to her tonight, but tomorrow they'd officially start his rehab and he'd have no choice.

At least, she hoped he'd cooperate. Otherwise, she'd have no choice to do exactly as her father wanted.

Van cut a piece of steak and shoved it in his mouth while pretending to watch the game. He wasn't a fan of basketball, but he wasn't about to talk about the fight either. Just the thought made his leg ache.

He swallowed the steak, barely tasting it as the memory of that night came barreling back into his head. He closed his eyes for a moment, trying to keep himself from reliving it. But as always, he failed.

The manticore shifter had been a ferocious opponent, and one of the most interesting he'd faced in a while. A bat-winged lionesque creature with rows of venomous teeth like a shark, Ronan was a relatively new fighter on the TFL circuit. He'd won the pairing with Van only because the originally slated fighter had been disqualified for missing his weight class.

And Ronan had only won because Van had been distracted.

Nothing like it had ever happened to him in a fight before. For the briefest of moments, he'd been compelled to look up. Then a flash of light had caught his eye, holding his gaze.

That was all the opening Ronan had needed. He'd bitten Van, paralyzing him long enough to claim victory.

Van stared at the steak on his plate without really seeing it. The move wasn't dirty or underhanded. In the TFL, there were no rules except for no fatal blows. But the manticore's bite had incapacitated Van, and the powerful venom would take a minimum of two more weeks to completely clear from Van's system.

Such were the consequences of fighting in a league where mythological supernaturals ruled the highest ranks.

As a dragon, Van was nearly unstoppable. And in that form, he was the largest of all the mythologicals. It was why he never fully shifted in combat, relying instead on his sheer strength and speed to win. He liked a fair fight. Anything else was boring.

But not shifting was a big part of why Ronan had bested him. His manticore form versus Van's human one had been an equitable match. So long as Van stayed vigilant.

Which he had. Until the distraction.

He cut another piece of steak, this time tossing it to Grom, who caught it midair and devoured it without chewing.

Ronan's teeth never would have pierced the scales of Van's dragon form.

Van ate another bite, but his appetite wasn't there. He forced himself to eat, knowing his body needed the protein to recover.

He'd known he wouldn't be able to fight forever.

But he'd expected to last longer before his abilities began to fail him. He'd always thought his speed would be the first to go.

Not being able to concentrate? To maintain focus? He hadn't counted on that.

It made him feel...washed up. Useless.

Like quitting was his only option.

Grom whined, drawing Van's attention away from his troubles and back to reality. "What is it, pup?"

Grom got up and whined again.

"You have to go out?"

"I'll take him."

Van glanced back to see Lisa standing near the breakfast bar. Her plate sat on the counter, the steak only half eaten.

She'd had her dinner there.

He was a bad host. Not that he'd asked her to come, but still, his mother would be unhappy if she knew how he'd treated this woman who probably hadn't asked to be sent here either. "Thank you. That is very kind of you."

She gave a quick little half smile. "No problem. Where's his leash?"

"Closet by the door."

"Okay, I'll find it." She patted her leg. "C'mon, Grom. Let's go outside."

Grom looked at Lisa, then looked at Van and sat down.

Van pointed toward the door. "Grom, *gulyat*."

Grom got up and trotted toward the door like he'd been told.

Lisa's brows lifted like she was impressed. "Back in a bit."

He watched her go. She was very pretty. And kind. Which was more than he'd been since she'd arrived. He sighed. Changing his mood wasn't an easy thing to do, but he would do his best to be nicer. After all, she was just doing her job.

He leaned back, ignoring the game. It was only a few days. He would get through this. Then he could go back to being cranky and alone.

A few minutes later, the door opened and they returned. A happy Grom came running over to Van and started sniffing around.

Lisa closed the door. "He's a really well-behaved dog. He did his business and came right back in."

"For that, he gets a cookie. Jar on counter."

"Okay. The one marked *cookies*, I take it?"

"Yes."

She got the treat out. "Here, Grom. Come get your cookie."

This time, Grom went to her without hesitation.

Van snorted. Food apparently helped erase her stranger status in Grom's eyes.

She finished up with Grom, then walked toward the stairs. "I'm going to head up. I know it's early, but I'm a little tired from traveling. I'll see you in the morning. Thank you for dinner."

He nodded. "Good night."

"Good night." She climbed the steps, giving him another chance to admire her form.

He liked women. Loved them. But he wasn't sure

why he'd developed this sudden fascination with Lisa. Maybe it was just because he hadn't been this near to a woman, other than Pandora, in a long time.

If so, that was a sad commentary on his life. Had he really been alone so long that the first pretty woman who entered his domain brought his desires to life?

He turned the sound down on the television.

As a dragon, he was two things. A protector and a destroyer. It made for a hard life at times. A life many chose to live alone because it was easier.

But those of his kind who had found someone to spend their days with…they were happy. He'd seen it with his own eyes in the lives of his parents.

He'd never really contemplated such a future for himself, and yet now, hours after Lisa had shown up, he found himself doing just that.

Pandora would have a lot to say about that. Which was why he wouldn't be telling her a word of this.

He turned the television off, grabbed his crutch, and stood up. He took his plate into the kitchen. Lisa's was already in the dishwasher. Appetite gone, he put the other steak away, then limped back out to the living room. "Grom, bed."

The dog followed him into the guest room and settled onto the big cushion Van had brought along from the upstairs move, turning three times before lying down.

Van brushed his teeth and got ready for bed, chucking his T-shirt into the hamper. He sat down on the edge of the bed and went through the tedious task of taking off the brace, keeping his leg straight. He shucked his sweat pants, then stared at his injured knee.

Purple bruising was visible at the edges of the bandages meant to help with the swelling. Under that wrapping, he knew exactly what the skin looked like. Two large, matched semicircles of puncture wounds, the marks of Ronan's bite.

The scars would look the same. Not angry and red, but they'd remain. A permanent reminder of the day he'd become…less.

He turned the light off and lay down on the bed, putting one arm under his head. He gazed up at the ceiling and repeated the ritual that had robbed him of a decent night's sleep every evening since the injury. Reliving the fight. Each move of his, each move of Ronan's. The pull to look up. The flash of light. The intense pain.

Then a new thought crept in, one he probably would have had sooner had he not been so wrapped up in his own misery. One that probably wasn't going to help him sleep either.

Directly above him, the very pretty Lisa was in his bed.

Monalisa had never slept in such a large bed. Well, she wasn't sleeping now, but that was the end goal. Exhaustion pulled at her, making her feel like she was processing everything at an incredibly slow speed, but somehow it wasn't enough to help her sleep.

Instead, she just sprawled there, trying not to think about how this was where Van slept. The strange man she just met hours ago. The very man she was supposed to be bending to her will.

Trying not to think about him meant that was all she *could* think about, and it was just so odd her brain couldn't let go of it. Finally, she gave in, hoping her brain would get tired and shut down.

Van wasn't as bad as she'd imagined he'd be, but he wasn't the nicest person she'd ever met either. She wondered if part of his temper wasn't just because he'd been dealt such a blow. She understood what it was like to be kept from the life you wanted. And she imagined how much more it must hurt to be kept from that life when you'd been allowed to experience it.

More than that, Van was kind of the rock star of the TFL, according to his file. He'd been undefeated until this last match, and the loss hadn't been by knockout or points or however fights were decided, but because he'd been so badly injured, there was no other option than to call the match.

An injury she'd caused.

She closed her eyes, but the pit in her stomach remained. She hated what her father had made her do almost as much as she hated her inability to ignore his commands. But it was even worse that someone else had been hurt because of what she'd been forced into doing.

Van might be a grump, but he was an innocent grump. He didn't deserve to have his life taken away from him.

She didn't blame him for not wanting to fight again.

Suddenly, she sat upright. What if he couldn't fight again? Was his injury that bad? She knew from his file that he'd been bitten by the other fighter, a manticore, a very deadly mytho, which was how her father referred to that class of supernaturals. She'd also read that manticore venom was incredibly strong and the effects would stay in the victim's bloodstream for up to a month.

Van was only two weeks out from the fight. Maybe the venom was making him cranky? That was definitely a possibility.

She felt for the guy. His career was over—as far as he was concerned. He was probably in constant pain, he'd lost his undefeated status, and the scars from that bite would stay with him the rest of his life, an ever-present reminder of the day his life had taken a dramatic downturn. For a moment, she thought about marching downstairs and confessing everything.

For the first time since she'd arrived, she smiled. That would be so nice.

But then she sighed and leaned forward, putting her face into her hands. Her father would never give her a coin then. He'd force her to bend Van to her will, and he'd end up back in the ring either way. Not to mention she couldn't even imagine how he'd respond to the truth about why she was here.

If he'd been cranky before, he'd go ballistic hearing that. Considering his general mood, it was kind of amazing he'd even let her into his house. Especially since she no longer thought he had an ulterior motive due to recognizing her.

She flopped back down to stare at the ceiling some more. It was nice he had Grom. He was a good dog, and he'd been so well behaved when she'd taken him outside. He'd really changed her mind about dogs. Especially when she'd discovered he liked his ears rubbed. The look on his face, eyes closed, mouth partially open, could only be described as euphoric. It was sweet and silly, and when she'd stopped, Grom had pushed his big head into her hand as if asking for more. He'd won her over big-time.

Maybe when she had her own life, she'd get a dog

too. Just a small one, though. The companionship would be nice. So would the unconditional love.

She sighed again. Getting that life meant forcing Van into the ring one more time. How on earth was she going to do that without using her powers?

Maybe things would be different tomorrow. Maybe they'd have some kind of breakthrough in pretend therapy and he'd suddenly want to fight again.

She snorted softly. And maybe her father would just give her a coin like he should have done years ago.

The image of the coin floated elusively in her mind, the shiny gold mesmerizing her with the promise it held. She clung to that promise. It kept her going. Because without it, she'd be just as miserable as Van.

No, one day she'd have a life, with her own apartment and friendly neighbors and a dog and...

She opened her eyes and saw daylight. She'd actually fallen asleep. But the light was strong, stronger than it ought to be for first thing in the morning.

She checked her phone. It wasn't first thing in the morning, it was a quarter after nine. Swamp water! She should have been up and moving by eight, at least. She hopped out of bed, grabbed some clothes, and ran to the shower.

Seven minutes later, she was out, had some makeup on, and was dressed for the day. Her hair was damp, but that couldn't be helped. She couldn't afford to take any more time getting ready, or Van would think the League had sent him a slacker of a therapist.

She hit the steps, and soft voices met her ears. Van's and someone else's. A woman. Pandora?

Monalisa jogged the rest of the way down to the living room.

Van and an older woman were in the kitchen. He was seated at the breakfast bar, his back to Monalisa, and the older woman leaned against the center island.

Van turned as Monalisa walked toward them. "Morning."

"Morning. Sorry I slept so long, I—"

He raised his hand. "It is not a problem. Time change, yes? Also, unfamiliar bed. Understandable."

Wow. That was unexpected. She nodded. "Yes, it was a combination of those things."

He gestured toward the older woman. "This is Norma Turnbuckle. She is my housekeeper."

"Hi, Norma. I'm…Lisa." She'd almost said Monalisa. "I'm Ivan's rehab therapist."

"He told me." Norma gave Monalisa a smile. "And this morning, I'm also the short-order cook. What'll it be? Eggs? Pancakes? Frittata?"

"I, uh…" Monalisa looked at Van. "Did you eat already? What did you have?"

He smiled a little. "What else? Steak and eggs."

"Of course." She laughed. "Whatever's easiest, really. Or I can cook my own. That's not a big deal. I don't want to be a burden."

"*Pfft*. No burden. I'm a hobbit, taking care of people is what we do," Norma said. "How about a veggie omelet? Van said you like the green stuff."

"That would be great, except I don't think those ingredients exist in this house."

Norma laughed. "Not normally they don't, but I did the shopping this morning according to what Van told me."

Monalisa looked at him again. "That was so kind of you."

He shrugged and sipped his coffee. "You are my guest, and I was not hospitable. All different today."

"Thank you."

"And please, call me Van. Everyone does."

"Okay. Van it is."

Norma pulled out a pan, then pointed with her spatula toward the end of the breakfast bar. "Fix yourself some coffee, and I'll have this whipped up in a jiffy."

"I don't suppose you have creamer." She didn't remember seeing any in the fridge last night, but then, she hadn't specifically been looking for that.

"In the icebox," Norma said.

Monalisa couldn't help but smile as she found a mug, filled it with coffee, and stirred in some sugar (from a bowl she also hadn't seen last night). Norma might have said she was a hobbit, but she seemed more like a magical house elf to Monalisa.

The fruit dish on the island was new too, because there was no way there'd been a giant platter of bananas, oranges, apples, and pears in here last night. Next to it was another bowl with tomatoes, onions, and sweet and regular potatoes.

Ivan—no, *Van*—wasn't kidding about today being different. At least from a dining perspective.

She went to the fridge for creamer and sucked in a gasp as she opened the door. The thing was stocked with all kinds of food that wasn't just slabs of meat. Three types of lettuce and a whole slew of other salad fixings. Plus, two kinds of juice, bags of carrot and celery sticks, an assortment of cheeses, olives and pickles, lunch meat, a container of deli coleslaw, and in front of it all, a large container of creamer.

Monalisa took it out, added some to her coffee, then put it back, finally turning to face Norma again. "You really stocked this place up."

Norma nodded as she tipped a bowl with beaten eggs into the pan where an assortment of veggies sizzled away. "There's more in the pantry too. Chips, cookies, bread for sandwiches, muffins, granola bars, popcorn. Snacky things. I didn't know what all you liked, and Van wasn't much help beyond vegetables, so I just took a stab at it."

"That's amazing. Thank you both." Monalisa glanced at Van. Hmm. Calling him that was going to take some getting used to. It wasn't so different sounding, but it was so much more casual. Like they were friends. And that felt like such a lie on her behalf.

But she would try, because it was what he wanted.

He looked pleased with himself, and she thought that was fitting. He had a right to after doing all this for her. She couldn't remember when someone had made such an effort on her behalf.

Someone who wasn't trying to win favor with her father.

The thought sobered her, and she drank her coffee to cover the sudden loss of her smile. Van doing all this for her seemed to underline how awful her true motive was.

"Oh, one more thing," Norma said, adding cheese to the omelet. "Van, I got that champagne you asked for. It's also in the pantry." She turned to see him. "Or did you want that cold?"

He looked stumped. "I don't know." His gaze shifted to Monalisa. "Should champagne be cold if it is a gift?"

"I feel a little lost. Who is it a gift for?"

"Pandora. For the housewarming tonight."

"Oh, that's a nice gift. If it's for them to drink tonight, then probably cold. If it's for them to drink any time, then I don't think it matters."

"Hmm. I do not know what they'll want. Maybe it should be cold."

Monalisa set her coffee down. "I'll get it. Where's the pantry?"

Norma pointed with her elbow. "That door there."

Monalisa had thought that was for the downstairs. There was definitely a lower level, but as she hadn't been given the tour, she had no idea how to get there. Not that she needed the tour. She went into the pantry, once again amazed by the amount of food that Norma had brought in, and looked for the champagne.

Her eyes widened in surprise when she spotted it.

Two bottles of really, really good stuff. But what else would Van want for his friend? Money was clearly not an issue when it came to looking after those he cared for.

She picked the two bottles up by the necks and hesitated. For a second, she'd included herself in that group. But that was ridiculous. He didn't care about her any more than he cared about the man on the street. He was just being hospitable, in his own words.

With a shake of her head, she came back out, nudging the door shut with her foot. "I'll stick these in the fridge."

"Good," Norma said. "Then you can eat. Your omelet's ready."

Van drank the last of his coffee, watching Lisa over the top of the mug. She looked a little different this morning than she had last night. He couldn't quite figure out what had changed, but she seemed…more approachable.

Prettier than he remembered too. Which was odd, because he'd thought her pretty as soon as he'd seen her. But today she looked softer. Maybe it was her hair. It was drying in loose, fiery waves that hadn't been there yesterday, and they framed her face like one of the women in the portraits painted by the old masters.

Whatever it was, he was pleased that he'd had the idea to text Norma last night about getting groceries and making breakfast, because if it had been up to him, it would have just been coffee and last night's steak with half a dozen eggs. Which was what he'd had anyway, minus the chunk of steak that had gone into Grom's bowl.

He put his cup down as Lisa came to sit by him at the breakfast bar. Norma was bustling around the kitchen, cleaning up and putting things away. Grom sat near Van's feet and sighed loudly every once in a while in hopes of becoming the center of attention.

Lisa set her plate, utensils, and coffee cup at her place, then pointed at his mug. "You want a refill? I'll get it for you."

"Yes. Thank you." He reached down to pat Grom on the head. Silly dog.

She smiled and took his cup, returning a minute later with it full of the strong black coffee he so enjoyed.

She took her seat and dug in. After the first mouthful, she put her fork down. "That's a great omelet, Norma. Really good."

Norma was drying a pan. "I'm glad you like it."

Lisa went back to eating. Norma threw the towel over her shoulder and came over to the counter. "You need anything else, Van?"

"No. Everything is good."

"All right. Same time tomorrow?"

He shook his head. "Little later."

"You got it." Norma gave Lisa a nod. "Nice to meet you, Lisa."

"You too, Norma."

Norma left the towel on the counter, then picked up her coat and purse. "See you tomorrow."

"*Do svidaniya*." Van drank his coffee as Norma departed, leaving him and Lisa in the sudden silence.

His house had never seemed small until now.

Thankfully, Lisa was much better at making

conversation than he was. She cut her omelet into bite-size pieces with the edge of her fork. "Does Norma come every morning?"

"Usually once a week, but since my troubles, now four times."

"She's very nice. And a good cook."

"Yes." He frowned. Yes and no answers did not a conversation make. "She brings groceries. Takes Grom out. Cleans also. Very good help."

Lisa nodded. "I'm sure she is, especially with you not being so mobile. Speaking of..." She glanced at his knee. At the brace. Then back at him. "What sort of exercise does your doctor have you doing?"

He grunted and stared into his coffee. "Stationary bike."

"How's that going?" She ate another bite.

He shrugged.

She swallowed, then the right side of her mouth curved up in the kind of smile that was a little bit know-it-all and a little bit sympathetic. "You haven't been using the stationary bike, have you?"

He frowned and stared at her defiantly. "Once. Very painful."

"But isn't the idea that as your strength and healing improve, the pain lessens?" She blinked and straightened, her expression growing slightly more serious. "That is how it works, you know."

He sighed. That was exactly what Dr. Martinez had said.

"If you don't do the physical therapy, you could lose mobility permanently."

Something else Dr. Martinez had told him. "I will be fine."

Her skeptical expression said otherwise. "It's a good thing I showed up."

"No bike."

She tilted her head and gave him a slightly confused look. "I know it's painful, but that's part of the process. I would have thought a guy like you would be a little…I don't know, less concerned about pain. You are the undefeated TFL heavyweight champion, after all. Achieving and maintaining that title had to come with a tremendous amount of effort. Some of it painful. Maybe a lot of it."

"*Was* undefeated. No more." He grabbed his crutch and pushed to his feet, the anger and self-doubt he'd been struggling with rearing its ugly head again. The self-doubt was easy enough to shove down. The anger wasn't. And he didn't want that coming out around her.

She reached toward him like she was going to try to stop his departure, but pulled her hand back at the last second. "Van, I'm sorry if I upset you. That wasn't my intention."

He ignored her, unable in that moment to explain that the pain wasn't the problem. It was the memories associated with it. The feelings. And the way they came flooding back. The humiliation of defeat. Or losing everything he'd worked so hard for. His career. His life. His purpose. The weight of it had crushed his drive. "Grom, *ko mne*."

The dog jumped up and trotted along as Van

limped toward the coat closet. Getting down the steps would be difficult. Getting back up them would be a major undertaking. But he could do it, even if it took an hour. He didn't need therapy.

"Van, one more match and you can retake your title as champion."

He opened the closet and took out Grom's leash before answering her. "But I will never again be undefeated. I am done fighting."

"The League told me you have one more fight on your docket. A rematch."

He snorted as he hooked Grom's leash to his collar. "The League can get scorched."

Before she could respond, he yanked open the front door and stormed out. Well, as much as a person in a thigh-to-calf brace could storm while leaning on a crutch. It wasn't nearly as dramatic as he'd hoped.

He got the door shut behind him and stood there, sucking the cold air into his lungs in deep gulps.

Miserable. That was the only word he could use to describe his current state of being.

And he hated it. Hated feeling this way. Despite so much of his young life, he'd grown up to be a pretty content guy. He'd made a good life for himself. He loved what he did, made good money, and he'd been genuinely happy. Until that last fight.

Grom whined, eager to run and burn off some energy.

Van reached down and unclipped the leash. Grom took off, a streak of black and tan racing through the woods around the house with a look of utter happiness on his face.

Van understood. He got cabin fever himself. But forget running, he could barely walk. And what he really wanted to do was fly, but the manticore venom in his system prevented him from shifting. That inability added to his frustration and fueled the simmering anger in his belly that seemed to be a constant these days.

If only he could fight. That would—

Lisa opened the door and joined him on the landing. "I'm sorry. It really wasn't my intention to upset you. I can't imagine what it must have felt like to lose that night. I'm sure it was devastating. And I'm really sorry you had to go through that."

He stared into the woods surrounding his house. Grom zipped past on his second time around. Van gave Lisa points for following after him. Few would do that. And more points for apologizing again. And for saying she couldn't really understand what it felt like. Too many people had acted like they'd understood, but they'd made light of it. Told him to get over it. That it happened to everyone. Not Pandora, but the people at the League. His manager. The League doctors. The promotions team.

They all thought he should just suck it up, get through the therapy, get back into the ring and on with the next fight.

But this wasn't about sucking it up. This was about accepting how deeply his life had changed. Nothing would ever be the same again.

"Anyway, I was going to offer to walk Grom, but I see he's walking himself pretty well. I'm happy to stay out here and watch him until he's ready to come in, if you'd like. But I'm thinking after that, I should probably change my ticket and leave you alone."

That got his attention. He turned to look at her. "You would quit?"

"You can't quit a job you haven't been allowed to start."

He stared at her. There was a heaviness in her gaze. As if the weight of the universe lay upon her shoulders. Was that what he looked like?

Maybe. But what mattered was that he was the cause of that look. He took a breath and shifted his gaze back to the woods. "What happens first?"

"I don't know what you mean."

"Therapy. What happens first?"

Her mouth gaped as she blinked at him. His profile was a rather amazing series of rocky angles and hard bone. But then, he was a dragon, and they were built as tough as the mountains they called home. "You mean you're going to do the therapy?"

His mouth pursed for a moment. "*Da*. Yes."

"So we can start today? Right now? As soon as you come inside."

He glanced at her, eyes narrowed like he suspected she might have a screw loose. "That is what I mean."

She blew out a breath of relief. She really hadn't thought that was going to happen. "Excellent news. Thank you."

Grom skidded to a stop in front of the porch. His tongue was hanging out, his sides heaving from the exertion, and Monalisa could have sworn he was smiling. Could dogs smile? She wasn't sure. She could, though. And so she did. "Where is your stationary bike?"

"Downstairs. But I do not—"

"Great, I'll just go run down there and check that out while you—"

"*Nyet*. No bike. No downstairs."

She swallowed her smile. The fire had returned to his eyes. It vanished as quickly as it had appeared, but there was no doubt it had been there. "Okay." She got it. He hated the bike. And clearly wasn't a fan of stairs. "But the physical component of the therapy requires you to exercise your leg."

"Fine. We walk."

She looked over his shoulder. Outside of the parking pad, the land surrounding his house was a rolling, hilly, rocky scape thick with trees and brush. It might be fine for Grom, but Van could easily make his injury worse on that kind of ground. Maybe the paved part of the driveway would be okay, but it was still sloped, and he'd have to go down the porch steps to get to it. "Where?"

He gestured around. "The deck. It goes all the way around the house."

"It does?" She walked past him to look around the corner. Sure enough, the porch went past the front of the house and bent again to disappear on the far side. She glanced back the way she'd come and saw the same thing. She'd been so nervous when she'd arrived, she hadn't really paid attention to it. "Okay, we can make that work."

Van whistled to Grom, who trotted up onto the deck and sat at his feet. "Then let's begin."

A new set of nerves kicked in. And they were all related to the pressure put on her by her father. She needed this to work. "Okay, I'll just go upstairs and get my notebook, and I'll meet you in the living room."

He squinted at her. "No walking?"

"Yes, we'll be walking, but this rehab isn't just about repairing you physically. It's about your mental and emotional state as well. The League wants you whole in every way."

He snorted. "I do not recall the League ever being interested in much more than whether or not I would make weigh-in."

She knew that was essentially true. She shrugged and dug deep for a plausible explanation. "You're a very valuable member of the team. They really consider you the face of the organization, and they're just concerned about you. That's why I'm here, after all."

"Very interesting."

She had no idea how to take that. Did he think she was lying? Supposedly, her father had bribed all the right officials so that if Van called to check up on her, they'd agree she was here on League-approved business. Supposedly. But then, her father was pretty good about covering his backside in these kinds of dealings, and there was no way he'd jeopardize his potential payday by not having all possibilities covered.

Knowing that gave her a little boost of courage. "Do you want to talk to my boss?" She pulled her cell phone out of her back pocket. "I'm sure he can explain the process better."

Van stared at her phone for a second longer than she would have liked before saying, "Let's just get on with it."

She almost exhaled in relief. She tucked her phone away and smiled. "See you in the living room."

She didn't wait for an answer, just hustled back upstairs, grabbed her notebook and the list of questions she'd jotted down, and returned to the main floor.

He was sitting in his big chair, waiting, Grom at his feet.

She lifted her chin. There was no more time to pretend she was a rehab specialist. Now she had to *be* a rehab specialist. She took a seat on the couch perpendicular to him, flipped open her notebook, and clicked her pen. "All right. Let's get started."

He lifted his brows as if to say he was waiting on her.

She read off the first question, pen poised to write. "What would you say is the main thing holding you back?"

That earned her a hard look and a sharp tone. "I was bitten by a manticore."

She let her pen drop. "Yes, you were. But I'm talking about in the bigger sense of things."

He frowned. "How much bigger could that be?"

"Let's try a different question." She scanned the list. "How would your ideal self create a solution to this?"

His expression didn't change. "I would not have been bitten." He hesitated, like he had more to say, finally adding, "What is my ideal self?"

Yeah, what was his ideal self? She really had no idea. "I guess what I'm trying to uncover is how, in a perfect world, would you have avoided the thing that's holding you back?"

More glaring. "Same answer."

Okay, this wasn't working. "Next question." She bit the inside of her cheek. "Here's one. If your money could talk, what would it say to you?"

He jerked back slightly, a shadow of suspicion clouding his eyes. "Why do you ask about my money?"

"It's just a question." She flattened her notebook on her lap. "I'm trying to start a dialogue so I can see where your head's at and how to help you overcome this…" She didn't want to say depression, because that wasn't really the right word. Or was it? "This difficult mental state the injury has put you in."

He laughed, which was not at all the response she'd expected. "Difficult mental state? I am fine. I am happy. I have my house and my friends and Grom. What else do I need?"

She stared back at him. "Your career, maybe?"

His mood compressed again. "My career is over."

"Because of one injury?" Forget whatever script she'd been following, this time she had to answer with her gut. "I just can't believe a guy like you would let one injury take away everything you've worked so hard for."

"Believe it."

She glanced at her questions again, finding one that fit. "How does that decision square with the man people think you are?"

His mouth opened, then closed. He sat farther back in his chair, gaze darkening. Little shimmers of heat rose off him. "No more questions."

"You agreed to do this."

He tipped his head back and stared at the ceiling. His chest rose and fell for three breaths before he looked at her again. "Fine. Next."

"How does your decision to quit square with the man people think you are?"

He looked through her. Past her. And said nothing.

She sighed. "Van, I know these are tough questions, but I'm here to help. And if you can't talk to me about this, is there someone else you can talk to? Pretending like this injury hasn't drastically changed your life is just…silly. Of course it's changed your life. And it's awful and crushing and probably the worst thing that's ever happened in your charmed, dragon existence, but maybe, just maybe, if you stop acting like you're a tough guy who doesn't need any help, you might find that talking about it makes you feel better."

She took a breath, trembling slightly, and waited for him to throw her out. She shouldn't have said half of those things, but he was a very frustrating man, and she was tired of holding back when it came to frustrating men.

His brow crinkled, and he stared at the brace imprisoning his leg. "This is not the worst thing that has ever happened to me. But it is close." He shook his head and looked away. "Talking about feelings is not the Russian way. It is not the fighter's way either."

She stayed quiet, letting him talk. This was the most communicative he'd been since she'd arrived.

His arms were outstretched on the chair, and he flexed his hands into fists. "The answer is, it doesn't."

She tilted her head. "What doesn't?"

"My decision to quit. It doesn't square with the man people think I am. But that man..." He swallowed once and seemed to be collecting his thoughts. "That man isn't really me."

"Then who are you?"

He let out a long, slow breath. "I do not know anymore."

Her heart clenched at the sadness in his voice. She hadn't imagined how deeply this injury had affected him. It was staggering. Especially because of her part in it. In that moment, there was nothing she wanted more than to genuinely help him. "Maybe we can figure it out together."

He didn't say anything. Just sat there. Grom shoved his head under one of Van's big hands, looking for attention. Van scratched the dog, and Monalisa found an opening.

"Why did you adopt Grom?"

"Because I am settling down. And I always wanted a dog. They're loyal."

"And loyalty means a lot to you?"

He met her gaze again. "Without loyalty, what is there?"

She nodded. "Then you've been planning on settling down. This fight wasn't really the cause of it."

"I wasn't planning on it this soon."

Finally, they were having a real conversation. "Did you like fighting?"

"For a creature like myself, fighting is like breathing. I was born for it. Not because I am an angry man, or because I want to cause pain or destroy things, but because I am a dragon. We are protectors."

"What were you protecting by fighting in the League?"

"My name. My rank. My people." He put his thumb between Grom's eyes and rubbed, sending the dog into a heavy-lidded state of bliss. "Can you understand that?"

"Honestly, I'm not sure."

He looked at her. "Think about how your parents

protected you growing up. That instinct is the same in me. Just with a different focus."

She laughed bitterly and glanced away. If he only knew the truth.

"Why does that make you laugh?" he asked.

"No reason."

"I answered your questions. You answer mine."

She stared at the notebook in her lap. "Let's just say protecting me wasn't high on my parents' to-do list and leave it at that."

He was quiet a moment. "I am sorry. No child should feel that way about the people who gave them life."

She forced a smile as she looked up. "Yes, well, we all have our burdens to bear, don't we?" She cleared the emotion from her throat and brought the conversation back around to him. "If you feel that way about fighting, why not heal from this injury and then come back stronger than ever? Why not accept this rematch and show the world it was just a fluke?"

Something flickered in his gaze. He put his hands on the arms of the chair and pushed himself up, grabbing his crutch as he did so. "How much walking until you're happy?"

Van stood on the porch. He didn't want to think about anything but walking. One foot in front of the other. And he would do it until Lisa was satisfied. Then he was going into his office, shutting the door, and working on his accent until it was time to get ready for Pandora's housewarming party. And if his accent magically righted itself before it was time to get ready, he'd play solitaire. Or start tweeting. Or watch cat videos.

Anything to be done with today's therapy.

He was about to get the walking underway when the door behind him opened and Lisa came out. He glanced over his shoulder, wondering if she was going to keep up with the questions while he exercised, but she was no longer carrying her notebook. "I know how to walk."

She crossed her arms. "So let's see."

He started forward, more to put space between them than anything else.

"Nope."

He stopped. "I am walking wrong?"

She came side by side with him. "You're using the crutch."

"Because I must."

"Not for therapy to work. Remember the old stationary bike? You need to start bending your knee. It will hurt, but it will help work the venom out quicker. And that means you'll heal faster."

"I am wearing a brace."

"And yet, I know you can bend if you want to. You did it in the kitchen when you tried to help me up."

He stifled the urge to roll his eyes. "That hurt as much as it did because I was fighting against the brace."

She pursed her lips. They were full and pouty and only inches away, making it difficult for him to look at anything else. "I'm pretty sure that brace is adjustable. Let me check."

She crouched at his side to examine the brace.

He looked down. And straight into the valley of her cleavage. Her skin was pale and lightly freckled. And looked very, very soft. A deep, guttural sound left his throat before he could stop it.

She looked up. "What?"

He jerked his head up to stare into the woods. "Nothing."

"I heard something."

"Clearing my throat." He kept his eyes straight ahead as she went back to work. He felt a small tug on the brace.

"There." She stood up. "I adjusted the little

stabilizer knob. It was turned all the way up." She held her hand out.

He looked at her palm. "What?"

"Crutch, please."

"And if I fall, you think you can get me upright again? All…" He gave her a hard once-over. "Hundred and ten pounds of you?"

"You're not going to fall." She put her hand on the crutch and leaned in. "And my weight is my business, but if it makes you feel better, I weigh a hundred and thirty. Say anything about it, and that fall might happen sooner than you think."

He smiled at her feistiness, unable to help himself. "Threats, eh? Now that is how to get a Russian to respond." He handed her the crutch. This was going to be extraordinarily painful, but he could manage.

"We Irish are a stubborn lot." An odd look came over her face as she stepped out of his way.

He didn't give it much thought, because it was time to move. He put a little weight on his injured leg. Pain twisted around his joint and tightened his muscles, causing him to curse under his breath.

"I don't understand Russian, but that's probably for the best." She winced in sympathy. "I'm sorry it's so painful. I promise it gets better."

He limped forward, gritting his teeth against the onslaught of electrified nerves. The venom felt like fire, and not the good kind. It burned with every step, until the edges of his vision started to dim. He grabbed the hand railing and leaned against it to catch his breath.

Lisa raced to his side. "You did great. Wow, you walked the whole way to the end. That was amazing. That's enough for now. Here." She stuck his crutch under his arm. "I'm going to tighten up the stabilizer again, okay?"

He nodded. Her perfume teased his nose with its sweet, earthy smell. Maybe catching his breath wasn't such a good idea.

She crouched down like she had before.

This time, he didn't look at the woods. Instead, he very subtly shifted his gaze toward her and allowed himself to enjoy just how pretty she was.

Even better, though, was how beautiful she was inside. As a person. She was pushy and stubborn and unafraid. In that way, she reminded him of Pandora a little. But he'd never wanted to kiss Pandora.

He lurched a little as that thought filled his brain.

"Sorry, did I hurt you?"

"*Nyet*." He did *not* want to kiss Lisa.

Did he?

She stood. "Okay, you're stiff again."

He stared at her. "What?"

Her cheeks went pink, and she became suddenly preoccupied with getting a loose strand of hair behind her ear. "I mean, the brace is tightened. I, uh, I need to go record today in my workbook. You want help getting inside?"

"*Nyet*. No."

"Great. Good. I'll, um, okay. Later." She disappeared into the house.

He closed his eyes and stood right where he was,

letting the cold air wash over him. Something his father used to say ran through his head. *The appetite comes with eating.*

Van hadn't had the slightest desire to be involved with a woman. And now he was thinking about kissing Lisa.

Was it just her nearness? Because she was smart and pretty and interesting? Or because he was lonely? And pathetic?

She was probably only being nice to him because it was her job. He was injured too, which could make her feel sorry for him.

He opened his eyes, his jaw clenched tight. He was no one's pity case. She'd no doubt laugh if she knew what was going through his head right now. Well, that was done with.

He wheeled around and went into the house, then straight to his office, calling Grom to join him. The dog seemed to know where Van was going and ran ahead into the office to stand on the bed Van kept in there for him.

"Good dog," Van said as he shut the office door.

Grom turned around three times before flopping down with a sigh.

Van nodded. "You and me both."

He eased into his big leather chair, leg outstretched to the side. His knee ached worse than it had in days, but deep down, he felt a small sense of accomplishment at walking as far as he had without the crutch.

But then, he'd never doubted his ability to recover.

He just hadn't planned on being forced to do it this soon.

Whatever. Pain was only weakness leaving the body.

He turned on his computer and fired up the program he'd been using.

A woman's perfect American voice trilled out of the speakers. "I would like an orange soda."

Van repeated. "I would like an orange soda."

"This soda tastes good."

He echoed the sentence back. "This soda tastes good."

But soda wasn't even close to what he really wanted a taste of.

Monalisa stood in the middle of the guest room, which was more clearly Van's than ever before. His smoky scent lingered, and now that she'd gotten to know him a little, she could picture him here. Sitting in the reading nook with Grom at his feet, lounging on the bed watching fight videos, taking long hot, showers…

She shook her head and remembered she was here to do one thing and one thing only. Get him to agree to the rematch.

But knowing that and doing it were two very different things. The more she became acquainted with Van, the more she felt for him. And the more she liked him.

She hadn't counted on that at all.

Being in such close proximity didn't help either. She'd always had her reasons for avoiding the fighters, but being around Van was knocking those reasons down. He wasn't remotely like what she'd thought he'd be. Sure, he was gruff and sort of cranky, but the man was in a lot of pain. And he was dealing with the loss of his career.

You couldn't expect someone in that situation to be the picture of cheerfulness. If anyone understood that, it was her. She knew better than most how hard breaks could crush your spirit. Not that she considered herself crushed, but it was difficult some days to find the energy to keep fighting for what she wanted. Giving up and giving in were easy. Maintaining the courage to face down your fears, that took some doing.

And maybe that understanding of what Van was going through was part of why she was starting to feel something for him. It wasn't necessarily that she was attracted to him, although he was attractive in his own way. If you liked big, fit guys who loved animals and books and felt their purpose in life was to protect those they loved. It was just that he was so much more than what she'd thought a fighter would be.

He was smart. Funny. And had a smile that could light up a room—as cliché as that sounded. She had to wonder too, if being kept away from the world for so long by her father had resulted in a heightened curiosity about the opposite sex.

After all, Van was the first man she'd spent time with who wasn't her father or one of his underlings. And more than that, he was the first man she'd ever been alone with. Could that be making her feel something? She certainly hadn't expected to like the guy. Especially when he represented something she didn't really understand. Fighting.

Van had already told her that fighting was so much a part of him that it was like breathing. Was that really so much different than who she was? After all, she'd been fighting for her independence since she turned eighteen. She thought about it for a long moment.

Yes, they were very different. Van wasn't just a fighter, he was a protector. And she? She was a destroyer. Her gifts gave her the ability to do one thing with great power. To persuade, with the end result being complete ruination. Her kind had been the destroyers of men since there had been light and darkness in the world. And it was something her father loved to exploit.

If only she'd been born powerless, her life would be a very different one.

Monalisa dropped her head and stared at her feet. What was she doing here, besides the obvious? Yes, she was here to get Van to do her father's will. And beyond that, she was here to get the coin that would give her freedom. But this mission, this job her father had given her, it was one more chip out of the crumbling wall of her life. One more small effort on her father's part to tear her down and keep her for himself.

She couldn't run. She couldn't hide. She had no real means of escape. Once again, she was faced with the truth that she had no options. She either did what her father wanted, or she suffered the consequences.

She glanced toward the first floor. Maybe she should just go downstairs and tell Van the truth. She'd thought about it once before. Maybe if she explained everything, really *explained*, he would give in and agree to the rematch. She'd promise him anything to help her.

Well, not *anything*. Or…maybe she would. But Van didn't seem like the kind of guy who'd demand such a high price from a desperate woman.

But then again, maybe he would send her home to her father to deliver the message that Padraig's precious rematch was never going to happen.

She sighed. This was her life. A series of difficult decisions capped off with this, the granddaddy of them all. She thought some more about going downstairs and talking to Van. Who knew? Maybe he'd come up with a solution. That thought gave her a small glimmer of hope, even though she knew there was no real solution outside of the obvious one.

Her feet started moving before she could rethink it. She went downstairs slowly but deliberately. She thought she'd heard Van's office door close earlier, so she went in that direction. It was shut, but she could hear him talking to someone. Was he on the phone?

She went a little closer and listened. She heard a woman's voice, then him. He seemed to be repeating the woman over and over. What was he doing? The sentences didn't make a lot of sense. Then she realized that with each word he spoke, his accent diminished. Like he was deliberately trying to sound more American. How odd. She didn't think he was difficult to understand. In fact, his Russian accent was sort of charming.

Maybe even a little bit sexy.

Van was such an interesting person. And she realized that despite what she'd learned about him so far, he was still an onion with many layers to be peeled. It intrigued her that someone with his level of success, fame, and fortune would continue striving to better himself. It made her like him even more. And although she didn't think he needed to do anything about his cute accent, he clearly thought he did.

She smiled and shook her head. A guy like that had to be willing to help her, right? She reached out to knock on the door, but her cell phone vibrated in her back pocket.

She pulled it out and checked the screen. Her father was calling. She was supposed to have called him when she got in last night but, like always, he was the last person she wanted to talk too.

Avoiding him would only make things worse, something she'd learned the hard way.

She backed away from the door as she tapped the screen to answer, keeping her voice down until she put a little more distance between herself and Van's office. "Yes?"

"You were supposed to email or text me with an update. I've gotten nothing. What's going on?"

She climbed the stairs to the bedroom. "What's going on is I'm here and I'm doing the job I was sent to do."

"Good. How's it going?"

"You know I've barely been here a day, right?"

"More than enough time to bring him under the sway of your gifts."

She closed her eyes and clenched her teeth until the urge to hang up passed. "You want him to fight, then his heart really needs to be in it, not just his head and not just for magical reasons. I'm working on it."

"See that you do. The clock is ticking."

"I'm aware."

"Don't be afraid to use your feminine wiles."

"I'm going to pretend I don't know what you're implying."

"Then you're wasting a lot of natural resources."

"How are you actually my father?"

"I guess you were just born lucky." Cackling, he killed the call.

She stuffed the phone back into her pocket, anger coursing through her. There was no escaping the man and his control of her. She walked to the French doors, opened them, and went out onto the bedroom's balcony to breathe in the cold air.

It was beautiful here, and so different than Vegas. She liked the hilliness, the tall, majestic pines, and the smell of wood smoke in the crisp air. Even though the sun shone down on her, it didn't have the same oppressive feeling as it did in the desert.

She tipped her head up, letting the rays warm her face. It was nice, and for a moment, she forgot everything else.

But just for a moment. Because her life was impossible to ignore for long. What she would have loved more than anything was to shift into her supernatural form and disappear into the wilderness. In that form, she was the living embodiment of energy. She was light.

Beaming, pulsating light, with the power to draw men into oblivion. She could avoid the darker side of her nature very easily, unless, of course, her father was forcing her to use it.

Which brought her right back to the task she was here to do. With a sigh, she went back inside to go over her notes. She had a few hours until they had to leave for the housewarming party.

It would be nice to be around people who didn't know who her father was. People who weren't afraid of her or trying to win her favor. For once in her life, she could be a regular person. Wow, what would that be like?

She had no idea. But it would be fun to find out.

She settled on the bed with her laptop to dig into her work, but her gaze drifted toward the closet. What was she going to wear tonight?

On one hand, she wanted to disappear into the crowd, which ought to be easy enough since she wouldn't know anyone there. But on the other hand, she wanted to make Van take a second look. Not because her father had told her to use her feminine wiles, and not because her mother loved to tell her that men could be brought to heel with a dazzling smile and a few inches of cleavage, but because…she just did.

She didn't want to think too much about what that

might mean, but there it was. She wanted Van's attention. At least a little of it. At least enough to know what it felt like to be *noticed*.

She pushed her laptop to the side and padded over to the closet to look through the few things she'd brought. Her hand went to the dress her mother had secreted away in her bag. But no, there was no way that would be the right thing to wear. Unfortunately, the dress she'd packed was a simple navy day dress, and not all that snazzy.

She tried on the slim black skirt and ivory blouse she'd brought. She looked nice, but very secretarial. She swapped the skirt for jeans. That was a possibility. Then she tried on her black trousers. Very professional. And very boring. And not the right look, unless she planned to wait waiting tables somewhere in town.

Jeans again, this time with one of her sweaters. That looked nice.

Nice was the kiss of death, wasn't it? What about this outfit was going to make anyone look twice? She could be going shopping at the mall or running errands.

Tonight was a special event. A party.

Her gaze returned to the little black dress.

Van frowned at the brace on his leg. There was no way he was going to put that wretched thing on over any of his suit pants. Those suits cost too much to be mangled by that evil contraption. Instead, he settled for a dark pair of jeans with a crisp white shirt and a nice sport coat. It was still a good look. Not as dressy as he would have liked for Pandora's party, but she would understand.

Stupid brace.

He put on one of his gold watches, his dragon-self enjoying the feel of the valuable metal against his skin. Gold was a precious thing. Especially to a dragon. A thing to be hoarded, along with other fine metals and gems. And hoards had to be protected for times of need. Which was why Lisa wasn't allowed to go downstairs. No one was.

Well, Pandora. But she'd helped him build the house. She'd had to know about the vault. Even so, she hadn't seen the inside of it since he'd taken possession of the house.

Thinking of her made him take a moment to check himself over in the mirror. This was about as good as he could do. There was no way to erase the bend in his nose from being broken so many times or the resting scowl his face seemed to settle in without trying. Was it any wonder people were intimidated by him? He looked like a thug.

He supposed that was exactly what people thought of him. He knew his profession—*former* profession—as a fighter didn't help. But so what if people didn't want to take a chance to get to know him? He was fine being alone. Always had been. The few friends he had were plenty.

He grabbed his crutch and went out into the living room. Grom trotted along. No sign of Lisa. He called upstairs, "Are you almost ready? The car will be here."

"On my way down," she called back.

"All right." He let Grom out to do some business. "Stay close. No rolling in bad things either."

Grom snorted and took off.

Van shook his head as he went into the kitchen to get the champagne. Heels clicked on the stairs behind him. Lisa was on her way down. Good. Her timing was perfect. He was going to need help with the champagne. Two bottles and a crutch didn't mix well.

The heels clicked into the kitchen while he was taking the bottles out of the fridge.

"Can I carry those?"

It was nice of her to ask before he'd even said anything. "Yes, thank you. Just one will help."

He turned to hand her a bottle and almost dropped it. He stared, fixated, mouth open.

She took the champagne from his hand, her brows knitting. "You okay?"

He took a moment because he wasn't sure. His immediate answer would have been no. Not with her standing there in a black dress that was at once heart-stoppingly sexy and extremely ladylike. The neckline dipped off of her shoulders just enough to expose her collarbones, plunging slightly at the center in a vee that pointed toward her breasts. Like he didn't know where they were. The dress hugged every curve of her body, stopping just above her knees. Her legs were bare, and she wore shiny black heels that exposed her toes.

They were painted glittery gold. His gaze stayed on her toes a long moment. "You look nice."

Nice? That was the best he could do? Grom in his new collar looked *nice*.

Lisa looked…hot. Like an inferno. Like a metric ton of lava. Like the surface-of-the-sun *hot*.

She glanced down at her toes. "I realize now my shoes weren't the best choice for the weather here, but I wasn't thinking. Things are different in Vegas."

He nodded. Then looked at her. "You are from Las Vegas?"

Her eyes went blank for a second. "I, uh, yes. I work at the League offices there. Well, not at the offices, but out of those offices. That's where I report to, I mean."

He nodded again. He wasn't entirely sure what she'd just said. Her collarbones were too distracting.

She set the champagne on the island. "Is this dress too much? I wasn't sure what to wear. Everything else I had looked too businessy or too casual."

"*Nyet.* Is good." And his English was bad. He took a breath and tried to remember what he'd just been practicing. "Your dress is very good. You look very pretty."

Pretty was better. And as far as he was willing to go. If he told her what he really thought, she'd run screaming into the woods, thinking he was about to maul her.

She leaned her hip on the counter, her fingers loose on the neck of the bottle. "You look really great too. Casual but dressed up, and that jacket is perfect on you. Probably custom-made, right? With your shoulders, I can't imagine you can buy anything off the rack."

Did that mean she'd been checking out his body? Did she like the way he looked? Not every woman appreciated this many muscles on a man. Why was he having the thoughts of a high-school boy? What was wrong with him? Were naked collarbones all it took to shove him into puberty again?

"*Da.* All my suits must be made." He shrugged. "A small price to pay for what my body allows me to do." He cleared his throat. "Allowed."

"Not to mention that you're probably going to look a hundred times better than the rest of the guys at this party who aren't wearing a custom-made jacket." She smiled at him and picked up the champagne. "Did you say the car was here?"

His phone buzzed, no doubt the driver announcing his arrival. "Just now."

The first part of the ride was spent in silence, the addition of the driver somehow making Van self-conscious about anything he might say. It was all right, though. Lisa seemed occupied with the town as soon as they turned onto Main.

"Hey, this place is really cool." She stared out the window, the shop lights reflected in her pretty eyes. "Hah! Look at that. Hats In The Belfry. That's funny."

She kept up a running commentary even as they got onto the residential streets. "The houses here are so pretty. And so different from what I'm used to. I love them."

The driver pulled in front of Pandora and Cole's and parked.

Lisa sucked in a breath. "Is this seriously their house?"

"Yes." That much Van could say.

"It's amazing. I'd be throwing a party too if I lived here." She snuck a look at him. "I can't imagine cleaning it, though." She laughed. "It would take days."

He studied her as the driver went around to open her door. What did a woman like Lisa want out of life? She'd been concerned about losing her job. He understood that. But the women he'd met in the last few years had been focused on *things*. Or at least, what things he had and what things he might be able to provide. Expensive gifts, nice cars, big houses, posh trips, lavish meals.

He got out of the car as she did too. She'd already grabbed both bottles of champagne from the driver, who'd gotten them out of the back. Van walked to her side and offered her his arm. The one not piloting the crutch.

She took it, guiding the champagne carefully through. "That's very gentlemanly of you."

"Hand me one of those bottles. You should not carry both."

"You sure?"

"Yes." He opened his hand for her to place one of the bottles in it.

She did, but her smile seemed to lessen a bit.

"Something wrong?"

Her gaze shifted to the house. "It's nothing. Just a little nervous. Parties do that to me, I guess."

He nodded as he looked around. Cars lined the street in both directions. Every window in the house blazed with light, showing off just how packed it was inside. And more people were walking up the driveway. He understood how intimidating it must feel. "Everyone is very friendly."

"I'm sure they are."

"But you do not know anyone."

She smiled brighter as she made eye contact, but the crinkles around her eyes betrayed her nerves. "Just you."

"I'll introduce you. You will see. Very friendly." His dragon instincts kicked in a little, the urge to protect impossible to resist. But she wasn't in any grave danger. Being uncomfortable wasn't life threatening.

Still, he would do what he could. Normally, Pandora would take over in a situation like this, but tonight she was the hostess. She couldn't spend her evening making sure Lisa was all right. "Ready to go in?"

"Yes." She lifted her bottle like a soldier wielding a sword before heading into battle. "Let's do this."

Monalisa's nerves weren't a put-on. She really *was* nervous, and for a whole host of reasons. One, she was worried she'd be recognized. Yes, she was miles and miles away from home, but her father entertained a lot, and she was always expected to make an appearance, so her face was fairly well known in the upper classes of the supernatural community. She was the daughter of the king of the leprechauns, after all. And there was no way of knowing who might be here.

Two, she'd slipped up twice already by admitting she was Irish and saying she was from Vegas. She couldn't afford a third time, and with all the small talk she would have to make, there was no telling what might accidentally come out of her mouth. She was, apparently, not that great at lying.

Her father would be so disappointed.

And three, there were the normal nerves of going to a party where she didn't know anyone. Van would no doubt be busy with all his friends. They'd have their own stories and inside jokes and had probably known each other for ages. Meanwhile, she was not only a stranger, but she couldn't even be herself.

She'd be walking a fine line all evening between not saying too much while still trying to appear social. A night like this should be fun, but she doubted it would be for her. More like work.

Regardless, she was going to make the best of it, because for all those reasons to be nervous, there was the huge benefit of no one knowing who she was. With any luck. No leprechaun pun intended. Could there be someone in this town who'd hobnobbed with her father? Maybe. But it was probably unlikely, even with as many people as seemed to be here. She hoped. And so, clinging to that hope, despite the rest of her worries, she put a big smile on her face and prepared to face the evening.

They walked into the house, and Pandora greeted them almost instantly, even though there was a crowd milling about.

"I'm so glad you could come." She hugged them both, Van first, then Monalisa.

It shook Monalisa. She wasn't accustomed to much physical contact. People didn't generally touch her, being royalty, unless she touched them first. And her parents certainly weren't the affectionate kind.

Van held up his bottle of champagne. "For you."

Monalisa offered the one she was holding as well.

"Thank you so much! That's so fabulous. Who doesn't love good champagne? And that looks like exceptional bubbly." Pandora took both the bottles. "Now you two get in there and get something to eat and drink while I stick these babies in the fridge. I won't take no for an answer. There's too much of both, and I need help getting rid of it. Food's in the dining room here. Drinks are in the kitchen. Which is where I'm headed."

She winked at Monalisa and took off.

Van looked at her. "Eat or drink?"

She had no appetite for either, but a drink might take the edge off. Just one, though. No point in tempting fate. "Drink."

"Come," Van said, patting Monalisa's hand. Then he took hold of his crutch and moved them forward.

Oddly, other than a few nods of the head and some interesting looks, no one paid much attention to Van as they made their way deeper into the house. They finally stopped in the kitchen, where the party was especially boisterous around the table. Small groups of people were clustered together, laughing and talking and enjoying short glasses of something pink. The punch on the table, from the looks of it.

She let go of Van's arm. The heat from his body had sunk into her, making her almost shiver as it began to dissipate. "Why don't I get us some of that punch? Seems to be the thing to drink. Unless you want something else?"

"No. That is good."

"Okay, I'll be right back." She made her way to the table and the enormous crystal bowl sitting there. The pink punch had slices of citrus floating in it, and there were bottles of top shelf vodka and rum sitting in chillers nearby. Maybe so guests could add their own spirits? She watched as someone came up to the table and did just that.

That was a great idea. She put a splash of vodka into two clear plastic cups, figuring that was what any reasonable Russian would prefer, then filled the cups the rest of the way with punch. Thankfully, not a single person spoke to her the whole time. So far, so good. She picked up the drinks and turned to head back to Van.

A teenage girl with earbuds draped around her neck stood in front of Monalisa. "Hi, I'm Kaley, and my dad said I need to work on my social skills by actually talking to people in person and not by text. So, like, this is me doing what he said. Who are you?"

Monalisa almost laughed. "I'm Lisa. Nice to meet you, Kaley."

"Are you a friend of my dad's or Pandora's?"

"Technically, neither." Monalisa lifted one of the punch cups in Van's direction. He was talking to a tall, distinguished older man. "I came with Mr. Tsvetkov over there."

Kaley glanced his way. "Oh, cool. I like Van. He's like the toughest guy I know in real life. His dog is super cool too. Have you met his dog? I'd like to get a dog, but Pandora's got a cat, and well, you know." She rolled her eyes.

This kid didn't have any trouble being social. "Sure, that could be tricky. And yes, I've met Grom. He is definitely a cool dog."

Kaley's eyes narrowed. "So, are you Van's girlfriend? That would be good. Because Pandora said he could totally use one to snap him out of this funk."

Monalisa almost choked. "No, I'm his rehab therapist. I'm just here to help him recover from his injury."

"Oh." Kaley thought about that a moment. "Then your job is to, like, get him happy again?"

"You could say that." Happy enough to get back into the ring.

A big smile broke out on Kaley's face. "Then you're kind of like his girlfriend, right?"

"No, it's strictly a professional relationship." She tried to catch Van's attention to see if he'd pick up on the signal that she needed to be rescued, but he was still talking.

"Well, your aura's pretty cool. And based on that, I think you two would make a good couple, so if you like him, like *like* him like him, you should go for it."

"I don't—what did you say about my aura?" The tiniest panic alarm went off in Monalisa. So small, it probably wasn't even worth listening to. Not much anyway.

Kaley preened. "I'm a witch like Pandora. She's my mentor, actually. She's teaching me all about witch stuff, and that's my gift. Reading auras. She says no one can do it as good as I can. And yours is, like, super interesting."

"Oh? How so?" The alarm got a smidge louder.

"I don't know what kind of supernatural you are, but..." Kaley leaned in like she was about to share something top secret. "You're kind of dangerous, aren't you?"

The alarm turned into full-fledged panic, freezing Monalisa. She had no idea how to respond. Admitting the truth wasn't going to help. Especially not if this kid decided to share her new-found info with everyone she knew. Like Pandora, who would undoubtedly tell Van.

Monalisa had no choice but to keep up the lie she'd begun. But what if Kaley could see the dishonesty in her aura too? She tried to come up with an answer that stayed clear of both sides. "Aren't we all in our own way?"

Kaley nodded. "Totally. And it's cool with me. I mean, I dig that you and Van both have that dark and light thing going on. You even share some of the same colors. His has a lot deeper greens and sparks of gold and red—like scales, which makes sense, right? But his aura also has the dark edging like yours. There are some definite similarities, for sure."

Intrigued, Monalisa had to know more. "What does mine look like?"

"It's pale green with streaks of blindingly bright light, plus a thin inner band of gold, and then the whole thing fades to black at the edges, which is what Van's does. Your black is thicker, though, so you must be a little more dangerous than he is. Which is super cool."

"That is very interesting. No one's ever read my aura before. Thank you for sharing that with me." She wasn't sure what to do with this new information. It *was* interesting. Thankfully, she felt like this was a good ending to the conversation. "I'd better get this punch to Van. Nice meeting you, Kaley."

"You too, Lisa. And I better go see if my grandfather needs anything. Oh, if you see my dad, tell him I was totally social, okay?"

"Will do." Monalisa made her exit. She got the feeling Kaley's dad was Pandora's boyfriend, so that made him Cole. She hadn't been introduced to him yet, but it would probably happen before the night was over.

She joined Van and almost breathed a sigh of relief that she'd gotten out of the chat with Kaley without revealing more about herself than she wanted to. Maybe she had a little of that paternal luck after all. If so, that was all she wanted from her father. Ever.

She held Van's punch out to him without interrupting the conversation he was still involved in.

Van took the cup. "Lisa, this is Bartholomew Stanhill."

The older man stuck his hand out. "Pleasure to meet you, miss. Please, call me Stanhill. Everyone does."

"All right." His British accent added to his charm. "Nice to meet you too. Are you a friend of Pandora's too?"

"You could say that." He smiled. "I'm sweet on the mother of the girls, Corette."

She shook her head. "Is that Pandora's mother? Or are the girls someone else? I just met Kaley." She laughed. "I'm Van's rehab therapist, so I'm a little clueless as to who's who."

"Not to worry, love. Corette Williams is the girls' mother, and the girls are Charisma, Marigold, and the hostess of this party, Pandora. Kaley is Cole's daughter."

"Oh, I see. And Cole is Pandora's boyfriend. That much I know."

"Righto, now you've got it. I think Cole's father, Jack, is around here somewhere too."

She was never going to remember all these names, but there probably wasn't going to be a test either. "So you and Corette are an item. How nice!"

His grin expanded. "We are. And it is. Engaged and the whole bit. Wanted to lock that down, I did."

A handsome older woman sidled up to them, slipping her arm through Stanhill's. "Did I just hear you say you wanted to 'lock me down,' darling?"

Stanhill made a face like he'd been caught. "Speaking of the most gorgeous woman I know, here she is. My lovely partner, Corette Williams. Corette, this is Lisa. She's here to fix up Van."

Van snorted at that, but said nothing more.

Corette's expression turned curious as she looked at Monalisa. "You're a matchmaker?"

"No. I'm not fixing him up that way." Monalisa couldn't begin to imagine having that job. "I'm his rehab therapist."

"Ah, I see." Corette smiled. "You have your work cut out for you, then, don't you? Lovely to meet you, Lisa."

"Very nice to meet you. Your daughter has done a wonderful job on this house."

Corette looked around. "Cole did the heavy lifting, but Pandy did the design side. They make a great team."

Stanhill nudged her. "That reminds me, I need to talk to that boy about his intentions with Pandora. Been long enough, don't you think?"

A mysterious gleam filled Corette's eyes. "I do think. I also think it's going to be remedied very soon."

That got Van's attention. "What do you know?"

Corette shrugged ever so slightly. "I've been sworn to secrecy."

The bell-like chiming of silverware being tapped on a glass rang out above the hum of the crowd.

Everyone turned toward the living room. A tall, dark-haired man with black eyes and glasses stood in the center, a fork in one hand and a nearly empty glass of beer in the other. "If I could have everyone's attention for a moment."

He scanned the crowd. "Where's Pandora?"

"I'm here," she answered from deep in the throng.

"Well, come up here next to me."

Monalisa leaned over to whisper to Van, "Cole?"

He nodded.

Pandora joined Cole. He slipped his arm around her waist before he began again. "We want to thank all of you for coming out tonight to help us celebrate our house being complete. It's been a long journey and an awful lot of hard work, but I think you'll agree with me, well worth it."

The party guests murmured their agreement.

He smiled. "I think you'll also agree with me about something else I believe to be well worth it."

He set the fork and glass down, then pulled out a small velvet box from his pocket. A moment later, he disappeared from view as he bent down on one knee.

Gasps arose all around them, and Corette put her hand to her mouth, her eyes damp with happy tears.

"Pandora Williams, will you make me the happiest man alive and be my wife?"

Pandora, who looked a little weepy herself, nodded, then squeaked out a "Yes."

The crowd erupted in cheers. Cole jumped to his feet, picked Pandora up, and whirled her around.

Monalisa felt like she'd just witnessed something amazing, but also very personal. There were no proposals in her future, that much she knew. Not unless her father ordered a man to marry her. Which seemed highly unlikely since he'd been set on keeping men away from her since she'd turned eighteen. Not that it was much of a task. No man in his right mind would fall for her. Not when her father controlled her life the way he did.

And who could blame a man for steering clear of her? She didn't even want the life she lived, so she understood why no one else would want to share it with her.

The proposal, for all its romance, had left her a little sad.

She glanced at Van. He was smiling and clapping along with everyone else. She did her best to shut down the pity party welling up inside her. This was a happy moment and absolutely not about her or her crappy life. Her feelings could wait until she was alone. Or maybe she'd just ignore them altogether.

Stanhill and Corette pushed their way forward to congratulate the couple.

Van threw back the remaining punch in his cup, then set it aside. "Come. You can meet Cole."

Monalisa took his lead, downing what was left of her drink, then put on a bright smile. "Lead the way."

"I think you had too much champagne."

"*Nyet*." Van leaned on Lisa more than he intended to, but getting up the steps was hard. And she was soft in all the right places.

The next step looked very far away. Hmm. Maybe he had had too much to drink. Even though he felt fine. Better than fine, in fact. Except for the ache in his damn leg. "Maybe too much vodka."

She laughed softly. "Maybe."

He cut his eyes at her as they climbed together. She smelled so good and looked so pretty. "Too much celebration."

Her arm was around him. It was a nice feeling. "But your friend got engaged. If there was ever a time for too much celebration, that was it."

"*Da*, that was it. But still, maybe, too much."

"You'll be fine in a couple hours. Dragons have impeccable metabolisms." She got him onto the landing and let him lean on his crutch.

He scowled. "Not with venom in my system." That stupid bite had ruined everything.

"Oh, yes, right. I forgot about that."

"Is why I am *p'yanyy*."

"I'm going to assume that means inebriated."

He smiled and winked at her. She was so smart. And pretty. "You learn Russian very good."

"Thanks." She laughed again, dipping her head so that her hair partially covered her face.

Her coat looked thin to him. She must be cold. "We should go inside."

"We should," she agreed. "But you have to unlock the door first."

"Mmm, *da*…" He wrapped his good arm around the porch post as the floor beneath him seemed to tilt. Damn venom. "Key in pocket."

Her brows lifted as she looked at him. "Are you asking me to get it out?"

"*Da*. Right pocket."

"I'm not sure you're that sloshed, but seeing as how you're an injured man…" She pursed her lips, then gave him a stern look and came closer. Her fingers wiggled into the pocket of his jeans, sending a bright jolt of electricity through him. She pulled her hand free, stepped back, and her stern expression deepened. "There's nothing in there."

"Other right."

Frowning at him in a way that made him want to laugh, she came close again and dug her fingers into the opposite pocket.

He felt them hook the key ring and drag it out.

Before she could step away, he turned his face into her hair and inhaled. "You smell good."

Her hand left his pocket, but the rest of her stayed where she was. "Thanks. You smell like smoke. But I guess you know that."

He nodded. "Does it bother you?"

She shook her head slowly, her sparkling green eyes alive with something needy. "No. I...like it."

And he liked her. Very much. Impulse took over. His pulse amped up at the thought of what he was considering. It was reckless and foolish, but he'd done worse in his life, and the drinks he'd had said go for it. So he did.

He bent his head and brushed his mouth over hers. The barest hint of a kiss. A test, really. To see what her reaction was. And if she'd let him do it again.

He watched her, his heart thumping, heat rushing through his system like gasoline had just been dumped on his internal furnace. That wasn't the vodka, that was Lisa.

She blinked her eyes open and stared at him, her lips slightly parted and her cheeks flushed. She didn't say a thing. But she didn't push him away either.

So he tried it again.

This time, she kissed him back. She pressed her mouth to his as a gentle moan left her throat.

The sound spurred him on. He put his free hand on the small of her back and pulled her closer as the kiss deepened. The world spun around him, but he was focused on her and her alone. She was as soft and sweet as he'd imagined.

Her tongue traced the seam of his mouth, teasing him, then she suddenly sucked in a breath and stepped back. Her eyes flashed with light for a moment as she put her hands on his chest. "We shouldn't do this. This is supposed to be a business relationship."

He smiled. "Says who?"

"Says the League. I'm here to rehabilitate you. Not climb into your bed."

Now there was a thought that gave him pause. Did her saying that mean she was thinking about it too? "I feel very rehabilitated right now."

She shook her head. "You've had too much to drink. And I'm on the borderline. We should just get inside and go to sleep."

He grinned.

"Separately." She turned around, key in hand, and unlocked the front door, giving him a chance to admire her backside. She pushed the door open, and Grom came charging out. She pointed toward the yard. "Go ahead, go do whatever you need to."

Finally, she looked at Van again. "I'll stay out here and watch him. Unless you need help getting in?"

"*Nyet.* I can do it." A new idea filled his head. "But maybe help changing."

She snorted. "Nice try."

"Just with brace. That is all I mean." He limped past her into the house and turned around. "Cross my heart."

"I guess I can do that. But we do it on the couch, not your bed."

"I am happy to do it wherever you want." He was on the edge of laughing, his mind putting far more meaning into her words than she was implying. He knew what she meant—and most certainly what she didn't—but in the moment, he just wanted to enjoy teasing her.

She gave him a look that said she was wise to what he was thinking. "Okay, fine. Just let me get Grom in."

"Good. *Spasibo*." He made his way to the couch, leaving the door open, but didn't sit. When she turned around to keep an eye on Grom, Van went over to the fireplace and lit the logs inside. Nice of Norma to get a fire ready when she was here earlier. It was almost like she knew he was going to need to set a romantic mood. The flames leaped and crackled, the sound soothing him.

Fire did that for dragons.

Grom's nails clicked on the steps outside. Van limped back to the couch and sat, waiting for Lisa.

She followed Grom inside, closed the door, then walked toward Van. "We should maybe talk about this."

"About my brace?"

She pursed her lips. Her sweet, soft lips. "You know what I mean."

"The kissing?"

"Yes, the kissing."

He shrugged. "We are adults. Adults sometimes kiss. What else is there to talk about?"

She sat beside him, exhaling softly. "That's all this

104

was, then? Just a sometimes kiss? A kiss because we both overindulged?"

He nodded, the crackling of the fire singing him to sleep. But he wasn't ready for bed yet. Not with Lisa so close. "And if it was more?"

"It can't be."

He studied her. She was holding something back. Hiding something. Her business, to be sure. But it made him feel sorry for her. Whatever it was, could it be so important that it would prevent her from experiencing a little pleasure? Was she worried this kiss would affect her job? "I won't say anything to the League. I promise. I am sure many of their employees have become friendly with some of the fighters. It would be natural, no?"

She fixed her gaze on his brace. "I suppose so."

Was that it, then? He wasn't sure. There was no relief in her face. "What else is bothering you?"

She looked up. "Nothing." The smile that followed seemed there only to cover her true feelings.

He let it go. If she didn't want to tell him more, that was her right. He would leave her alone. As much as he didn't want to.

The surprise of that thought would be enough to occupy his thoughts all night. And then some.

Monalisa couldn't explain what was going on inside her no matter how much she wanted to spill everything. Van would throw her out if she did. There was no other possible reaction for him to have when he learned that the woman he'd just kissed—who'd just kissed him back and enjoyed it—was the same woman who'd used her gifts to ruin his life. And was here to do it again.

He would be livid. And he would have every right to be.

Which was why the kissing stopped now. It had to. She couldn't get involved with the man she'd been sent to dupe. Because, eventually, the truth would come out. And if he had feelings for her, those feelings would just make things worse.

So whatever had just happened between them on the porch? That was absolutely, completely over.

Even if kissing him was the best thing she'd ever experienced.

Keeping her cool on the outside required serious work right now, because on the inside she was jumping up and down and melting into a puddle and screaming like she'd won something while giggling as if she was eight years old again. Possibly floating a little too.

The man could *kiss*.

No, she didn't have anything to compare it to, but she was pretty sure she would have known if the kiss had been bad. Which it wasn't. Not even a tiny bit. A bad kiss wouldn't leave her wanting more. A *lot* more.

Van was such a surprise. He was gentle while still being strong. He'd made her shiver as he'd set her on fire. And with only the touch of his mouth on hers, he'd lit up every nerve in her body.

He put the super in supernatural.

And with that one kiss, she was smitten. Ruined, really. Because for the rest of her life, he would be the ruler all other men were measured by. And if she lived to be a thousand years old, she was always going to wonder…what if?

She swallowed down the growing lump in her throat and looked at him. "I guess we should get that brace off, huh?"

He nodded, eyes a little heavy. She was tired too. Tired of all the pretending. Tired of her father. Tired of not getting to live her own life.

She bent to work on Van's brace. The straps were Velcro, and there were plenty of them. She dug her nails beneath the first one, trying to shake the lingering questions in her head: What would it be like in this instance if her life was her own?

She ripped the first strap open, the sound gratifying. If there were no constraints on her, she wouldn't have stopped kissing him so soon. That much she knew.

But there *were* constraints on her. More than there were straps on this brace. So she'd stopped and done her best to dissuade him not to do it again.

No matter how much pleasure the thought of more kissing brought her.

She tore the second strap open.

No matter how much misery her life caused her.

The third strap followed. Then the fourth. Each

tearing sound underscoring her wretched existence.

She needed to get away from Van before she stopped caring and blurted out everything. Or started rage-crying.

There was only one way to fix this mood. Shifting and allowing herself the freedom of being in her true form. It made her happy when all else failed.

She freed the last strap and pushed to her feet. "All done. I'm going to bed."

She didn't wait for his response, just ran upstairs. She stepped out of her heels, then ditched the dress her mother had bought her. She was antsy, but it was too soon to shift. She'd have to wait until Van was asleep to be sure that he didn't come looking for her for any reason.

In his current state, that was definitely a possibility.

As if on cue, he called out for her. "Lisa? Are you all right?"

She tipped her head back to stare at the ceiling. No, she wasn't all right. And she might never be. She blinked back the threatening tears. "Yes. Just tired."

More lies. What did it matter?

Her phone buzzed from the nightstand where she'd left it plugged in. She knew before looking at it who was calling.

She grabbed it and punched the answer button. "What?"

"No hello? No 'Hi, Daddy'?"

"Not for you. What do you want?"

"You know what I want. An update."

She walked to the railing overlooking the living room. Van wasn't on the couch, and Grom wasn't around either. Maybe they'd gone to bed. She went into the bathroom and closed the door just to be sure. "I'm working on it."

"I want specifics."

"Even if I can get him to agree to fight, he still needs to heal."

"I understand that. And time will be allotted. But there is no if about getting him to agree to fight. That *will* be the outcome. Do you understand?"

"I understand I have no choice. Do you understand what a horrible person you are?"

He sighed. "Monalisa, you are never going to get anywhere in this world."

"Not with you holding me prisoner." She hated him. Hated what he'd done to her. What he kept doing to her.

"I'm enabling you to fulfill your true purpose."

"You're a vile little man with a soul as black as night." She hung up. *Enabling you to fulfill your true purpose.* What a crock.

Trembling with anger, she tossed her phone on the bed and walked out onto the balcony in nothing but her bra and underwear. There was no one to see her. She stood there, gulping down the cold night air in an effort to calm herself.

It wasn't working that well.

She wanted to shift. She needed to shift. So she closed her eyes and gave in.

Van was nearly asleep, dreams of Lisa already leading him into a blissful fog, when a flash of light and Grom's sharp, sudden bark snapped him awake.

Whatever intoxication he'd felt was gone now. He blinked into the darkness. In a split second, his dragon eyes adjusted. He pushed onto his elbows. Grom was standing tensely, ears at attention, his entire body looking poised for action.

Van sat up. "*Ko mne.*"

Grom relaxed, walked over, and settled his big head on the bed beside Van, letting out a little woof as if to say, *Shouldn't we go see what that was?*

Van stroked the dog's head, scratching his ears. "Is all right, pup."

What had that been? A trick of his mind? Like when the sensation of falling sometimes woke him? Was this his mind playing games with him? Instead of falling, would he now be reliving the burst of light that had caused him to lose against Ronan? Maybe it was the venom in his system doing it. A side effect of that poison.

Seemed logical.

Grom whimpered and nudged his head forward.

Van sighed and patted the bed. "All right, you big baby."

Grom crawled up, turned three times, then flopped down beside Van. Snores fluttered out of him within minutes. Van, on the other hand, couldn't go back to sleep that easily. And not just because there was a beast of a dog now taking up half the bed.

He slid himself out the other side, wincing as the movement caused fresh pain in his leg. Once he reached the edge of the bed, he put his feet on the floor and reached for his crutches. He kept a pair by the bed for emergencies, because there was no way he could get that brace on quickly.

Hoisting himself up, he went out to have a look around. Maybe the flash had woken Lisa too. At least then he'd know it hadn't just been in his mind.

But all was quiet and nothing seemed disturbed. He stood at the bottom of the stairs leading to his bedroom that Lisa now occupied. Not a sound. Not even the faintest bit of breathing. That was odd. But maybe the covers were muffling them.

He went to the windows on the side of the house and looked into the dark. Nothing unusual out there either.

Maybe that flash *had* just been in his head. Seemed like it more and more. He should go back to bed. Sleep was important for healing.

He was halfway through the living room when he heard a sound he recognized. The French doors on the upstairs balcony quietly opening and closing.

His entire body went on alert just like Grom's had at the flash of light. Could that flash have been related to something sinister? Only a fool would break into this house, but considering what the level beneath Van contained, the temptation existed. As did fools. And if Lisa had left that door unlocked…

The thought of her in danger charged him to act. The stairs would take too long and cause too much pain. But there was another option. One potentially more painful. But it would be quick, and it would give him the element of surprise.

He dropped his crutches onto the couch. Then he braced himself for the pain and jumped.

The burst of movement took him up and over the second-story railing and onto the landing just outside the bedroom.

Lisa shrieked and flattened herself against the French doors, her eyes sparking with the same flash of green he'd seen once before. Her scream set Grom off, filling the house with barking.

She had only underwear on. Two small strips of black lace and silk.

The sight caused Van's breath to catch in his throat, and the pain in his leg became a memory. At least temporarily. Her skin was luminous in the dark. She was stunning. Like a wild creature. He somehow found his voice. "What are you doing?"

She covered herself with her hands. "I should be

asking you that question. Why are you up here?"

"I heard the door." He gestured to the balcony. Grom was still barking. "I thought someone was breaking in."

"Well, they're not."

He yelled down for Grom to hush, before turning back to her. "What were you doing outside in your underwear?"

"You could turn around, you know."

Turning would hurt. Instead, he stared at the ceiling. Didn't matter. The image of her in those two flimsy scraps of black were seared into his memory now.

She let out a frustrated sigh. "I was just getting some air."

"I see." He didn't exactly. She could have opened a window.

"I thought you were asleep."

"I was, but—" Telling her what he thought he'd seen probably wouldn't help him with whatever rehabilitation was supposed to be happening. "I woke up. Grom climbed on the bed. I was restless."

"Well, everything's fine. You can go back downstairs now."

Except he wasn't sure he could. Not without help. He glanced toward the steps. "I do not think I can."

"You jumped up here. Can't you jump down?"

"Too much pain." He looked at her again, forgetting that he was supposed to be averting his eyes.

"Right." Her brows rose, and she pointed at the ceiling. "Do you mind?"

"*Prosti*." He lifted his gaze again. "I need my crutches. That is all."

"Where are they?"

She was moving toward the closet. Getting clothes. "On the couch."

"Okay, I'll get them." A hanger chimed against the closet's metal bar. "You can stop staring at the ceiling."

He did. Only to see she was wearing one of his shirts. A green and blue flannel that was worn soft from years of washing. One of his favorites. Never more so than now, with her long pale legs peeking out under the hem. It skimmed the tops of her thighs.

She tugged at it. "I hope it's okay I put this on. I forgot to bring a robe."

He nodded, lost for words. It was very, very okay.

"I'll be right back." She jogged down the steps, returning a minute later with his crutches. She handed them over. "I'm sorry I made you think someone was breaking in. I won't go out at night anymore."

"Go out whenever you want. *Do* whatever you want. I just didn't realize…" He shrugged as he got the crutches under him. "My instincts are hard to ignore. I thought you were in danger."

She put her hand on his arm. "You jumped up here and endured that pain because you thought I was in danger?"

He nodded, staring into her eyes and the depth of new emotion there. "I told you. I am a dragon. We are fighters, and we are protectors. You are in my house.

My guest." He hesitated. "My friend. I will not let harm come to you."

The muscles in the slender column of her throat worked as she whispered his name. "Van..." She shook her head, her eyes suddenly liquid.

She planted her hands on his chest, leaned in, and kissed him.

This kiss was nothing like the first. It wasn't cautious or hesitant or the slightest bit timid. This kiss was hungry and needy and almost knocked Van off his feet.

Heat erupted inside him, kindled by her demanding mouth and her hands on his bare chest. Three points of contact. Three brands burned into his skin. The heat turned into fire and lit him from within. His fire, her light. Together, they caused a combustion of his senses unlike anything he'd ever felt before.

He leaned on the crutches for support so that he could touch her. His hands went to the curve of her waist, as comfortable there as if her hips had been under his grasp a thousand times before. And yet, touching her like that was utterly new, thrilling him down to his soul with the intimacy of it.

She was warm beneath his flannel. Not at all like a woman who'd just come in from the cold. But very much like a woman who was as on fire as the dragon she was kissing.

He lifted his hands to thread his fingers through the silk of her hair, and he whispered against her lips, "Lisa, you are so beautiful."

A soft noise, part sob, part gasp, left her. She eased

back, sucking her bottom lip between her teeth. "I know I said no kissing. And I know I started that. But…"

She took a breath and shook her head like she couldn't quite find the words.

He smiled gently. "No need to explain."

He expected her to back away, but she stayed close to him a little longer. "Thank you."

"You are welcome." He wasn't sure what she was thanking him for—the kiss? Trying to protect her? Not judging her after she'd told him there could be nothing between them? Whatever it was, it didn't matter nearly as much as her being safe and happy. "Now you must go to sleep so you can rehabilitate me again tomorrow."

She laughed softly. "After seeing you jump up here, I think you're probably capable of more than you've been letting on."

"Ah, but you have not seen me get back down." That was going to be a lengthy, painful process.

She glanced at the stairs, then back at him. "Can I help?"

"I will be fine." He kissed her forehead. "Good night, beautiful Lisa."

She blushed. "Good night, Van."

He left her standing there and slowly worked his way down the stairs with his crutches. The pain was excruciating. But her kiss lingered on his lips, numbing the worst of it most pleasurably to the point that he was still smiling when he reached the bottom, still smiling when he climbed back into bed, and still smiling when Grom crawled up and joined him.

The delicious aromas of coffee and bacon woke Monalisa, along with the hushed sound of voices. Van and Norma.

Monalisa smiled and stretched and yawned. Everything about today felt better. And not just because she'd gone to bed with Van's kiss still warming her lips. But that probably had a lot to do with it.

And even though she knew that kiss had been the last one—it had to be—she was okay with that, because that kiss she'd taken for herself. The impulse had been so strong she'd been unable to avoid it, just like the impulse to shift and spend a few moments in her true form outside last night.

She blinked up at the ceiling, but Van's face was all she saw.

No one had ever acted so selflessly to protect her. Yet, he had done it without a second thought. And he barely knew her.

Kissing him had been the only way she'd been able to express how deeply moving that was. Words would not have done it. Words would have only revealed how lacking her life was. How sad and pathetic and awful.

Although it didn't feel that bad this morning.

She'd fallen asleep in his shirt, so she left it on now as she got out of bed and padded to the railing.

He was in his seat at the breakfast bar, his broad back to her, his crutches leaning on the counter. Unlike last night, he had a shirt on. But his body was no less amazing.

An indulgent smile curved her mouth at the memory. "Morning," she called down.

Norma looked up as Van swiveled the barstool around. "Morning," they both answered.

Norma went back to stirring some sort of batter. Bacon sizzled in a pan behind her.

Van stayed right where he was, staring up at Monalisa. He was in sweat pants and a T-shirt, both of which fit him remarkably well. And she wasn't sure, but it seemed like he checked out her legs before meeting her eyes again. "How did you sleep?"

"Good." So good. "No brace this morning?"

He shrugged one shoulder. "Not yet. Breakfast is almost ready."

"I'll be right down." No brace could be a good sign. Maybe he was feeling better. That would be wonderful. She put on some leggings and a pair of thick socks meant for boots, then took the stairs. She fixed a cup of coffee and sat next to him, elbows on the counter as she had the first sip. Delicious. And perfect, like this day was going to be. "What are you working on over there, Norma?"

"Syrniki. They're one of Van's favorites."

Monalisa shook her head. "I have no idea what that is."

"Cheese pancakes," Van said.

Monalisa couldn't stop herself from making a face.

He laughed. "They are good. You'll see."

Norma carried two plates over. Both held stacks of small, round pancakes that were toasty brown and drizzled with red sauce and a creamy syrup. "Cottage cheese pancakes, to be exact. With jam and sweetened condensed milk. Try them. If you don't like them, I'll make you something else."

"No, I'm sure they'll be great." They actually looked pretty good, especially the way Norma had prepared them. And there was always the side of bacon.

Van gave her a look. "Grom loves them."

She snorted. "I'm not sure that's a ringing endorsement. I've seen Grom lick his privates like it was an ice cream sundae."

His mouth twitched like he was trying not to smile. "Syrniki are very good."

"We'll see."

Van dug into his with great enthusiasm, letting out a long, loud, "Mmm" as he chewed.

Monalisa tried a bite. The jam was raspberry. And the pancakes were really good. Creamy and sweet and tender. She swallowed the mouthful. "Okay, I was wrong to be skeptical. These are great."

"Told you," he teased.

"Yes, you did." She ate some more, and before she knew it, her plate was clean. "Wow, I can't believe I ate all that."

Norma looked up from the dishes. "You want more?"

"No, I'll burst."

Norma looked at Van. "I know you do."

He held his plate out and smiled.

Norma filled it, then added a single pancake to Monalisa's plate. "Eat, you're too skinny."

"I won't be if I keep eating like this." But she cut into it with her fork anyway.

"That's the point." Norma smiled. "I'm doing laundry today, Lisa, so if you have any, I'm happy to add it to the load."

"No, I'm good. Thank you." Even though Van had already seen her in her underwear, something about mixing them with his in the wash was far more intimate.

"All right. I'll let Grom in, then I'll be in the laundry room if you need me. Unless you need anything else, Van?"

"No. All good."

"All right. Holler if you need me." Norma went to the front door to get the dog, who came galloping in a few moments later. He walked over to Van as Norma headed to the laundry room.

Monalisa leaned toward Van, who was scratching Grom's head. "She's not going to spend all day in the laundry room, is she?"

120

"Only until the laundry is done. There's a television in there and a nice chair. She likes to watch her stories while she works. And sometimes, she naps."

Monalisa laughed. "That doesn't sound so bad after all."

"She gets her work done, so why should I care?" Van pushed his plate away and wiped his mouth. He turned his head to look at Monalisa. "I suppose you want me to walk today."

"I do. But I also think you really need to get on that stationary bike."

He frowned. "It is downstairs."

"But the stairs can be part of the therapy. You live in a house full of them, so you need to get back to using them anyway. Plus, the more you do, the faster you'll heal. And really, don't you want to sleep in your own bed again?"

"I do." A wicked gleam passed through his eyes. Like he was imagining himself in that bed, and not alone.

She cleared her throat, but let it pass. Then she realized that her father might have been a little bit right. Unfortunately. But using her feminine wiles wouldn't be the worst thing in the world, especially if they got Van to exercise and heal. And regardless of whether he ever fought again, she should help him to get better if she could. It was her fault he was in this mess to begin with. "Well, I'll be downstairs, then."

He scowled. "What?"

She got off the barstool. "Yep. Downstairs. Waiting

for you. It's the door right across from the pantry, right?" It was only a guess. She didn't really know.

He put his hands flat on the counter. "No one goes downstairs."

She edged toward the door in the kitchen. His response had pretty much told her this was the right one. "And you're going to stop me how? Run after me with your crutches?"

"Lisa, I mean it." His eyes glowed red, and his brow furrowed.

It was enough to stop her in her tracks. He was really serious about this. It couldn't be that he was just that dead-set against getting on the exercise bike. "What's the big deal about downstairs? You afraid I'm going to break your precious gym equipment?"

"No, I..." He huffed out a breath. "I will walk the deck as many times as you—"

"Is there even any gym equipment down there?" She crossed her arms and decided to test him a little. "You're not hiding some weirdo porn collection down there, are you? Or a freaky sex dungeon? What is it down there, all red velvet and black satin with matching his and hers whips and chains?"

"No." Van looked flustered. "Nothing like that."

She nodded and pursed her lips. "If you say so. Wait, are you secretly into Hello Kitty? Do you store your massive collection downstairs?"

He stared at her. "Hello what?"

She held her hands up. "No judgment."

"What is downstairs is very personal." Then he narrowed his eyes a little. "Just gym equipment."

Something smelled. "Gym equipment is personal?"

He sighed. "I also keep some valuables down there."

She rolled her eyes. "I don't care if you keep all the gold in Fort Knox down there. I just need you to work out and get better."

His eyes widened at the word *gold*, then he regained his composure. "Why?"

"Why do I want you to work out?" She shrugged. "Just like your urge to protect me last night when you thought I was in danger, I have this drive for you to get better so that your life improves. So that you're not in pain. We're friends now, right? I want to help you. I feel compelled to. I don't want my time here to be wasted."

His eyes narrowed like he was thinking that over. Then he nodded. "You are a healer?"

That was the last thing she was, but what else could she say? "Sure. I like that. For you, I'm a healer." She smiled brightly. "Does that mean we can go downstairs and get a real rehab session in?"

He sighed and shook his head and was about to answer, when a sly look came over his face. "With one condition."

"You need to put your brace on first?"

"No."

"Then what's the condition?"

His grin expanded as he got up, grabbed his crutches, and made his way around to her side of the counter, stopping only when he was right in front of her. "Kiss me again."

That wasn't a hardship, but it also wasn't part of

123

her plan. "Van, I don't think that's such a great idea."

"It is a very good idea." He paused, brushing a strand of hair off her cheek. His touch sent a shiver through her. "Or did you not like kissing me as much as I thought?"

Oh, no, she'd liked it very much. She smiled and felt her cheeks go warm, among other parts of her. "No, I liked it."

"Then why is more a bad idea?"

Because there was so much at stake. He was already going to hate her when he found out the truth. How much more would he despise her if he felt like she'd led him on? But if it got him to work out and exercise that leg… She made herself smile. "I just don't want you falling for me, that's all. You know, a therapist and a fighter. It's just not done."

"But I am not a fighter anymore."

And there it was. Her reason for being here, underlined in black and white. "I don't know how you can give that up."

"Because I can." He bent forward like he was going to kiss her.

She stepped back, grinning.

He looked confused. "No kiss?"

"You can kiss me." She kept backing up until she reached the door that led to the lower level. She opened it, reached in, and flipped the switch. There wasn't much to see beyond the steps. She glanced back at Van. Grom stood next to him, ready to go but watching for his master's command. "I'll be on the stairs. Halfway down."

Van laughed and limped after her. Truth was, he hadn't put his brace on because it was a huge chore, but also because his leg wasn't bothering him this morning nearly as much. After last night's activity, he'd expected serious pain today, but that wasn't the case at all. Which told him that Lisa was right about exercising the leg.

Didn't make him happy about letting her downstairs, but he trusted her. So far anyway. She seemed like a good person. Something about her told him that she was a fighter too. Someone who has dealing with her own obstacles in life. She was able to stand up to him, that was for sure. To him, that alone was a mark of a strong person.

And yes, she was an incredible kisser and smart and beautiful, and he liked her company. All of that made for a very appealing package. So much so that where he had once wanted to be left alone, now he just wanted to be left alone with Lisa.

It was funny how much things could change in just a couple days.

Grom walked along with Van to the door, then stopped at the first step. Van motioned for the dog to head down. "Go ahead, Grom."

But the dog stayed at Van's side.

Van lifted his gaze to Lisa. "Call him to you. I don't want him underfoot when I'm on the steps."

She patted her leg. "Come on, Grom. Good dog. Come here."

"You have to say *ko mne*. It's Russian for come."

She repeated the word. "*Ko mne*, Grom."

Her accent wasn't quite right, but it wasn't bad either. Grom's ears perked up, and he trotted down the stairs. She scratched his ears. "Good boy."

Her gaze shifted to Van. "Now you." She patted her leg again, her voice low and saucy. "*Ko mne*, Van."

He laughed and shook his head. "A little knowledge is a dangerous thing." But there was something oddly arousing about a woman who felt comfortable enough to talk to him that way. Again, he was reminded what rare company that put her in. Besides Pandora, and perhaps Norma to some extent, he couldn't imagine another who would do that.

The stairs loomed before him. He wasn't afraid of the steepness or the pain now so much as he hated looking weak in front of her. It was ridiculous, and he recognized that it was male ego more than anything else, but he knew himself well enough to know what else it meant.

He cared what Lisa thought, because he liked Lisa. In a way, that was very different than just being friends with someone. He could see the possibility of a future with her. Just in a daydream sort of way, but still…he'd given it more than a minute of thought. How about that? And two days ago, he'd been decided on turning his back to the world. He grunted out a little laugh.

"What was that?" she asked.

"Nothing. Coming." He maneuvered himself carefully onto the first step. It was a balancing act with the crutches. Too far forward and he'd pitch down the stairs. Too far back and taking the next step became even more difficult. Right in the center, that was where he needed to be.

Step by step, with the speed of a geriatric snail, he progressed, until he finally joined Lisa where she stood. He commanded Grom to go lie down. This time, the dog listened to Van and trotted the rest of the way down the steps and into the gym.

Van faced Lisa. He wasn't breathing hard or feeling it in his muscles, but he couldn't deny he'd been too long away from his regular fitness routine. "Here I am."

She smiled. "Here you are."

She leaned up, kissed him on the mouth, then practically skipped the rest of the way to the bottom. "Again."

He groaned and tipped his head back. "You're playing games."

"And you're making progress."

He leaned on the crutches. "Is there another kiss for me?"

Her smile was sly but sweet. "Do you want one?"

"Yes." Very much he did. But this time, he wanted more than just a quick peck.

"Then get moving, comrade."

He snorted at her sass, genuinely happy for the first time in many days. "*Da, komandir.*" He started moving again with the same care.

She leaned against the wall. "Can I ask you something sort of…personal?"

He kept his eyes on the steps. "Sure." He'd seen her in her underwear. It seemed only fair to answer a question or two about himself.

"Are you working on getting rid of your accent?"

He looked up. "Why do you ask?"

"I wasn't trying to eavesdrop, but I overheard you in your office yesterday, and that's kind of what it sounded like."

He worked down to the next step. "*Da.*" He sighed. "I mean yes, not *da*. But some habits are hard to break."

"I think you should say whatever you want to." She was quiet a moment. "Can I ask why you're trying to get rid of it?"

He kept moving. "So I am easier to understand. So I fit in better. Because this is my country now."

"I don't think you're hard to understand. In fact, I kind of like your accent."

He glanced at her. Two more steps. "You do?"

"Yes." She smiled. "It's sort of sexy."

The word sent a bolt of pleasure through him, and suddenly, the steps were taking way too long. He balanced on his good leg, leaned forward, planted his crutches on the bottom step, and swung down to join her in one fast movement, putting them face-to-face. In this light and at this distance, he realized there were flecks of gold in her eyes. How perfect. "I have been told that before."

She stared up at him confidently. "I'm sure. Just like I'm sure you're used to having women all over you at the fights." Her expression grew a little smug. Like she knew his type.

He moved closer. "*Da.*" If she liked his native tongue, he'd use it. "But they are rarely the kind of women I want to spend time with."

"Oh? And what type of woman do you want to spend time with?"

"Petite redheads with green eyes who like to go outside in their underwear." He bent and took the kiss he'd been promised.

Her palms coasted up his arms to settle on his shoulders. The feel of her delicate hands exploring his body rocked him to his core. She touched him as if she'd never touched a man like him before. He doubted that was true, but she had the most amazing gift of making him feel that way.

She leaned into him, but only a little. Maybe she was unsure of how stable he was on the crutches.

He was plenty stable. He freed one hand and planted it on the small of her back, pulling her closer.

The kiss deepened for a few more perfect seconds,

then her hands slipped off his arms to his chest and pushed, breaking them apart. Her gaze held an odd gloominess. Not at all the response he'd expected from that kiss. "Don't fall for me, Van. We can't be a thing. It's too complicated."

"There is nothing complicated about it. Unless you do not like me the way I like you?"

She stared at the center of his chest, finally shaking her head. "Feelings can't play into this."

"That is like trying to discuss how lights work without using the word electricity."

She laughed, a soft, melancholy sound. "You're a smart guy, you know that? All I can tell you is, I'm not the kind of woman you want to spend time with either. Trust me."

"I do trust you, but…" None of that made sense to him. And after that kiss, he couldn't let it go. "At least tell me why?"

She hesitated, taking a long breath before answering him. "I've already told you. I work for the League, you work for the League—"

"And I told you, I am retired."

She lifted her chin, and a hardness he'd never seen before filled her eyes. "No, you're not. By your own admission, you're a fighter. You'll go back, even if you say otherwise now. If we were a couple, I'd want you to go back, because frankly, it's where you belong. I know you feel defeated and you're dealing with this injury, but inside, you need to fight. It's part of who you are. And getting involved with me would only sidetrack that. At some point, you'd end up breaking things off so you could fight again without worrying about the conflict of interest. Or worse, you'd really and truly quit and then, in time, come to resent me as the reason you never stepped into the ring again."

He couldn't deny that in his heart of hearts, he would love to fight again. He swallowed, trying to find the words to tell her that everything she'd just said had hit the mark.

"Your silence tells me I'm right." She stepped around him and walked into the gym, forcing him to turn. "All I am is a convenient distraction, Van."

He followed after her. "I do not feel that way."

"I'm sure you don't right now. But next week? Next month?" She sighed. "You really want to prove that I'm more than that to you? Then complete your contract. Fight that rematch. Then, when you're standing in that ring, with your championship belt back in your hands, tell me you're quitting and maybe I'll believe you. Because until then, you're always going to be wondering what if. And I don't want to be the thing that stopped you from answering that question."

He stared at her, searching his head and his heart for what he really desired. Two answers came over and over. He wanted her.

And he wanted to fight.

Monalisa stood there in the middle of Van's workout room, waiting for him to answer and wondering if this would be the moment when he threw her out.

Then the muscles in his jaw flexed. "You're right."

Her mouth opened in surprise. She snapped it shut. She hadn't expected that to work. Her smile came naturally. "I'm glad."

He moved toward her. "But I'm not willing to give you up for the ring. I want both."

Her belly twisted. That was not supposed to be part of his decision. "I don't see how that can happen."

"I do. We'll keep our relationship a secret until after the fight. Then, no matter if I win or lose—"

"You'll win."

He smiled. "And I will retire for good afterwards. Regardless of the outcome. Then you and I can do what we like, and it won't matter who knows about it."

There were a thousand reasons why that wouldn't work, but arguing any of them would be pointless if she wanted to earn her freedom. All she had to do was nod and agree. Van didn't need to know she was dying inside, mortified by her own actions.

For the thousandth time, she thought about telling him everything and hoping for the best, but she was already so deeply in. And he'd just agreed to fight again. The coin was within her grasp.

Soul sick at her own ability to deceive such an amazing guy, she somehow smiled and nodded. "Sure, we can give that a try."

Saying those words made her feel even worse. How was she going to get through the next few days of pretending everything was fine when all of this was to get herself free? Sure, getting Van to fight of his own accord was better than her compelling him to do it against his wishes, but it was still all so awful. She hated herself. Almost as much as she hated her father.

"Good. You will help me with this rehab. Then I will be healed and able to train again to prepare for this final match."

"Exactly." She turned away, unable to face him, but masked her true feelings by looking around the room. The downstairs was an enormous space filled with every kind of workout machine and piece of equipment imaginable. There was even a practice ring in the center. The end walls were mirrored. She avoided looking into those, unwilling to see her lying, treacherous face.

On the stair wall, there was a large steel door that

looked like something off an old World War II bunker, but it probably went to the garage. "You sure have everything you need down here, don't you?"

"I do. I will get started on the bike."

She fixed her smile in place. "Great. Hey, would you mind if I went upstairs and took my shower while you got your time in? I hadn't quite gotten that far with my morning routine."

"Go ahead." He winked at her. "And I promise not to cheat."

The smile got harder to maintain. "I'm going to hold you to that." She turned and walked back up the stairs. As soon as she set foot in the kitchen, her smile flatlined and she sucked in a hard breath.

She was a horrible person. With no options. Her father would force her to do what he wanted, no matter what she decided. She stared at the ceiling and tried not to cry.

The hum of the bike started up, muted by the distance between them. Now was as good a time as any to text her father the news.

She marched up to the bedroom and dashed off a text to him. *Everything's a go.*

Then she tossed her phone on the bed and climbed into the hottest shower she could stand. Her skin was pink when she got out, but the heat hadn't done anything to erase the guilt riddling her.

She couldn't do this to Van. She liked him. *Really* liked him. He was such a good man. The kind of guy she could see herself with, if she ever got that lucky again. He didn't deserve this. She wrapped up in a towel and grabbed her phone off the bed.

Her father had responded. *That's my girl.*

"Not anymore," she whispered as she dialed his number.

He answered immediately. "My darlin' girl, I knew you could do it."

"I am *not* your girl. And I am *not* doing this. I'm going to tell him everything, and then you can deal with that."

Silence answered her. But only for a second. "You *will* do this, Monalisa. We've discussed it. And now I command you to do it. And you know the consequences of ignoring your father's command."

A sharp pain pierced the back of her skull, just a phantom recollection of what was to come, for sure, but she winced at the memory all the same. "I don't care anymore. I'd rather be dead than your slave."

He laughed. "You may get your wish, then, girlie. But we both know you won't last. The pain will get too much like last time, and you'll cave. Then Sean will have to come out there and bring you home. What's left of you anyway. You'll be a quiverin' mess by then. But if that's what you want…"

She hung up on him, and a sob racked her body. So much for today being a good day.

Getting dressed, putting makeup on, and drying her hair were exercises in endurance. She felt numb and sick and disgusted with herself. And her father.

But she also felt helpless. Because she was.

She went out and stood on the balcony for a moment, drinking in the cold air and trying for just a second to forget the mess she was in. She couldn't, of course, but the fresh air made her feel a little better.

Maybe once this was all over and she was free, she could come back here and explain everything to Van. She didn't really expect him to forgive her, but at least she'd get to tell him her side of the story and explain why she'd lied to him.

That made her feel a little better. Enough that she was able to head back down to the gym.

She stopped at the bottom of the steps, unable to do much else but ogle.

Van stood in front of one of the big hanging punching bags. It was easy to see that he was bearing most of his weight on his good leg, but he wasn't using crutches, and that was impressive. But not as impressive as the sight of him shirtless and pounding on the bag.

Each hit showed off the muscles in his back and arms as they flexed and moved. He'd land a punch, then balance himself. Over and over. The sheer size of him was remarkable, but the power of his strikes was stunning. The bag jumped each time he struck it.

She could only imagine what he could do to an opponent in the ring. No wonder the manticore had bitten Van. There was probably no other way to stop the force of a dragon shifter.

He grabbed hold of the bag, steadying it.

"Very impressive."

He looked over his shoulder and smiled. "I did my time on the bike, I promise."

"I believe you. How does your leg feel?"

"Pain is weakness leaving the body."

She laughed. She'd experienced real pain. That wasn't what it had felt like to her. "If you say so. But does that mean you're hurting?"

He shrugged. "Is okay."

Obviously, he wasn't going to admit how badly he hurt. She got it. Men were like that. "Why don't we call that done for today, then?"

He nodded and limped to a nearby bench and sat. His crutches and T-shirt were there. Grom came running over from where he'd been lying near the wall. Van picked up his T-shirt and pulled it on. "Let's go into town today."

"Sure. Do you need help with some errands?"

"No. I thought you might like to see more of it. We can have lunch. Stop by the pet store and get Grom a new bone."

At the word *bone*, Grom's ears perked up.

"That would be great." And a nice way to distract herself. She crossed her arms and raised her eyebrows. "You are going to shower, though, right?"

He laughed as he pushed himself up on his crutches. "I will not end up looking as nice as you, but I will try."

An hour later, they were on Main Street, courtesy of a Ryde driver. Van had put his brace on over jeans, which he'd paired with a fisherman's sweater and lug-soled boots. The bulk of the sweater made him look even bigger. Maybe because of that and his shaved head and resting serial killer face, people gave them a fairly wide berth on the sidewalk.

If he noticed, he didn't say anything. Could be he was used to it. She wasn't. It was hard to see the looks on people's faces and not tell them to stop judging Van. Because it seemed like that was what they were doing.

She didn't like it. Just because she was going to end up hurting him didn't mean she wanted anyone else to do it.

The face of one approaching woman was frozen in a fearful grimace, her gaze stuck on Van.

Monalisa did the only thing she could think of. She linked her arm through his and smiled at him. The woman's expression changed to shock, and Monalisa felt a little vindication. "This is a great town." Some of the tourists weren't so fabulous, but the place itself was pretty cool. He'd explained before they left the house a little more about how supernaturals could live here without issue, being themselves all the time thanks to the enchanted water and the year-round celebration of Halloween.

"It is. Building my house here was an easy decision."

"Where's the pet shop?"

"Farther down. We will do that last. After lunch."

"Okay. Where do you want to go now?"

"Wherever you like." He smiled back. "I don't come to town much, so this is new for me too. But I do like to shop. Once in a while." He laughed. "What good is having money if you can't spend it, right?"

"Right." She couldn't really relate to that. Her parents kept her on a pretty tight budget, all part of controlling her. It worked too.

"Let's go in here." He grabbed the shop's door and opened it, waiting for her to go through.

She glanced up. Hats In The Belfry. She'd seen this shop on the drive to Pandora's. "Okay, cool."

It was toasty inside, so she loosened her short jacket. There were rows and rows of foam ovals attached to the wall, each one sporting a different hat. One wall was men's, one was women's, another kids', and in the center of the store, three spinning racks were devoted to silly hats of all descriptions.

"What do you think?"

She turned around to see Van in a gangster-style fedora. She laughed. "Now you really look like a tough guy."

He took the hat off. "Which one, then?"

"You really want a hat?"

He nodded. "One that makes me look…less like me."

She squinted at him. "I think I know what you're saying, but I don't like it. There's nothing wrong with the way you look." There was a lot right with it, in fact.

His jaw tightened. "I see the way people look at me. They are afraid. I do not like that."

"Those people are idiots."

He snorted. "I'm sure they would disagree with you."

"They're judging you based on what you look like. That makes them shallow and superficial."

He stared at her, a knowing glimmer in his eyes. "Did you not judge me when you saw me?"

She had. She'd judged him just like she judged all fighters. "Yes, but I got over that pretty quickly. And I'm sorry about that. I was an idiot too."

"You were never an idiot."

"I'll decide that. Now let's find you a hat." She scanned the rows behind him, finally settling on a newsboy style in herringbone tweed. "Try this."

He put it on. "Well?"

She adjusted it, giving it a little slant. She stepped back and smiled. "I like it. And it goes with your sweater." Truth was, he looked more Irish than Russian right now, but there was something very charming about the hat on him.

He looked at himself in the mirror. "I like it." He turned back to her. "Now you."

"A hat for me?"

"*Da*. My treat."

"No, I can't let you—"

"Lisa." He grabbed her hand. "You got me out of my funk. You got me to see that I cannot turn my back on fighting. Not yet. I am grateful. Please, let me say thank you."

He wouldn't be saying thank you when he found out the truth. She made herself smile. "I'm not sure I look good in hats."

He winked. "Let me be the judge of that."

He picked out a deep green wool felt hat with a slightly floppy brim and a black ribbon band. She put it on, angling it to one side, then faced him. "Is it me?"

"Definitely. See for yourself."

She looked in the mirror. He was right. It was her, much more than she would have guessed. She felt a little mysterious in the hat. Like a secret agent. "Wow, it's pretty cute."

"You are pretty cute. The hat is just lucky to be on your head."

She laughed, flattered and unsure of what to say to such kind words, besides, "Thank you."

He paid for the hats, and they headed back onto the street wearing them. They stopped at a few more stores, looking and laughing and having a great time.

Monalisa's stomach rumbled as they left the last shop.

Van took her hand. "I know that sound. Time to eat."

She flattened her hand against her stomach. "I guess I am getting hungry."

"Good. I am starving. And I know just the place." He tipped his head toward something farther up the street.

She followed his gaze. "A biker bar?"

Van shook his head at Lisa's comment. Howler's was a lot like him. It looked like one thing on the outside, but on the inside, it was so much more. "It's not just a biker bar. You will see."

He guided Lisa to the door, opening it for her. As soon as they were inside, he spotted Bridget Merrow behind the bar and gave her a wave.

Bridget came over. "Van, how are you? I knew you were back in town, but I figured you were holed up recovering. Bum deal, man."

He nodded, but didn't want to dwell on that. He slipped his hat off. "Bridget, this is my friend Lisa. Lisa, this is Bridget Merrow. She owns Howler's."

Lisa and Bridget shook hands. Bridget was all smiles. "Nice to meet you, Lisa."

"You too, Bridget."

He could tell what Bridget was thinking, that Lisa was the first woman outside of Pandora that he'd ever come in with so they must be more than friends.

Bridget gave him a look that confirmed that. "Van, where have you been hiding her?"

"I am not hiding anyone. We were at Pandora's housewarming last night."

"Ugh," Bridget said. "I couldn't make it. Had to work. But I heard Cole finally put a ring on it."

"He did," Van confirmed. "It was very nice."

"It was," Lisa said. "And Pandora was nice enough to invite me."

Bridget nodded. "She's cool like that. So what brings you to town, Lisa?"

"I'm here to help with Van's rehab. I work for the Titan Fight League. That's the organization Van fights for."

"Oh, we know all about TFL in here. We're all fans of Van's in town."

"You wouldn't know that by the way people look at him."

Bridget shifted her gaze toward the street. "Tourists, honey. The rest of us, the locals in the know, we like Van very much." She gave him a big grin.

"Thank you, Bridget." Van smiled. This was a good place to live.

Bridget peered past them. "Is it snowing out there yet? Weatherman keeps saying it's imminent."

"Not yet," Lisa answered. "But it is chilly." She took her hat off and fluffed her hair.

"Well, let's get you warmed up with some lunch." Bridget grabbed two menus. "You guys want a table or a booth?"

"Something private." Van wanted to be able to talk to Lisa.

"I've got just the spot." Bridget led them to the back corner. "Here you go. Specials are chicken pot pie, beef stew, and apple cobbler. I'll send your waitress right over."

"Thank you," Lisa said. "And nice to meet you."

"You too." Bridget narrowed her eyes a little, and for a moment, the gold gleam of her inner werewolf peeked out. "You take care of our guy, now."

Lisa straightened. "I will."

Van laughed as Bridget headed back to the bar. "She did not mean anything by that."

Lisa's gaze stayed on Bridget. "I'm not so sure. Wolf shifter, right?"

"Yes. Very good."

"It's the eyes. Gives it away." She looked around. "So does the name Howler's, frankly."

"I suppose it does."

She made eye contact with him again briefly before opening her menu. "It was nice to hear her say that everyone in town likes you. That was sweet. She obviously likes you very much too. Were you two ever a thing?"

Her question surprised him. Was she a little jealous or just curious? Either way, her interest intrigued him. "Just friends. She is dating one of the local firemen. Very serious. Another werewolf."

"Good for her." She went quiet as her attention shifted to the items on offer.

"There is someone for everyone, don't you think?"

"I don't know. I've never really thought about it that much." She looked up. "What are you getting?"

But he wasn't ready to change the subject. "Don't you want to get married? Have a family?"

She didn't say anything, glancing down at her menu again, then finally lifting her head. And then, as if it was an afterthought, she smiled. "Sure. Who doesn't?"

Her answer would have been more convincing if not for the sadness in her eyes. He couldn't understand it, and she didn't seem eager to talk about it. That had never stopped him before. "That is not very convincing."

She put her menu down. "I do want those things, but there's a lot of other stuff in my life I need to work out first. I don't know how else to explain it." She started to pick up her menu again, then hesitated. "And my parents haven't set such a great example either."

Based on what she'd already told him about them, that wasn't surprising. "They are divorced?"

"No, they're together. But most of the time their relationship seems more like it's based on a business deal than a love match." She shook her head. "I'm not sure why I'm telling you all this."

"It's okay. Talking is good. We get to know each other."

She smiled a little. "How about your parents? Are they together?"

His turn to stare at the menu. "Passed on. I miss them."

"I'm so sorry."

He nodded, suddenly unsure himself of how much to share. "My father died getting us safely out of Russia. My mother died of a broken heart. She missed him so much."

"Sounds like they were very much in love."

"They were. Very good parents. My brother and I were very lucky."

"You have a brother? I'm an only child. Does he live here too?"

"Boris lives in Japan. Has for many years. He is married and has a child. He teaches mixed martial arts."

"Is he a fighter too?"

"For a little while, but he liked teaching better. He retired from the ring when he met Shiori."

"Have you been to visit him?"

"Many times. Travel with the League was always one of the perks."

An older woman in a Howler's polo shirt approached the table. The name badge under the logo said Phyllis. "Afternoon, folks. I'm Phyl, and I'll be taking care of you today. What can I get you to drink?"

"Just water for me," Lisa said.

"Same here," Van answered.

"All right. Do you know what you want to eat yet?"

He glanced at Lisa. "You need more time?"

"No, I'm good. You?"

"Also good. Go ahead."

Lisa looked up at Phyllis. "Chicken pot pie special, please."

Phyllis scratched a note on her tablet, then asked Van, "And for you?"

"Steak sandwich." He handed her his menu. "Rare."

She took it and Lisa's, then tucked them under her arm. "I'll get that right in."

As she left, Bridget returned with a shallow dish resting on a flat plate. "Here you go, fresh from the kitchen so the plate is super hot." She laughed. "Not that that will bother you, Van."

"Those look yummy. What's under all that cheese? Stuffed mushrooms?"

Bridget nodded. "They're new on the menu so you guys get to be guinea pigs. They're Philly cheesesteak-stuffed 'shrooms. Eat up, I want a report."

She left as quickly as she'd arrived.

Lisa's brows lifted. "That was nice."

"Bridget takes good care of the locals."

"This town just gets better." She stuck her fork into one of the mushrooms and lifted it onto her side plate. Steam wafted off it. "She wasn't kidding about them being hot."

Van looked at Lisa, really looked at her, and realized how nice it was being with someone. This was what settling down meant. Being around to do things like window-shop on Main Street or go out for lunch.

He'd never really done much of that. Or any of it,

really. But today was showing him just how enjoyable it was.

One more fight was exactly what he needed. Closure, Pandora would probably say. Then he'd be ready to retire.

Ready to live this kind of life. He laughed softly.

Lisa looked up from her mushroom. "What's funny?"

He shook his head. "Nothing. I just…I'm having a good day. With you. This is good."

She smiled. "I'm having a nice day with you too. Thanks again for the hat. You're a very kind man." She looked a little sheepish. "I really did expect you to be such a different kind of guy."

"What did you think I would be like?"

She shrugged. "I'm embarrassed to admit it, but I thought you'd be…less…smart."

He barked out a laugh. "I get that a lot." He stabbed one of the mushrooms for himself, popping it into his mouth. Hot food wasn't an issue for him any more than heat of any kind was. Dragons could handle it.

Her smile disappeared. "I'm sorry about that. Not just that I thought it, but that other people think it. It's not fair. You're clearly a very smart guy, and you don't deserve to be judged like that."

He swallowed. The mushroom was very good. "Life is not fair. Is no big deal."

"That's for sure. About life not being fair, I mean."

He squinted at her. "What would you be doing if you could do anything? Where would you live? Who would you be?"

She blinked at him, and her mouth opened and closed, but no words came out. She took a breath, then finally answered him. "I love my job."

Said with all the enthusiasm of someone who didn't want word getting back to her boss. He laughed. "I'm sure you do. But come, tell me what dreams you dream."

She stared at her fork, her fingers tracing the handle. "I stopped dreaming a long time ago. Dreams turn into disappointments when they don't come true."

That made him sad for her. "But you must think about doing something beyond your life now."

She nodded slowly. "I would like the freedom to do whatever I want."

"Money, you mean?"

She laughed bitterly. "Sure, that's part of it, I guess."

"What else?"

Her gaze turned distant for a moment, then she brought her eyes up to meet his. "Van, there's something I need to—"

"Here you go." Phyllis arrived with their food. "Chicken pot pie for the lady and a steak sandwich for the gentleman."

She put their plates in front of them. "What else can I get you? Ketchup for the fries? Side of anything? Horseradish for that steak?"

Lisa's smile turned oddly bright. "I'm good. This looks great."

"Nothing for me." Van left his food untouched as

the waitress left. He was waiting for Lisa to finish her sentence.

She broke the pot pie's crust with her fork, releasing a cloud of steam. "Food sure comes out of that kitchen hot, huh? Yours looks good too. Can I steal a fry while I wait for mine to cool down, or are you one of those people who hate to share?"

"You can have a fry." Had he imagined her about to say something? Maybe it hadn't been important, but in the moment, it had felt like she'd been about to unburden the weight of the world from her shoulders. "Was there something you were going to say?"

She squinched up her face like she was thinking hard. "Um, not that I can remember. Oh, I need to go by the post office. Maybe that was it. Unless you have stamps?"

"I might. We can stop by." He picked up one half of his sandwich and started eating.

He was pretty sure she hadn't been about to tell him she needed stamps. Obviously, she'd changed her mind about whatever she'd been on the verge of revealing. Something too personal maybe. Something hard.

He felt for her. Carrying a burden like that was never easy. Maybe someday she'd feel comfortable enough to tell him. Maybe not.

Whatever it was, he wished he could explain that nothing she told him was going to make any difference about how he felt toward her. In fact, it might even make him like her more.

But that was a bridge they would have to cross together.

Monalisa had never been happy about all the parties her father had forced her to attend until now. Those parties had given her a backlog of small talk to pull from, hundreds of inane questions to lob at Van in an attempt to keep the conversation focused on him.

And away from the fact she'd almost found the courage to tell him the truth.

Almost. Thankfully, their server had arrived with their food before she'd gone too far. And in those few moments, she'd wised up and realized that telling him in a public place wasn't going to be any better than telling him in a private place. It could be worse, actually. He might stop her from going back to the house to get her things. Or his friends might band together with him and drive her out of town.

If she had any money, she'd leave an extra tip for the waitress, because the woman's interruption had saved Monalisa's hide.

What had she been thinking? Telling Van was a bad idea. Bad. She didn't think he'd physically hurt her. He wasn't the kind of guy to lay a hand on a woman, that seemed pretty clear. But one of his friends might. Bridget, for example.

She looked like the kind of woman who wouldn't shy away from backhanding someone she thought deserved it. Or did werewolves just bite?

Either way, Monalisa didn't want to find out.

She needed to remember that this was all temporary. This wasn't some new life she was living, being shown the town and treated to lunch. And a hat. This was all part of the game she was playing. This was what Lisa Devers, rehab therapist, got to do.

Because Monalisa Devlin, pawn of the leprechaun king, had to earn her freedom before she could even think about living this kind of life.

This wonderful, peaceful, do-whatever-you-want kind of life. She stabbed a hunk of chicken. Where you could date someone and spend an afternoon with him doing normal things, like eating chicken pot pie and having the best time you'd ever had.

She had a long way to go to get there. Which was also why she needed to stop falling for Van.

She could already tell her feelings for him were developing into something more than just friends. He was sweet and kind and clearly generous. But that was because he didn't know who she really was, or what she was here to do. He would change the instant he found out. There was no way he'd feel the same way about Monalisa once the truth surfaced.

It killed her inside. She'd never known a guy like him. Never had the chance, really, with the way her father kept men away from her. And whatever was happening between them would be utterly destroyed when her real purpose here came to light.

Maybe she'd write him a long letter and leave it behind for him to find. Explain everything that way. Because she couldn't bear the thought of him not knowing that she'd had no choice.

"You okay?"

She jerked her head up. "What?"

Van pointed a French fry at her food. "Is something wrong with your meal?"

"Oh, no. It's just…hot." She blew on the hunk of chicken stuck to the end of her fork, then popped it into her mouth. So much for making small talk. She launched into a series of questions then, old standbys that always worked at parties. Seen any good movies lately? What are you reading? Where did you go to college? How are the kids? Your wife? Your dog? Can you believe the weather? Who does your hair? Where did you get that dress? That suit? That glass of wine?

Not all of them worked in this situation, obviously, but there were enough to start a conversation and keep it going.

And she did. All the way back to the house.

They stood on the porch, watching Grom race around since he'd been let out. She leaned against one of the railings, sad but happy at the same time. Even if she never got free from her father, a real possibility considering his history, she would always have this day as an example of what life could be like. It might be enough to get her through. A sliver of happiness to cling to when all else was bleak.

She smiled at Van from under the brim of her hat. How easy would it be to fall crazy in love with a guy like him? Too easy. Her heart ached a little at the thought, and her smile wavered. She forced herself to snap out of the melancholy she was quickly sinking into.

"That was so much fun today. Thank you for lunch and the hat and the walk around town. I know that had to be a long day for you. Especially after you were on the bike this morning. How's your leg?"

"You are welcome. I enjoyed it too." He glanced toward the brace. "My leg, not so much."

"You should get some rest. Take a nap. Sleep is great for healing, you know."

He smiled. "I know. I think I will."

"Good. I might take one too. After I write up a few reports." She pulled her jacket tighter. The sun was going down, the temperature was dropping, and the clouds definitely looked like snow.

His eyes narrowed. "Telling the League how I am doing?"

"Something like that." She pointed. "I think Grom got you a present."

Grom trotted toward the porch carrying what looked like a small tree in his mouth.

Van snorted and shook his head. "Drop it."

Grom growled playfully but held on to his treasure.

"Van, I have the b-o-n-e you bought at the pet shop. You think he'd make a trade?"

"Good idea. Show it to him."

She pulled the big rawhide treat out of the bag and wiggled it at Grom. "Hey, puppy, you want this instead?"

Grom dropped the dead tree instantly, effectively blocking the stairs with it. He climbed over it to sit in front of Monalisa.

"Okay to give it to him?" she asked Van.

He nodded. She held it out to Grom, who took it gently but eagerly. Then he whined to go inside. She opened the door. "What are you going to do about that tree?"

"Toss it into the yard." Van froze. "Unless that is not respectful."

She squinted. "Respectful?"

"To your…kind. I have never known a dryad before. But I know that trees are sacred to your people. Is that not true?"

Bollocks. She'd told him she was a dryad and completely forgotten about it. Of all the… "Not sacred, exactly." Like she had an actual clue. *Think fast.* "And this one was clearly dead already, so there's no disrespect. In fact, the best thing you could do would be to put it to good use now."

"Good use?"

"You know, use it for kindling or something like that. Maybe build us a fire with it tonight." *Please let him buy that.*

"That does sound like a purposeful end."

Thank the heavens.

Van used his crutch for support and bent, picking up the enormous length of wood in one hand. He straightened and leaned back on the railing so he could put both hands on the tree. Then he snapped it in half like it was a twig. He kept going until it was in small, manageable pieces stacked beside the door. "There. Now we have kindling."

Seeing his strength demonstrated like that was impressive. "Excellent. A fire will be nice this evening."

"And I will build you one."

"After a nap. Or maybe we should just go to bed early." She went halfway inside, then looked back to see Van's eyes twinkling. "You know what I mean."

"*Da*." He chuckled to himself.

"Oh, behave. You're like a teenage boy." She walked into the house, smirking.

He followed her. "Perhaps that is the effect you have on me."

She took her hat off, suddenly feeling shy. She finger-combed her hair. "So, maybe we could watch a movie or something tonight?"

"Sounds good. Norma left meatloaf and mashed potatoes in the refrigerator. And some green thing for you."

She laughed. "Okay, I'll take care of heating dinner up after we rest." She backed toward the stairs. "See you in an hour?"

"An hour is plenty."

"Perfect." She jogged up the steps. She hung the hat on one of the bedposts, then sat and pulled out her phone. She'd heard it going off all day but had ignored it. She knew who'd been calling. Her father.

The screen showed five missed calls and three text messages, all the same. *Call me. Call me. Call me.*

She didn't want to. He would only threaten her again, and she'd heard all his threats a thousand times. Why should she subject herself to that?

Instead, she sent him a text back. *No need. I'm doing what you want. Leave me alone.*

His response was almost instant. *All I needed to know.*

She rolled her eyes. If he didn't give her the coin after all this, she might end up in jail on assault charges. Or attempted murder. And real jail, not the familial one she was in now. How much worse could it be? With a sigh, she set her alarm for forty-five minutes, then lay down and closed her eyes.

She woke up to the soft chirp of the timer she'd set. She hadn't expected to sleep, but the day out had definitely tired her a bit. She got up, stretched, and went down to see about heating up dinner.

No sign of Van, but if he was still sleeping, she'd let him. He needed the rest. She quietly opened the fridge.

Norma had left an assortment of containers, each one labeled with clear instructions about how to reheat it. The woman was kind of amazing. Monalisa set the oven temp, then put everything in except for the green beans and gravy, which Norma's directions said to microwave.

"Did you sleep?"

She yelped and turned to see Van standing on the other side of the counter. "You startled me. Yes, I did. You?"

"Yes." He was on his crutches again and back in sweats and T-shirt. The man could make anything look good. "I feel better. Ready to eat."

He also had an insane appetite. "That's great. Dinner will be warmed up in about half an hour if Norma's instructions are right, which I'm sure they are."

"I will find us a movie. What kind?"

"Whatever. I'm easy. You pick."

He narrowed his eyes. "Is this a test?"

She laughed. "Maybe."

He made his way back to the living room, Grom happily accompanying him, and fired up the television.

A wave of intense longing came over her. This was all so perfect. This house, this man, this happy life. She wanted it to be hers for real, but there was no way on earth to make that happen. Playing house was the best she was going to get.

Maybe she should stop holding back and give herself entirely over to the fantasy. See what it was like to be loved by a man like Van.

They were both going to get hurt when the truth came out anyway. But that wouldn't be fair to him.

No, she would just enjoy the few days she had left here and hold on to the sweet memories she was making and pray that Van didn't hate her too much when this was all said and done.

She wasn't sure she could bear that.

Van flipped through the On Demand selections looking for a movie he thought Lisa would like. His interests, which typically ran to action flicks or moody thrillers, weren't important. He wanted something that would make her laugh. Too many times today, when she hadn't realized he'd been looking, he'd seen sadness in her eyes.

It hurt him to see such pain in her. Especially now that he was coming to care for her. It was his instinct, he knew, his inborn urge to protect. And it was especially strong around her.

He understood what that meant. His dragon wanted her. Hell, his dragon had already pretty much decided she was his. Didn't matter that they'd only known each other a few days. His dragon side didn't need a lot of time to make those kinds of decisions. It wanted what it wanted. So while his human side might be uncertain, his dragon side was already wondering what kind of ring she'd like.

He shook his head. A dragon and a dryad. Had there ever been such a pairing?

He laughed. Despite what his dragon side was planning for, he was getting ahead of himself. There was no telling where things would go between Lisa and himself. He was assuming a lot. Such as her liking him as much as he liked her. That she'd be willing to give up working for the League just like he was. That she'd want to live here in Nocturne Falls.

Maybe he should take her back into town again tomorrow. Really make her fall in love with the place. That should be easy.

He stared at the remote in his hands. If only he could make her fall in love with him the same way. But she had reservations about him, he could tell.

Maybe once this last fight was over and she saw that he really was ready to retire and settle down, maybe then they could make a go of things.

"Find anything?"

He glanced up to see her standing next to him. "Have you seen *Choir Life*?"

She snorted and popped one hip to the side. "You really want to watch a movie about college girls trying to find themselves through an a cappella group?"

He shrugged. "It might be good."

"Pretty sure you would hate it." She tipped her chin toward the screen. "Scroll a little."

He did as she asked, paging through the selections.

"Ooh, there. That one. *Red Widow*. Helen Mirren

and Tom Hardy take on the Russian spy world as a mother-son team." She pursed her lips. "Or maybe that's not your thing, seeing as how I'm pretty sure the Russians are the bad guys."

He smirked. He'd already seen it twice. It was a great flick. "I am American now. This is a good choice."

"You're sure?"

"Positive."

Something beeped in the kitchen. She jerked her thumb in that direction. "Cool. I'll go get the food and be right back."

He put his hands on the arms of the chair to push himself up. "I will help."

"You'll do no such thing. Sit there and rest. I've got this." She took a few steps toward the kitchen, then stopped and looked at him again. "What do you want to drink? I saw beer in the fridge."

He nodded. "Yes, that."

"Okay, be right back."

He watched her, smiling and feeling like this was the most perfect moment of his life. He wanted things to be like this all the time. This easy. This comfortable. This contented.

Whatever it took to keep Lisa around, he would do it. And whatever it took to make her happy, he would work on that too.

How hard could that be?

She returned with a cold beer, a plate of food, and utensils. "Dinner is served."

He took the plate and utensils from her, then the beer, setting it on the side table. "Thank you."

She hesitated. "Say it in Russian."

"*Spasibo*."

She grinned. "I like that."

He smiled, so charmed by her in that moment. "Get your dinner and join me." He wanted her close to him.

"On my way." She sauntered off, returning a few seconds later with her own plate and beer. She settled onto the couch and lifted her beer, leaning toward him. "Cheers."

"Cheers." He met her halfway, clinking his bottle against hers. "Thank you for heating this up."

"No problem. Norma did the hard part."

He sipped his beer before putting it back on the table. "You're not going to have a very good view of the screen from there."

She shrugged as she forked up a piece of meatloaf. "I can see okay."

"Is not good enough."

"It's fine, really."

It wasn't. He lifted his plate, then scooted over. "This chair is big enough for both of us."

"It's not that big." She laughed. "And I'm not sitting on your lap to eat my dinner."

"Not on my lap. Next to me."

She seemed to be considering it. "We'll be squished in."

"You do not want to be squished with me?"

She grinned. "There are worse things." She thought a moment. "How about I join you after dinner?"

"Good." Then maybe he could talk her into sitting on his lap. Or at least across it. He dug into his meal. The thought of having her that close to him, touching him, was very appealing. He put his fork down to click back to a channel. He picked the first neutral thing he saw, a game show.

"Aren't you going to start the movie?"

"After we eat. You cannot see it."

She took a sip of her beer, which she had on the floor by her feet. "You're a stubborn guy, you know that? But sweet."

"Like candy."

She laughed, slapping a hand over her mouth. "I almost snorted beer through my nose, thank you very much."

He preened a little. "Also funny."

She nodded. "You're a whole wealth of things, that's for sure."

But was it enough to keep her interest? To make her happy? He wished he knew.

Grom sighed and rolled over on his back, looking longingly at Van.

"*Nyet.*"

Grom huffed, making Lisa laugh again. "It's not hard to figure out what he wants, is it?"

"No. But he has kibble in his bowl, and too much people food is not good for him. And he knows it. Don't you, Grom?"

With a whiny, growly noise, Grom got up and went to lie by Lisa. Van laughed. She reached down to pet him. "Poor doggy. Such a hard life."

Grom finally gave up and went to lie near the fireplace. They finished their dinner, and then Lisa took the dishes back into the kitchen.

"Leave them in the sink," Van called. "I will do them later." He used his crutch to get up and went over to the fireplace. Grom stretched out as if anticipating. There was still kindling and logs in the basket, but Van would need what was stacked by the door if they kept the fire going longer than a few hours. He started arranging the small kindling, then larger pieces on top and finally a hefty log.

"You want another beer while I'm in here?" Lisa called out.

"*Da*. Yes." He really needed to get better about that. He shoved a starter stick into the kindling. If he'd been able to shift, even into his half form, he could have breathed the fire into being, but shifting was impossible with the venom in his system. He clicked the lighter and set the end of the starter stick ablaze. Blue flame licked the end, traveling quickly into the smaller twigs.

She padded in behind him, her shoes long gone. "Oh, that's going to be so nice." She stood next to him and handed him the beer.

He knocked his bottle against hers, happy she was having another one too. "This is a good day."

She stared into the growing fire. "Yes, it is."

He tucked his crutch under his arm, then shifted the bottle into that hand so he could put his other arm around her. She leaned into him a little, and he bent to kiss the top of her head. Her hair smelled nice.

Floral and herby. Her shampoo, no doubt. It suited her. Feminine but a little wild too. "What are you thinking about?"

She shook her head. "Nothing."

He knew that wasn't true, but he didn't want to ruin the moment by trying to get more than that out of her. "Movie?"

"*Da.*" She looked up at him and winked.

One word. One small gesture. And just like that, he knew this was the woman he wanted to spend the rest of his life with.

It staggered him, like a punch to the gut. He clung to his crutch. How could anyone know anything with such certainty? He wasn't sure. But his dragon side and his human side were no longer struggling to sync.

Lisa Devers was the woman he was meant to be with.

"This is going to be tight." Monalisa squeezed next to Van in the small spot between him and the arm of the oversized chair. Oversized, yes, but still a chair.

"Is good." He scooped up her legs and swung them over his.

"Your knee!"

"My knee is fine. You weigh very little. I know this because you told me." He smiled and put his arm around her. "Are you comfortable?"

She snuggled into the crook of his arm. "Yes." Believe it or not. She'd never been this intimate with a man before, but being with Van felt so right. Too right. The kind of right that was going to leave her miserable for months. But she would endure that pain in exchange for having these sweet memories of what could be.

He found the movie on the list and hit play, then set the remote aside and leaned back to watch. His hand settled on her thigh, a few inches above her knee. It was heavy and warm and felt possessive in a way she didn't mind at all.

If this was what being in a relationship was like, she prayed someday she'd get to experience it again. And get to hold on to that relationship for more than a few days.

The movie was fast-paced, funny in spots, full of action and snappy lines. She and Van reacted alike, laughing together, tensing at the same time, even gasping in unison once. He adjusted his arm around her shoulders so that he could thread his fingers through her hair. He played with the strands, twisting them around his fingers. It was a blissful sensation and one that threatened to cause her to drift off. Just when she thought she might, his hand moved to her shoulder and stayed there.

They spent the rest of the movie wound around each other like that. Snug and content. It was perfect.

Then he went oddly still in the last few minutes before the credits started to roll. She picked her head up and looked at him.

He was asleep.

She smiled, understanding completely. The crackling fire had made the house toasty, and the chair was like a giant leather-covered marshmallow. Being snuggled up had made her a little sleepy too. Or maybe it had been the beer. She kept her voice low. "Van?"

But there was no response. Except from Grom, who sat up and yawned, then gave her a look she was coming to recognize as him needing to go out.

"That makes two of us," she whispered.

She climbed out of the chair, careful not to wake Van, and went to the door. Grom followed and trotted outside when she opened it. "I'll be right back for you, promise."

She shut the door quietly, then jogged upstairs to use the bathroom herself. When she came out, she saw the light on her phone blinking. Her father. Who else?

Ignoring the phone until later, she went back downstairs and out onto the front porch to check on Grom. There was enough moon and starlight to see him rolling around in the leaves. And to see the snow that was coming down in fat, fluffy flakes. "You better have done your business already."

He jerked upright, tongue hanging out, and woofed at her, stomping the ground in his playful way.

"No, it's too late to play. You need to do what you need to do and get back inside. It's cold out here." And she hadn't grabbed her jacket. She hugged her arms around her body, desperately missing Van's heat. What was that Russian word he'd used to get Grom to listen? She couldn't remember it.

The door opened behind her, and Van limped out, eyes still heavy with sleep. "What is going on?"

She shivered. "Your dog is goofing off, and I'm freezing."

"I can fix that."

She expected him to put his arm around her, but instead his eyes glowed for a moment and the temperature started to rise. It got downright balmy. "What did you do?"

"I can radiate heat in my human form. It's about all I can do right now."

"Wow, that's a very handy skill." She dropped her arms. "Now what kind of magic do you have that will get that silly dog back up here?"

He leaned on his crutch, moving forward to the railing. "Grom, *ko mne*."

The dog straightened, then ran up onto the porch and into the house.

She laughed. "That really is magic." She went in after him, Van behind her.

He shut the door.

She stood where she was, letting him come to her. "We should back up the last couple minutes of the movie. You missed the ending."

He smiled sheepishly. "I've seen it."

"You have? And you wanted to watch it anyway?"

He pulled her close with one arm, the other hand occupied with holding on to the crutch. "It's a good movie. And I wanted you to see whatever you wanted. And to be happy."

"I am happy."

He stared down at her, shaking his head slowly. "I have seen the sadness that comes into your eyes when you think I'm not looking. I do not know what troubles you, but it hurts me. I want to make things better for you."

A lump settled in her throat. "I'm not sad. I just think a lot. That's my thinking face." Lying to him was awful. She leaned in and kissed him, hoping to distract them both with the press of her mouth.

It worked.

A long, hot minute later, she broke away with a smile. "I should go to bed. We both should."

"It is barely nine o'clock."

"I know, but we're both tired, and we have more therapy tomorrow. Plus, I don't want to be the reason you're not healing like you should."

He pursed his mouth. "I will not argue. But only because I see the end goal in all of this."

"What's that mean?"

"You'll see."

She glanced behind her. "Do we need to do anything to the fire?"

"No. It is almost out anyway." He kissed her once more, soft and sweet. "See you in the morning, *zolotse*." He snapped his fingers, and Grom followed.

She wanted to ask what the word he'd called her meant, but that felt like it might ruin the moment. Then she remembered that her father had probably left a thousand messages for her, which ruined the moment anyway.

She plodded upstairs and picked up the phone from the nightstand. As suspected, her father had left numerous messages and texts. *Call me now. No games. Important.*

For a second, she wondered if something had happened, but then she realized it was just his way of getting her to do what he wanted. Like always.

She texted back. *What?*

Her phone rang. It was him. She answered it as she headed out to the balcony to talk where she wouldn't be overheard. Once again, without a jacket. But this wouldn't take long. She'd hang up before she got too cold. "What now?"

"I need Ivan here in five days."

"Five? Are you insane? That's this Saturday."

"I know what day it is. Just do it."

"That's ridiculous. The venom won't be out of his system by then. Not even close." The heat of her anger made her forget the temperature and the thin blanket of snow already forming. "He needs at least another month."

"Five days. Make it happen. I have some whales coming in, and if they're here for the fight, they'll drop big money."

She didn't care what her father or his wealthy, gambling customers wanted. "It's not that easy."

"It is if you use your gifts. Which you should already be doing."

"I hate you."

"Five days."

She hung up. She wanted to pitch her phone into the woods, but if her father couldn't reach her, he'd send Sean out here, and that would just make things worse. She leaned on the railing. Five days was impossible. Van would never be ready to fight by then.

The tears she'd been fighting for so long finally came, streaming hot down her face. She wanted to scream and break things. But that wasn't her way.

Her way was just to suck it up and deal with the wretched hand she'd been dealt.

Because there was no alternative. No escape.

She picked up her head and wiped her face with her hands. There was one escape, however temporary. She could shift and take a few moments to drift through the forest. It would be so peaceful with the snow coming down. Quiet and serene and just what she needed right now. She'd done it once before without any issue.

And she already knew Van was off to bed.

She closed her eyes and called up her magic.

The voice Van had heard turned out to be Lisa on the phone. He watched her from inside the house, the triple-paned windows making it hard to determine exactly what she was saying, even with his keen hearing.

Whoever she was talking to, they were making her angry. That made him angry. But he shouldn't be eavesdropping. It wasn't right. If she wanted to share her troubles with him, she would. Someday, he hoped she'd be that comfortable with him.

She hung up and started to cry.

The sight of her tears made him want to hurt whoever she'd been talking to. He put his hand to the glass. He should go upstairs and comfort her. That would be okay, wouldn't it? He could say he'd heard her crying and—

A piercing flash of light blinded him. Grom growled. Van blinked, unable to see beyond a bright glaring spot left in his vision. He staggered back, gripping his crutch until the metal bent in his hand. That light. He knew that light.

That was the light that had cost him everything.

"Grom, *tiho*."

Grom quieted, and as the glaring spot faded, Van stared up at the balcony to see if Lisa was all right.

Snow drifted down in big flakes.

Lisa was gone.

His heart pounded in his chest, and a thousand thoughts flooded his brain. Was she hurt? Why had the person responsible for that light followed him to Nocturne Falls? Who were they? What did they want? His hoard? That was the only reasonable explanation he could come up with.

"Lisa!" He called out her name as he walked toward the stairs. No answer. He made his way up to the bedroom as quickly as he could. The pain was easier to ignore with adrenaline in his system. "Lisa, where are you? Say something."

But there was no response. Whoever had flashed that light had taken her. Anger burned white-hot in him, and his instincts to protect her married with his drive to hurt whoever had done this. Had he been well, he would have shifted immediately and taken to the skies to hunt them down.

And when he found them, he would have covered them in flames and turned them to ash. He turned back to the stairs. He could call Nick Hardwin. The man was a gargoyle, one of the class that could fly. He'd help Van search.

He put his hand on the railing to steady himself

when the balcony door opened behind him.

"Van? What are you doing up here?"

He pivoted. There was snow in her hair. "What happened? I thought someone took you. Or hurt you. Or worse. There was a flash of light and—"

She sucked in a ragged breath. It sounded very much like a sob.

The sound caused another possibility to click into his brain. One he didn't want to give room to. One that meant things he didn't want to be true. One that sent a chill through him so harsh, he felt cold for the first time in his life. He cursed in his native tongue before reverting to English again. "You are not a dryad, are you?"

She swallowed and shook her head. It was a small, timid movement.

His next words came out in a dark snarl. "What are you?"

She wiped a hand over her mouth, her eyes sad and desperate and tearful. "I can explain."

"I am listening."

She swallowed. "Can we go downstairs?"

"*Nyet*. Explain. Now."

She finished closing the balcony door, then she moved closer to the bed. Farther from him. "I don't know where to begin."

"Anywhere. Just start."

She took a breath. "I've wanted to tell you this so many times these last few days." She sat on the edge of the bed and twisted her fingers together. She stared at her hands. "I'm a Will-o'-the-Wisp."

175

She looked up. "Do you know what that is? We're a rare creature."

He just stared at her.

"That flash of light you saw, that was me." Her voice was quiet. Resigned. As if this conversation had been inevitable. Perhaps it had been.

"The one the other night?"

"Me too."

He asked the question he dreaded the answer to. "And at the fight?"

Another sob escaped her throat, and she nodded, silent tears washing her cheeks. "Yes."

The whispered answer echoed through the room like a scream.

He rocked back, unable to process more than the feelings of betrayal and anger. "Why?"

She shook her head. "I had no choice."

There was always a choice. "You need to leave."

She folded her hands in her lap. The tears were gone, replaced by a dull, blank look. "I know. I'm sorry."

He turned around and limped down the stairs.

The wheels of her rolling suitcase skipped and scudded over the snowy gravel road. She hadn't wanted to wait in the house until the Ryde driver came, and if she was going to wait outside on the porch anyway, she might as well use the time to put some distance between her and the mess she'd made.

So what if it was snowing?

She didn't blame Van. She blamed her father. Herself too, but just like she'd told him, she'd had no choice.

If he'd exploded in rage, or broken something, or screamed at her, she would have expected all those things. Almost welcomed them. But the way he'd responded had shaken her far worse. She'd never seen such hurt in someone. The pain in his eyes had been visible like a shining light.

Pain she'd put there.

Snowflakes hit her face. She wiped at them, and her hand came back wet. It wasn't snow. She was crying again. She was so numb it was hard to tell. Hard to care. Her movements were robotic and instinct driven, because if she opened herself up to the emotion just below that, she would collapse and die from the pain of it. That much she knew.

And maybe that wasn't such a bad option. But not here. Not where Van would have to explain what had happened. Not where she'd only be causing him more trouble. She could hold on until she got back to Vegas, then she'd melt down. And if her broken heart and destroyed spirit killed her, the mess would be on her father's head.

And wouldn't that serve him right?

With that singularly buoyant thought sustaining her, she walked all the way to the main road and flagged down the Ryde driver there.

He hopped out and put her suitcase in the back of

the SUV, while she took her purse, climbed in, and slumped back on the seat.

He got in and glanced at her in the rearview mirror. "Where to? Your check-in said the airport, but it's closed because of the blizzard."

"What? This isn't a blizzard. It's just a little snow."

He laughed. "Sorry, but the FAA thinks otherwise."

She looked outside. Really looked. Everything was covered in white. Bollocks. She couldn't go back to Van's. "Any idea when planes will be flying out again?"

He shrugged. "Tomorrow maybe? Who knows? You still want me to take you somewhere, or you just going home?"

"I was trying to get home."

"That's rough."

She thought for a moment, then came up with the only place she could think of that would probably still be open. "Take me into town. To Howler's."

"You got it." He took the SUV out of park and off they went.

It was slow going. The roads weren't plowed, but the car seemed to be doing okay. Maybe he had four-wheel drive.

She leaned against the door and stared into the swirling white beyond the window. It blurred together after a while, and her thoughts returned to what had happened. She wasn't surprised. The truth had been bound to come out.

She just hurt so much more than she'd expected to.

She sighed, and her breath fogged the glass. The pain was because she liked Van so much.

That had been a stupid thing to do. To fall for the guy she'd been sent to con. How dumb. She'd never done anything remotely that stupid ever. Not even the time her father had sent her to talk some internet billionaire into hosting his company party at the Shamrock. And that guy had been cute and wealthy.

She scowled. Van was handsome and loaded too, but that had nothing to do with why she'd fallen for him. Her feelings were about the way he'd treated her, the unexpected sweetness of his spirit, his kind soul, his generous nature, his way with animals and people, his wit, his intelligence, his fantastic body—okay, so maybe a little of how she felt had to do with what he looked like, but that was just human nature, right?

Just like it was human nature to tell yourself everything was going to be all right even when you knew that was a lie.

She sniffed and dug in her purse for a tissue. Her phone was blinking again. She'd missed a notification. She snatched it out of her handbag and checked it on the off chance it was Van wanting to talk.

It wasn't.

And her father could get lost.

She crammed the phone back down into her purse and pulled out a tissue, wiping at her nose. Hopefully, Bridget would be there and she could help Monalisa find a place to stay until the airport opened up again. She didn't remember seeing a hotel, but there had to be an inn or a bed-and-breakfast with a vacancy.

The car slowed, then finally stopped altogether. "Here we are. Howler's."

"Oh." She sat up and looked toward the bar and grill. The lights were on. That was a good sign. She slid out of the car, her feet sinking calf-deep into the snow.

She trudged around to the back where the driver had gotten her bag out. "Thanks."

"Sure thing. Hope you get home soon."

"Me too. I'll make sure to give you five stars."

"Much appreciated." He got back in and pulled away, leaving her in the midst of the snowpocalypse.

There was no way her rolling bag was going to make it through the drifts ahead of her, so she hoisted the whole thing on top of her head and waded toward the door.

She was almost there when it swung wide and a familiar face appeared.

Bridget.

The werewolf shook her head. "What are you doing out in this mess? Where's Van?"

Monalisa made it inside and put the suitcase down. She stomped the snow off her boots. "It's a long story."

"How about we start with a hot drink?"

"That would be great. I wasn't sure you'd be open. The airport's closed."

"Why didn't you go back to Van's?"

Monalisa sighed. "That's part of the long story."

"C'mon," Bridget said with a wave. "Let's get you that hot drink, and you can start from the beginning. Leave your suitcase behind the hostess stand. It'll be all right there. I don't think anyone else will be coming in."

"Thanks." She tucked it behind the counter that held menus and a seating chart, then followed Bridget. The place was almost empty. Because most people weren't morons. Like her. She took the first empty chair at the bar and settled in.

Bridget was already behind the bar. "What'll it be? Irish coffee?"

Monalisa made a face without meaning to. "No, thanks. That reminds me of someone I'd rather not be reminded of."

"How about an adult hot chocolate?"

Monalisa nodded. "Perfect."

She'd never been much of a drinker. The two beers she'd had at Van's had been unusual. But now, getting a little sloshed seemed like the best decision she could make. Maybe she'd pass out and wake up to find this had all been a dream.

A really, really bad dream.

Van stood fixed before the fireplace. The slowly dying embers burned red-hot under their coating of ash. Time ticked by. Their glow faded as he stood there. His gaze wavered as his mind grappled with what had just happened.

What had he done?

Essentially, he knew the answer to that question. He'd thrown Lisa out. Just like that, without asking any questions. Without letting her give her side of the story.

But then, she hadn't fought back. Hadn't tried to explain. It was like she'd known this was coming. Had been anticipating it.

How? Why?

He swallowed against the knot in his throat, but it stuck. His actions were unacceptable. He had to go talk to her. Had to get answers. But still he stood there, staring into the fire, mesmerized by the dying flames, unable to move for reasons beyond his leg.

He couldn't shake the sickening feeling of betrayal. Couldn't rid himself of the rest of the questions swirling around in his head. Why had she distracted him at the fight? She'd said she had no choice. But that didn't make sense to him. Why hadn't she had a choice? Had she been forced to do it? If so, by who? Or had she done it for some personal benefit? Could she have bet on the fight?

That must be it. She'd bet on the fight. Bet against him.

But then she would have had a choice. And why the hell had she come out here to his house? Did she really work for the League? That would be easy enough to find out with a phone call in the morning.

He blew out a long breath. The hard way was to talk to her. It was also the right thing to do. He tried to make his feet move. To go talk to the woman who had ruined his life. To find out *why*.

As angry as he was, how desperate had she been to come here? And why? What was her ultimate goal? His hoard? He had to understand why she'd done what she'd done. At least then he might have some closure.

He rolled his shoulders, at last breaking free of the fire's mesmerizing effects. Grom lay a few feet away, watching Van with a curious expression. Grom knew something was wrong. Van nodded. "*Da*, there is trouble."

How had he fallen for a woman who been hiding so much from him?

He'd thought she'd been keeping something from

him. Now he knew just how right he'd been. He'd just never expected it was something this awful.

He limped to the door and wrenched it open. "Lisa, come inside. We need to talk."

There was no answer. He stuck his head out and looked around. There was no sign of her on the porch. "Lisa?"

No answer. The car must have come for her already. But there were no tracks in the driveway.

Had she left another way? What would that way be? Could she have used her supernatural powers to disappear? What kind of supernatural did she say she was? A Will-o'-the-Wisp? He knew nothing about that sort of creature. What kind of powers did they have that would allow them to disappear into a snowstorm?

That just showed how little he knew about her. Her name might not even be Lisa. She had said she was from Vegas. Which was the right thing to say if he was supposed to believe she worked for the TFL. And she said she was Irish. She looked it. But what did that matter in the scheme of things? He would call the League tomorrow morning and ask some questions about her. At least get that much truth. But that would be hours from now.

At the moment, he had a different problem on his hands. He didn't know where she was, and the snow showed no signs of stopping. He sighed and looked at Grom. "I have to go look for her."

Grom tipped his big head at Van and woofed.

Van reached for his coat hanging beside the door.

"Don't worry, I will find her. I might be angry, but I can't let her get hurt because of this. She could die in this kind of weather."

He pulled his jacket on, grabbed his crutch, and headed onto the porch. Grom whined to follow, but Van shut the door. Then he stood on the porch and inhaled, searching for her scent, for some clue of where she might have gone.

But there was nothing. The snow had blanketed everything in a thick layer, taking with it any chance of finding Lisa.

And it was still coming down.

Frustration built in him, doubling what he already felt. He was angry now, not just with her, but at himself. He'd acted rashly, out of emotion. That was the dragon in him. But his human side knew better.

Didn't it? He wanted to think so. Trouble was, both sides liked Lisa a lot, and right now, both sides were hurting. It was impossible to separate man from beast when it came to matters of the heart like this.

He walked to the edge of the porch to look for tracks again. Nothing. No car tires, no footprints. Unbelievable. He peered down the drive, trying to see through the falling flakes for any indication of where she might have gone.

His phone vibrated. Could that be her? He yanked it out of his back pocket to check the screen.

Not her. Pandora. He answered. "Hello."

"Hi there. What are you doing?"

Standing outside, feeling like an idiot. "Nothing. What are you doing?"

"Watching your pretty rehab therapist get nice and toasted at Howler's. What did you do?"

"What?" She was at Howler's. That was good. Safe. Warm. But getting drunk did not seem like Lisa. Not that he knew her. "I did not do anything."

"Really? Because she told Bridget you kicked her out."

He squeezed his eyes shut for a moment and sighed. "I did."

"Are you serious? If I was there, I would punch you. And not in a kind, loving manner. Why on earth would you do that in this weather?"

"Long story."

"I'm sure."

"Why are you at Howler's? Shouldn't you be home with Cole?"

"Charisma came home when she found out about us getting engaged, so we're having a girls' night out. We came here so we could hang with Bridget for a bit too."

"We?"

"Me, Charisma, Marigold, Willa, and Roxy. We invited Delaney and Ivy too, but they're occupied with babies. Well, Ivy's not yet, but she thinks it could be any minute, so she bowed out."

He didn't care if she was hanging out with Elenora Ellingham herself. "Good. Keep Lisa there until I get there. I am on my way."

"Hold up, buddy boy. Stay right where you are."

"Why?"

"Because, smarty-pants, you kicked her out. She may not want to see you. Ever think about that?"

He hadn't. "But we need to talk."

"I'm sure you do, but you're not doing it here until I talk to her first and make sure she wants your company."

He groaned. Women.

"I'm serious," she said. "You walk into this joint before I tell you it's okay, and I'll turn you into a salamander."

His eyes widened. "You have such a mean streak, *kotyonok*."

"Don't call me kitten. I don't know what you've done yet."

"I did not do—" He groaned. "Fine. Talk to her. But I would like a chance to speak with her before she leaves town."

"Well, you've got some time. Airport's closed because of the weather. She'll be here at least another day."

"Good."

"I'll call you as soon as I know where her head's at."

"Thank you."

"Give my love to Gromit." She hung up.

He tucked the phone away, took hold of his crutch, and went back inside. Grom looked at him expectantly. "We are not going anywhere. Aunt Pandora is a pain in my *zhopa*. Also, she says she loves you."

Grom knew very well who Pandora was. He let out a little bark.

Van nodded. "Yes, just you. Me, she is not so happy with."

"Lisa?"

Monalisa looked up from her second spiked hot chocolate to see a familiar face. "Hmm? Oh, yes. Well, it's Monalisa, actually." No point in keeping up the charade now. "And you're Pandora. The woman with the ring." She smiled sadly. "How nice for you."

"Yep, that's me." She hooked her thumb toward the woman beside her. "And this is my sister, Charisma."

Monalisa glanced at the other woman. She was sharply dressed in a silk blouse and black riding leggings tucked into black riding boots. Her tweed jacket added a nice touch. Like she'd just stepped off the cover of some British horse magazine. Her sleek brunette bob was nothing like Pandora's red hair, but Monalisa could see the resemblance in the shape of their eyes. "Nice to meet you."

Charisma stuck out her hand and smiled. "Nice to meet you as well. Pandora tells me you're a rehab therapist here to get Ivan out of the dumps and back in the ring."

Monalisa barked out a laugh, startling them both. "Yeah, no."

"No?" Pandora asked.

Bridget came over before Monalisa could answer. "You ladies need another round back there? Might as well, seeing as how we're snowed in."

Pandora nodded. "Sure, and considering that we're basically the only customers in here, why don't you join us?"

Bridget laughed. "One of us has to be the adult here. Besides, I'm working." She tossed a bar towel over her shoulder. "Refills coming up. I'll run them back there in a second. Lisa, you ready for round three?"

She put her hand over the mug. "Yes, but no more hot chocolate. Something…stronger. I just don't know what yet."

Bridget gave her a nod. "I'll get it for you the minute you do."

Charisma leaned her arm on the bar. "Why don't you join us in the back room? We're celebrating Pandora's engagement, but you look like you need to talk, and we're all exceptional listeners."

Monalisa opened her mouth to explain why she couldn't, but nothing came out.

Charisma smiled. "And, as added incentive, Pandora's fiancé is footing the bill."

Finally, Monalisa found some words. "I don't think you want your fun evening spoiled by the sordid details of what just happened between Van and me."

Pandora hopped onto the seat between Charisma and Monalisa, her back to the bar. "On the contrary.

This is a girls' night out! We're here to laugh and cry and commiserate. Also, if I can be perfectly honest, we're not really the billiards and darts crowd. It's getting a little dull back there."

"Hey," Bridget said. "You knew what that back room was for before you got here."

Pandora looked over her shoulder. "True, but we came here for the cheap drinks more than anything."

Bridget snorted and shook her head as she kept mixing cocktails.

Pandora leaned her elbows on the bar. "So what do you say? Join us? We're a tame group. I'm a realtor, Charisma's a life coach, Marigold's a florist, Willa's a jeweler, and Roxy is a writer. But above all that, we're women, we're supernaturals, and we all know how awful—and wonderful—men can be. And you look like you could use some sympathetic company."

Monalisa stared at her empty mug. The urge to unburden herself grew stronger. But she didn't know these women. Although, that was sort of a plus. So was the fact that she'd never see them again after tonight.

Pandora elbowed her gently. "C'mon. You might feel better."

Monalisa glanced up at Bridget. "Shot of Jameson, neat."

"Coming up," Bridget answered.

Monalisa slid off her seat. "I'll have it in the back. With the others."

Van knew he was supposed to wait until Pandora called him. He decided the best place to do that was the back room of Howler's. That way he'd be right there when Lisa decided she was ready to talk.

He just had to figure out how to get to Howler's with eighteen inches of snow on the ground and more joining it with every passing second.

He also had his bad leg to contend with.

That meant driving was out. Not that the roads were passable anyway.

And he couldn't shift into his dragon form because of the venom lingering in his system. He'd tried right after the injury had happened and had succeeded only in causing himself so much pain he'd blacked out. So flying was out.

At least for him.

He dialed Nick Hardwin's number. He'd only met the guy once, at the Black & Orange Halloween Ball, but they'd hit it off talking about fighting techniques.

Nick was a former Army Ranger and had some interesting ideas about hand-to-hand.

Also, they were two of the largest supernaturals in town, both could fly, and Nick's girlfriend, Willa, was one of Pandora's best friends. The two women had decided Van and Nick should be friends too.

Right after the ball, Van had left for a round of training and fights. But he liked the guy. Now he just hoped Nick remembered him.

Nick answered on the third ring. "Hello."

"Nick, this is Ivan Tsvetkov. I was hoping you would remem—"

"Van, hey, man, what's up?"

Van let out a sigh of relief. "So much. I hope you are well."

"I am." Nick hesitated. "I heard about what happened at your last fight. Really sorry about that. I should have called you, but Willa said Pandora said you weren't up to visitors, so…"

"No problem. I was not feeling very friendly, that is true."

"Everything okay now? It's kind of late. But it's cool you called. I was up."

Van took a breath and uttered the second-hardest three words he could imagine. "I need help."

"Yeah? Okay, what can I do?"

"This is an odd request."

Nick laughed softly. "I was an Army Ranger. You wouldn't believe some of the stuff I've done."

"I suppose that is true." Van collected his thoughts, trying to figure out where to start. "My injury makes it impossible for me to shift right now. And the weather is very bad. Also, I cannot drive anyway. So, I was wondering…"

He couldn't quite make himself say it. It just sounded so odd. "That is, I was thinking…" Again, the words wouldn't come out. "Could you…" Disgusted with himself for wasting time, he spat out what he meant to say. "I need you to fly me to Howler's. It is an odd thing to ask, I know, but I am desperate."

"I'm guessing this involves a woman, because no one needs to drink that bad."

Van closed his eyes. Instantly, Lisa's pretty, deceitful face appeared in his mind. "Yes, it is about a woman."

"'Nuff said." There was a smile in Nick's voice. "You know the girls are over there having a night out?"

"Yes. Pandora is supposed to be keeping Lisa occupied until I get there."

"I see. This Lisa must be something else for you to want to see her this bad."

He grunted. "Something else is right."

Nick chuckled. "Okay, I'll be over. You live up near the ridgeline, right? That big chalet-style house?"

"Yes."

"I'll be there in about ten minutes. Dress warm, it's going to be a cold ride."

Van snorted. "I will be fine."

They both hung up, then Van got Grom to go out. "You must. I am leaving."

Grom stood at the top of the steps, staring into the white abyss. He glanced back at Van.

"Give me a moment." Van eased down the porch stairs and made his way a little deeper into the snow. Then he fired up his internal furnace and let the heat radiate out of him.

As the snow began to melt, he turned in a widening circle. When he was done, he had a patch about fifteen feet wide cleared. He looked up at Grom. "There." He pointed at the space he'd made. "Now you go."

Grom trotted down and started running around in the circle and biting at the falling snowflakes.

Van laughed. "You are something, dog."

Then Grom took off into the drifts with a big leap. He sank up to his chest, but he kept going, plowing through, and running around as best he could. The trails he left behind looked like they'd been made by a drunken lunatic.

Van frowned. "That is enough. Back in the house, silly dog."

Grom perked up at the word *house*. That seemed to motivate him. He came back into the area Van had cleared, lifted his leg and peed, then dashed back onto the porch.

Van laughed and went in after him. He grabbed an old towel from the stack in the closet kept there for this exact purpose and rubbed Grom down as best he could. Van threw another log on the fire and prodded the embers a little. Grom loved a good fire to sleep by.

Then Van headed outside to wait for Nick.

The gargoyle was already there, crouched in the open area Van's heat had created. He nodded. "Hey. Thanks for the landing zone."

It took a lot to surprise a dragon shifter. But seeing Nick in his supernatural form did just that. "You are welcome." He was staring, and he knew it, but it was the first time he'd seen a gargoyle of Nick's size in his true form. "You are leviathan class. Very impressive."

Nick nodded. "Yep. Big as they come." His voice was a gravelly rumble. "I'm guessing you've fought against my kind before."

"Only titan and ranger classes. Never yours."

"We are a rare bunch." He seemed to be studying Van. "You must be about my size when you shift, right?"

Van smiled. "Something like that."

Nick's stony brows lifted. "Bigger?"

Van nodded. "Yes." Then he shrugged lightheartedly. "I am a dragon."

Nick laughed, and the sound echoed through the stillness like a shot going off.

Van narrowed his eyes. "You ever think about fighting?"

Nick shook his head. "Not in a professional way."

"Good. Let's keep it that way. I do not need the competition."

Another deep laugh rumbled out of Nick, then he gave Van a curious look. "I thought you were retired."

Van opened his mouth, then closed it again to mull that statement over. "I was. But maybe one more fight."

"Cool. I'd love to see that. If I could afford the tickets."

"For taking me to Howler's, I will get you good seats."

Nick smiled and jerked his head toward Van. "So how are we doing this?"

Van lifted the crutch over his head, a hand on each end of the metal support. "Like a hang glider."

"Sounds good to me." Nick spread his wings and lifted into the air, treating Van to a new surprise. The gargoyle was nearly soundless in flight.

Van used the crutch to get into the middle of the circle, then hoisted it overhead again.

"Hang on. You fall off, and I may not be able to catch you."

"I will be fine."

Nick grabbed hold of the crutch and, with a few powerful beats of his wings, took them straight up.

The view was spectacular, but as they rose, visibility disappeared into a white blur.

"You can see in this?"

"Enough," Nick responded. "But I don't really need to. I have a decent mental GPS."

"Good." The wind bit into Van as Nick increased his speed. He turned up his internal thermostat until he barely noticed it.

A few minutes after he'd done that, they started to descend. Nick set them down in Howler's back parking lot. There were a few cars hidden under a thick draping of snow.

"You good?"

"Yes." Van balanced on his good leg until he got the crutch under him again, which was a little more difficult with the depth of the snow. "Thank you very much."

"I hope it works out for you, man."

Van nodded, then shifted his gaze to Howler's back door. "I hope so too."

A shot and a half of Jameson's later and the strangers Monalisa had just met were fast becoming friends. They'd listened with incredible sympathy and attention to her entire history with her father, all about the coin he refused to give her, and how he'd forced her to deceive Van. She felt now like they could be friends for life.

Too bad that was such an impossibility.

Almost at the end of her tale, she tipped back the last of the whiskey in her glass, then set it down on the table of the big booth they were crowded into. She took a breath and finished what she had to say. "And then he threw me out."

The women responded with a collective gasp.

Pandora shook her head. "Outrageous."

Charisma sighed. "Just like a man not to give a woman a chance."

"Not all men," Roxy said. "But I agree, Ivan should have let you explain."

Marigold nodded, making her blonde curls bounce. "*This* is why I don't date."

Willa crossed her arms and sat back. "And I thought my stint as queen was bad. Sister, you have a world of trouble on your plate."

Pandora leaned her forearms on either side of her wine. "Van will understand if you explain."

Monalisa ran her finger around the rim of her empty whiskey glass. "I'm glad you think that, but that requires him to listen, and I don't know." She shook her head, remembering the look on his face. "I doubt that's something he's interested in."

Pandora shrugged. "His reaction was just that. A reaction. I'll go back to the house with you, and I'll get him to listen."

Monalisa sighed and looked around the table. "But he has every right to be furious at me for what I did to him. I lied to him. A lot."

"You had no choice," Charisma said. "He's got to understand what an impossible situation you were put in."

The door at the back of the room opened, letting in a gust of cold, but Monalisa barely felt it as she stabbed her finger into the table. "I'm still in it. My father's command doesn't magically go away because Van kicked me out."

"What command?"

The deep, male voice turned all six of their heads. Monalisa, Roxy, and Willa had to push up to see over the back of the booth.

"Van." Nervous energy pinged through Monalisa's body.

He stared back at her, his gaze as steely as his expression was unreadable. "Lisa." He frowned. "Is that even your name?"

"Sort of. It's actually Monalisa."

His eyes narrowed as if he was calculating just how much of a lie that was.

Pandora slipped out of the booth from her end seat, and the rest of the women followed, forming a circle around Monalisa with Pandora at the front. "Don't tell me you walked here with that leg and this weather."

"No." He tried to look past Pandora to see Monalisa, but Pandora matched his every move, blocking him.

Monalisa almost smiled at Pandora's protectiveness, but then the realization set in about how pathetic it was that the best friends she had were women she'd known less than an hour. That said so much about her life.

Pandora held her ground. "Then how on earth did you get here?"

More frowning. Van ran a hand over his shaved head. Stalling maybe? "A friend."

"You must have wanted to be here a whole lot."

"Pandora, I am here. What else matters? I need to talk to Lisa now." He grunted. "*Mona*lisa."

"I'll say you need to talk. Throwing a woman out in the middle of a massive snowstorm?" She shook her head and clucked her tongue. "Not very gentlemanly."

A muscle in his jaw twitched. "I know."

She planted her hands on her hips. "What would your mother say?"

"Enough," Van grumped. "I will speak to Monalisa now."

Pandora didn't move. "What if she doesn't want to speak to you?"

Monalisa didn't want Van tortured anymore. He'd been through enough. All of it because of her. She put her hand on Pandora's arm, moving the witch aside so she could step forward. "It's okay. I want to talk to him."

When he saw her, his expression morphed from relieved to upset, then back to a hard blankness. Except for the tiniest hint of something that looked very much like hurt in his gaze, he was once again unreadable. "Good."

He cleared his throat and looked at the women behind her.

Monalisa understood. She turned and smiled at them. "Maybe we could have a little privacy?"

They all gave her sympathetic nods. Pandora squeezed her arm. "We'll be on the other side of the bar if you need us. Just holler. We all have exceptional hearing. Well, except for Roxy. Hers is just normal."

"Thanks," Monalisa said. But she wasn't worried. For all of Van's gruffness, he wasn't going to hurt her.

Pandora started to leave, but turned at the last second to point at Van. "You be nice."

He held out his hands. "I am always nice."

She snorted and left.

The room got uncomfortably quiet with just the two of them in it.

Monalisa dug her teeth into her bottom lip as she gathered her thoughts. "It was nice of you to come."

He grunted an acknowledgment. "It was wrong of me to throw you out."

"No argument here." She took a few steps forward and leaned against the nearest pool table. "You want to hear my side of things?"

He didn't move for a moment, then he nodded. "I want to understand what drove you to do what you did. Your act ruined me."

Guilt washed over her. She stared at her feet. "I know it did. I'm so sorry. I had no idea that the outcome would be so drastic. But even if I had, I really didn't have a choice." She took a breath. "I guess maybe I did. But I've never made it through the pain long enough to find out if I really can resist. Or if it will just kill me."

His brow furrowed. "I do not understand."

"Let me start from the beginning." She pointed toward one of the booths lining the wall. "Do you want to sit? It's a long story. And you don't need to stress your leg any further."

"I am fine. But we can sit."

So they did, on opposite sides. She folded her hands on the table, one on top of the other, took a breath, and told him exactly what she'd just told the women on the other side of the restaurant.

Every single awful detail.

Van had expected a lot of excuses, a sad tale about a life gone wrong, bad choices made, decisions that couldn't be undone.

He had not expected what Monalisa actually told him, and by the time she finished, he had to remind himself to shut his mouth, because it hung open in shock and disbelief. "Your father controls you?"

She nodded, her eyes bright with angry tears. "All my life. I'm nothing to him but a weapon in his arsenal."

"I cannot understand how your father can do this. I would never treat a child of mine in such a manner."

"Not many would, but he's a leprechaun, and his status as king has made him greedy, ambitious, and paranoid. Everything he does is a calculated move designed to protect or expand his empire."

"Does he not consider you something to be protected as well?"

She flattened her palms on the table and stared at him. "What do you think, based on what I've told you?"

He clenched his teeth for a moment, his anger now directed at the man who called himself Monalisa's father. "He does not."

"The worst part is…" Her gaze went back to the tabletop as her words trailed off.

"Tell me."

"I don't want to."

He thought about taking her hand, but wasn't sure if she would welcome that. "Are you afraid of me?"

That lifted her head. "No, not really. I don't have any concerns about you hurting me. You don't seem like that kind of guy."

"Good. I am not. So then tell me."

She sighed. "I still don't want to. It's awful."

"I cannot imagine how much worse it could be."

She combed a hand through her hair, pushing it off her face, then returned both hands to the table and looked at him. "You understand I am basically powerless to resist him? I can try, of course, but—"

"You cannot fight the pain it causes." He slowly reached out and covered her hands with one of his. She didn't flinch or pull away, so he kept it there. "I do not want you to suffer because of me. I know pain. And I do not want you to become as familiar with it as I have these last few weeks."

"Thank you."

He lifted her top hand and brought it to his mouth, kissing her knuckles. "I want you to know too that I do not blame you for any of this. And now that I know, my feelings for you are…as they were."

She sniffed, and her mouth bent in a tiny smile. "You're a good man, Ivan Tsvetkov. My feelings are the same for you too."

"Then tell me what this worse thing is, and we will figure it out together."

She stared at his hand, her gaze taking on a distant

gleam. "He has commanded me to bring you to Vegas for the rematch."

"I know that, *zolotse*."

She barely noticed that he'd called her by that strange Russian word again. "In five days."

He jerked back. "Less than a week? The venom will still be in my system. Fighting will be very difficult. Winning will be impossible."

She nodded, looking like she was on the verge of tears. "I tried to tell him that, but he has whales coming in—regular clients who spend huge amounts when they're at the casino—and he wants the rematch to happen while they're there so they can bet on it and up his take."

"What about Ronan? He has to agree to this too."

"Ronan's been staying in the Dublin Suite since the fight. I think he's as deep in my father's pocket as you can get without being part of the pants he has on."

Van sat back. "That is a conflict of interest. Does the League know?"

"A few of the officials do, but my father pays them off to look the other way."

"Your father does not deserve the power he holds."

"No, he doesn't. But what can I do about that? What can any of us do?"

Van tapped his fingers on the table. "I have an idea." He pointed toward the other side of the bar. "But we're going to need your new friends."

"Gang's all here," Pandora said as the women rejoined them. "I take it you two have made up."

"We have." Monalisa had swapped sides to sit with Van. They were hip to hip and thigh to thigh, and his radiating warmth was as welcome as his comforting presence and smoky scent. She knew she was basically in love with him at this point and how silly it was to be so crazy about someone she'd known for such a little amount of time, but she didn't care. He was the best man she knew.

And she wanted to keep him.

Van nodded. "What happened was not Monalisa's fault. And she needs my help. But first, I need your help."

"Mine?" Pandora asked.

"You and your sisters." He looked at the other two women. "And yours too, if you can help."

They all nodded.

"Sure," Pandora said. "What do you need?"

Monalisa wanted to know too.

He gestured to the empty side of the booth. "Sit. This is important business."

Pandora, Charisma, and Marigold slid onto the bench while Roxy and Willa pulled chairs over.

When they were all seated, he leaned forward. "I need you to find a spell that will rid me of this venom. I need you to heal me so that I can fight again. And I need you to do it now."

The sisters looked at each other. Charisma spoke first. "Can we do that?"

Marigold shook her head. "I don't know. I've never done it before. But I could make a tincture to dull the pain."

"Not good enough," Van said. "The venom must be gone. I must be whole. I must be able to shift."

Willa tucked her hands under her thighs. "You three are very powerful together. There must be something you can do."

Pandora nodded. "I'm not saying we can't, just that we never have. We'll have to dig into my mother's library and do some research. That's the best we can do." She smiled at Van and Monalisa. "We'll figure something out. I promise."

Roxy straightened. "Maybe I can help. I'm great at research."

Bridget joined them, bar towel still over her shoulder. "This has turned into quite the party, I see. You know, I could be closed right now. Y'all are the only ones in here. Besides me and Juan Carlos in the kitchen." She turned to look out the windows. "But seeing as how no one can go anywhere…"

Van slapped his hand on the table. "If Juan is here, we should put him to work. And make this worth your while. Who's hungry?"

Pandora grinned. "You buying?"

"Of course. I want you all well-fortified for the work ahead."

"In that case…" Pandora lifted a finger. "I'll have the petite filet and a side of the lobster mac and cheese. And truffle fries. Because, why not?"

The rest of the women started ordering and asking questions. Bridget laughed, pulled a notebook out of her apron, and began scribbling.

Monalisa tucked her arm through Van's and snuggled up close to whisper in his ear. "Thank you."

He turned and kissed her temple. "I told you, I am a protector. This is what I do. And you are who I want to protect. Always."

She leaned in and kissed his cheek. "I hope they can find a way to help you."

He patted her hand on his arm. "They will. You'll see." Then he smiled. "But first, we eat."

"And then I guess we figure out how to get home."

Bridget turned toward them. "That reminds me. The snow has stopped, and I just talked to my brothers. The plows are on their way. By the time you're done eating, the roads should be clear."

"Good," Van said. "Then one of you can take Monalisa and me home."

Willa grinned. "You mean you don't want Nick to fly you back?"

They all looked at her.

She laughed and held up her phone. "He texted me."

Van rolled his eyes while the women cracked up. "Maybe I will not buy dinner after all…"

Twenty-four hours of reading, researching, and talking to the most powerful witches in town and Pandora and her sisters had yet to come up with a solution to Van's problem. He punched the heavy bag in a one-two combo, trying to rid himself of this new frustration.

It helped, but not enough.

And while the pain in his leg subsided a little more every day, it wouldn't be gone enough by fight time. Five days. Four now. What a joke. He'd be the walking wounded and an easy target. Sweat trickled down his back as he continued to pummel the bag. All Ronan would have to do was land blows on the bite mark and Van would go down.

Monalisa's father might not care about the results of the rematch, but Van did. This would be his last fight. And he wanted to leave the ring victorious.

"Still at it?"

He turned to see Monalisa walking toward him. "Just a little bit more."

"You've been down here for two hours. How much more could there be left to do? Not that I'm complaining if you want to stay shirtless for a little longer."

Grinning, he used his forearm to wipe the sweat from his brow. "The rematch is only four days away. I need to be ready."

Her smile turned a little sad as her gaze slipped to his brace. "I know."

"Don't worry about me. I will be fine." He wasn't sure how, but Pandora would come through. She always did.

"Okay, well, I'll let you get back to it. I just wanted to tell you that I'm going to take Grom out for a bit, then I was hoping we could go into town. Maybe get some dinner?" Her smile brightened. "I do have my father's credit card, so whatever the most expensive place is, let's go there."

He laughed. "We can do that." A night out with Monalisa would be good, especially if they could forget about the rematch for an hour or two.

She started back toward the steps, then stopped in front of the vault door. "Where does that lead, by the way? The way the floor above this is laid out, it's like there shouldn't be anything there. Unless it goes into the side of the hill."

He stiffened. That was exactly what it did. Then he forced himself to relax. Monalisa had been brutally honest with him, laying her whole life out for him to judge. There was no reason he couldn't share a little with her. Even if it meant revealing one of his most closely held secrets. "It does go into the hillside."

She glanced over her shoulder. "For real?"

He nodded, then grabbed his towel to wipe the rest of the sweat off.

"Wow, that's cool. So is it like a fallout shelter?" She grinned at him. "I want to be on your zombie apocalypse survival team."

He laughed as he pulled his shirt on. "No, it is a vault. It's for…" How much was he willing to tell her? If he wanted a future with her, everything. "I keep my hoard in there."

Her face screwed up into a question. "Your hoard?"

"I am a dragon. We have hoards."

"You mean like treasure?"

"Exactly like that." He expected her eyes to light up or a big smile to come across her face. Clearly, he still had a lot to learn about Monalisa.

Because she frowned. "Oh."

"You think that is a bad thing?"

She shrugged. "My father has a hoard. Not saying you're anything like him, not at all, because you're obviously not. It's just…I don't know. Great wealth has a way of making people do things they might not otherwise." She gave him a brief smile. "Of course, for all I know, you could have a random stamp collection and an old Studebaker in there. Treasure is in the eye of the beholder, right?"

"No stamps. Or cars. Also, nothing that will change who I am. I promise. A dragon's hoard is for times of need, to enable them to take care of those they love and need to protect. It is something we fiercely protect as well, but things will never outweigh the value of a person. Not for a dragon."

Her smile returned. "That's nice to hear. My father certainly doesn't feel that way, but then, his hoard is pretty massive."

"Mine is…" Showing her would be easier than explaining. He limped over and put his hand on the bio scanner. The laser read his print, then cogs turned and the locks clicked. When the last one sounded, he grabbed the handle and pulled the enormous door open.

The lights inside flickered on automatically.

Her mouth rounded in amazement. She blinked twice, then finally pointed at the space in front of her. "Now *that* is a hoard."

Monalisa understood instantly what it meant that Van had shared this with her. He trusted her. It was a staggering revelation after all they'd been through. For him to put that sort of faith in her made her feel a little unworthy. And very, very lucky. "I won't tell a soul about this. I promise."

He nodded like he'd already known that. "You want to go in?"

More than she wanted to put a very expensive dinner on her father's credit card. "Can I? I won't touch anything."

He laughed. "It is no fun if you don't touch." He tipped his head toward the vault. "Come. I will show you my favorite pieces."

He held his hand out for her to go ahead of him. She walked in and took a look around. It was exactly what you'd imagine a dragon's hoard might be. Piles of gold coins, chests full of bejeweled trinkets, shelves laden with gold and silver objects, crystal bowls overflowing with precious gems. Everywhere she looked, things sparkled back at her in the low light.

She did a slow turn, taking it all in. "How can you pick favorites?"

"They are the ones that have meaning beyond their value." He walked to a glass case and stopped in front of it. "Like these."

She joined him for a better look. "Fabergé eggs." Three of them, each more spectacular than the next. "Of course you'd pick those. They're Russian, like you."

His eyes stayed on the treasures. "Yes, but these were also my mother's."

The significance of that hit her hard. He'd clearly had such a different childhood than she had. She looped her arm through his. "You must miss her very much."

"I do. She was a remarkable woman." He bent his head toward her. "Much like you."

She let out a soft, quick laugh. "I'm not remarkable."

"But you are. The burden you bear…many would have crumbled long before now. Or turned to the side of darkness. It would be easier, would it not?"

She thought about that. "Yes. If I was a team player and just happily went along with my father's plans, he'd be thrilled. He might have even given me that stupid coin by now. But I can't do that. I can't even pretend. He's so awful."

"We will find a way to make you free. That is my promise to you."

She smiled at him. "Thank you. I hope that can happen. I don't know how much more of life under his thumb I can take."

"It will happen. You will see." He tugged her forward. "Come, I will show you the crown jewels of a kingdom that no longer exists."

She followed him, but part of her was lost in the thought of what could be. If she actually got her freedom, she could do anything, go anywhere, be anything. Nocturne Falls would figure into all of those possibilities.

"This sapphire is nearly fifty carats and—"

"I want to move here." She stared at him. "When I get free, I want to move to Nocturne Falls."

He put the scepter down. "I want that too."

"I don't have any money, or a place to stay, and I don't have any skills, but if you'll help me, I promise I will pay you back."

"Of course, *zolotse*. I will help you with whatever you need. You can stay here."

She shook her head. "I don't want you to think I'm ungrateful for that offer, but I don't think that's the best way for us to get to know each other. We've been forced upon each other this week, and that's turned out okay, but I want…I need to know what it's like to live on my own. My father's never allowed it."

Van nodded. "That makes sense. I believe I know a place you can rent very reasonably."

"Thank you for understanding. And for helping." She squinted at him. "What is that word you called me?"

"*Zolotse*?"

She nodded.

He hesitated, looking almost sheepish. "It means *my gold*."

His explanation left her speechless.

He leaned in and kissed her. "You are a treasure to me."

She threw her arms around him in a hard embrace. "Thank you." She'd never known anyone so kind or so concerned with what happened to her. Even if she never got free of her father, Van had shown her that there was more to life than what she'd experienced. That there was compassion in this world, not just commands.

He put his hands on her shoulders, eased her back, and gazed into her eyes. "You helped me see that retreating from the world was no way to live. And gave me purpose again. Also, my dragon side has decided it wants you very much."

She laughed. "Oh really? Your dragon side wants a Will-o'-the-Wisp?"

He nodded. "And as you can see around you, what my dragon side wants, it usually gets. Of course, you are not just a priceless treasure, you are a person with feelings and your own mind, so if you do not want me…" He shrugged playfully.

She poked him. "I want you." She felt her cheeks get hot. "You're the first man I've ever said that to."

"Good." He beamed. "I would like to be the last."

"Sure, you say that now, but wait until you get to know me." She loved teasing him, this easy back-and-forth. It was new and fun and felt exactly like what she'd always thought falling in love would feel like.

"I will prove it." He limped toward one of the chests filled with coins, grabbed one, and limped back. "Your father may not have given you a coin, but I will." He held it out. "From me to you. A gift to prove my intentions are true and real."

She stared at the coin. It wasn't the one she'd always dreamed about, but it suddenly seemed so much better. "I don't know what to say. You don't have to do that. I was only teasing."

He leaned on the crutch, still holding out the coin. "Accept it, Monalisa. A dragon doesn't share his hoard with just anyone."

Smiling, she took the coin. The gold was warm from his touch. "Thank you. That's the best gift I've ever gotten."

The doorbell rang, and they both looked up.

"I'll get it." She could get up there before he could anyway.

"Thank you." He motioned for her to go ahead of him. "I'll close the vault and be right behind you."

"Okay, see you upstairs." She took a few steps toward the door, then went back and kissed his cheek. "Thanks again."

He grinned. "Go ahead, or I will give you everything in here."

She laughed and ran off, getting to the door a few seconds later. She opened it to see Pandora. "Hey, how are you? Come on in."

"Thanks." Pandora stomped the snow off her

boots before entering. "I'm good. How are you guys doing?"

"Pretty good. Van's on his way up."

"Great." She unzipped her coat. "Then I can talk to you both at the same time."

Grom came barreling up from the basement and practically knocked Pandora down. She laughed and crouched to love on him. "Hiya, Grommy, how's my boy? Did you miss me?"

He licked her face, making her laugh some more, then took off in an excited dash around the house, brushing past Monalisa and knocking the coin from her hand.

She scooped it up, slipped it into the pocket of her jeans, and started for the kitchen. "You want some coffee or something? I was going to make another pot anyway."

Pandora stayed by the door. "What did you just pick up off the floor?"

"Nothing." Then, realizing Pandora might not entirely trust her yet, Monalisa backtracked. "A coin. Van gave it to me. You can ask him when he comes up."

Pandora stood, her expression bright. "Is that from his hoard?"

"Y-yes. But like I said, he gave it to me, so—"

"Holy cats. He means business."

"What? Why?"

Pandora's eyes widened a little. "That is a *coin* from his *hoard*. Dragons don't give up parts of their hoard to just anyone. He's serious about you to give you that. Like, thinking-about-the-future serious."

The weight of the coin in Monalisa's pocket became a palpable thing. "Should I...what should I do?"

"Do you like him that way too?"

She nodded. "I do. I really do."

"Then nothing. Hang on to it. It's kind of like a dragon promise ring."

Monalisa glanced down at her pocket, impressed that Van thought so much of her. "Wow."

Van appeared at the top of the steps in the kitchen. "What is wow?"

Monalisa's head came up. "Um…"

"Hey, Van." Pandora waved and leaned against the counter. "I was just telling Monalisa that Charisma and I have finally talked Marigold into using an online dating site."

He frowned. "That is not a good idea. Those sites are full of weirdos."

Pandora rolled her eyes. "Hey, Mari's not getting any younger. And Saffie needs a male role model in her life."

"She has Stanhill."

"And he's a peach, but maybe someone who isn't several centuries old."

"Bring her around here. I will be her role model."

Pandora snorted and made a face at Monalisa. "We're not trying to frighten the child."

He sighed. "Then what is wrong with Cole? You did agree to marry him."

Pandora cut her eyes at him. "She needs a daddy of her own."

He nodded. "I suppose that is true." He grabbed a bottle of water out of the fridge, then held it out to them. "Ladies?"

They both declined.

He shut the fridge, twisted off the top, and drank half the bottle before walking over to them. He gestured to Pandora with the bottle. "So, have you come to tell me you can fix my leg?"

Her happy expression faded. "About that. I'm really sorry, but we've hit a dead end."

Van's heart sank. "This is bad."

Pandora held her hands up. "I know, it's not what I wanted to tell you, I promise, but we've scoured the books in my mom's library, we've talked to the rest of the coven, even consulted Alice Bishop—"

"Who's that?" Monalisa asked.

"She's the oldest, most powerful witch in town. Pretty much works exclusively for the Ellinghams. Namely, Elenora Ellingham. They're the family that founded Nocturne Falls. Anyway, Alice is kind of Elenora's assistant, seeing as how the grand dame saved Alice from the Salem trials way back when."

Monalisa's brows shot up. "Old *and* powerful. Got it."

He growled softly to get their attention. "I am going to lose this fight. How is it not possible for you to fix this?"

Pandora sighed. "It's like this. If you were a normie—" She glanced at Monalisa. "That's a nonmagical human."

Monalisa nodded.

Pandora continued. "If you were a normie with the venom of a supernatural, we could extract that without too much fuss. If you were a supernatural with some kind of regular poison in your system, we could most likely deal with that too. But you're a supe with supe poisoning. The only spell that we thought remotely might work also carried the risk of you ending up no longer a dragon."

Van jerked back. "Unacceptable."

"That's what we figured too."

The spot between his brows was starting to throb. He rubbed it. "I will lose again."

Pandora put a hand on Van's arm. "Listen. I know things seem bleak, but we have a theory. First, I need to ask—you've tried to shift into your dragon form, right?"

"Yes."

"So what happens?"

He shrugged. "As soon as the change begins, the pain intensifies. It's like I'm being bitten all over again. I cannot complete the change."

"What stops you?"

He looked at Pandora and wondered if she'd heard anything he'd just said. "The pain. Did I not explain that well? It was bad. I blacked out."

She sighed, pursing her lips like she was a little exasperated with him. "That's awful, but I get that. Is that all that stops you, or is there some supernatural shutdown that happens?"

He frowned right back at her. "Is that *all*? The pain

222

caused me to pass out. I do not think you understand what I am saying."

"No, I get it. Intense pain. And you're out like a light. But no other supernatural reason? At least nothing you can sense?"

"Pandora." Monalisa wrapped a strand of hair around one finger. "Where are you going with this?"

"Well…" She put her hands on the counter behind her and pulled herself up to sit. "We think you *can* shift. And by shifting, you'll force the venom to run its course. That's why it hurts so much. It's burning itself out of your system."

He dipped his chin to stare at her. "You want me to try to shift again?"

"Absolutely."

"I will just black out again."

"How long ago did you attempt to shift?"

"Right after the fight."

"Then it shouldn't be like that now. Time has passed. There's less venom in your system."

"But maybe I pass out because shifting would be worse. It could be my body's way of protecting me. Shifting now could be worse."

Pandora's smile went slack. "That probably won't…I mean, there's no way—"

"Wait a minute," Monalisa said. "Could his trying to shift injure him more? What's the worst-case scenario here?"

Pandora sucked her bottom lip under her top teeth. "That's the tricky part. We don't really know."

Monalisa shook her head. "Then he can't do it."

He took her hand, squeezing it for reassurance. "If it is the only way?"

Monalisa looked at him. "You can't. You have no idea what the outcome will be. What if it makes your leg worse? Or…hurts you in some other way?"

"I won't let it go that far."

"How will you know?" She blinked hard, eyes shining bright. "Please don't do this on my account."

"I don't have a choice. If I step into that ring unhealed, it will be very bad for me."

"Forget the fight," she pleaded. "This is my problem, I'll deal with it. I've been dealing with it for years."

He enclosed both her hands in his. "Monalisa, what you dealt with in the past, you did alone. No more. Going forward, we do this together."

"Van…" She swallowed, and took a deep breath. "I just don't want anything to happen to you."

"I know. It won't. I promise." He looked up at Pandora. "I need a safe place to do this. The clearing behind Sebastian Ellingham's. Do you think he would allow it?"

She nodded. "Absolutely. I'll call him and set it up. It's covered with snow, but that's no big deal."

"The snow will be gone when I'm done."

She hopped off the counter to stand beside them. "When do you want to do it?"

"As soon as possible. I have dealt with this pain long enough."

Monalisa's grip on his hand tightened. "You don't have to go through this."

"I do." He smiled, although he didn't really feel like it. "It will be good to be in my dragon form again." That much was very true.

Several hours later, they were trudging through the snow toward the clearing behind Sebastian Ellingham's estate. Monalisa had driven Van's Hummer quite skillfully, even if she hadn't exactly gone the speed limit. But he'd rather her feel safe and them be a little late, than for her to get upset about driving an unfamiliar vehicle in the snow.

They'd parked at the head of the trail and were now almost at the clearing. Van had been surprised to see so many other cars, but no doubt word had spread about what he was going to attempt.

The open space had been used for many things over the years. The first transformation of a young shifter, the combat necessary to settle certain disagreements, bouts of good-natured wrestling among shifters in town.

Today, Van hoped it would not become blackened by the combustion of a dragon.

He'd known of one such tragedy in his lifetime— Yuri, a distant cousin, was hexed by one of the witches in his village. Yuri had defied the witch by dating her daughter. Fearing Yuri would take her daughter and fly away, the witch had cursed him to remain forever in his human form.

Yuri had laughed at the witch and told her not to waste her breath, that her magic wouldn't work. Then, to prove to her how foolish she was being, he'd stepped back, spread his arms wide, and shifted.

Except, he hadn't shifted. The witch's magic *had* worked. The transformation had bottled up inside him, and with friends and family watching, he'd combusted into a ball of fire, turning to ash before their eyes.

The tragic event had left a lasting impression on Van, giving him a healthy respect for the women of the craft and an even greater fear of upsetting one of them.

But it had not been enough to keep him from working with Pandora, and his relationship with her was one of the best he had. She was an excellent friend, true and dear, and through knowing her, he'd come to understand that painting everyone with the same brush was a foolish way to judge people.

With that in mind, he hoped that what he was about to attempt would not result in the same catastrophe Yuri had suffered. He took some comfort in the fact that Yuri had been cursed, but he was here with the blessing and good wishes of some very powerful witches. That had to count for something.

As Van and Monalisa crested the small rise that led into the clearing, he stopped and tugged on her hand. "Look."

Standing at the tree line, surrounding the circle, were a host of friendly and familiar faces. Pandora and her sisters were close to the front. She gestured for them to join the group. "Come on."

Van and Monalisa started walking again. Seeing all those faces was a good surprise, but he worried that if things didn't go well, his friends would bear an awful memory of this day for the rest of their lives, as he did with Yuri.

Perhaps that showed on his face, because Pandora broke away to approach Van and Monalisa as they neared. "I hope you don't mind that everyone showed up. It's for support, I promise, not in hopes of some kind of spectacle."

Before Van could respond, Sheriff Hank Merrow stepped forward.

He cleared his throat. "Son, you want us gone, we're gone. But if you don't want to go through this alone, we're here. We even cleared the space for you. Anything we can do to help, we will."

Van looked past the sheriff. The snow was tamped down in a large area going all the way to the tree line. Van's throat tightened at the show of support. He swallowed against it. These were good people. "Stay."

The sheriff nodded. "In that case…" He held out his hand toward the crowd.

A pretty young woman separated herself from the group. She had blue hair and pointed ears. Elf, Van guessed.

She waved at him. "Hi. I'm Jayne Frost. I'm a winter elf, and my gifts tend to run toward the cold and icy." She wiggled her fingers and fresh snowflakes fell out of thin air.

"Impressive. And while it is nice to meet you…" He shrugged. "I think we are good on snow."

She laughed. "That we are, so I'm sure you're wondering why my skills matter to you right now."

He couldn't stop himself from nodding.

Her smile didn't diminish. "I can keep you from overheating, if it seems like that's going to happen."

He snorted, then realized he must sound derisive. He hadn't meant to. "That is very kind, but I don't think anyone can control the inner furnace that burns inside a dragon."

She arched her brows, narrowed her gaze, and pointed at him.

A wave of cold enveloped him with such force, he shivered. He held his hands up in surrender as he made a mental note that winter elves were not to be doubted. "I stand corrected. You are clearly more powerful than I imagined. Your help is most welcome, Miss Frost."

She blew on her fingers, then polished them on her coat as she grinned. "You got it."

"That's Princess Frost," Birdie Caruthers shouted out.

Jayne rolled her eyes, then shook her head at Van and mouthed a silent, "No, it's not."

Van glanced at everyone who'd shown up. The sheriff and his brother, the fire chief, and their sister, Bridget. Roxy, the writer he'd met at Howler's, was in the crowd, standing with a man in a deputy's uniform. Stanhill and Corette. Van was deeply touched by the gathering. "Thank you all for coming. I hope that I will not disappoint."

Nick and Willa were in the back. The gargoyle lifted his fist in the air. "You got this, man."

Van lifted a hand in acknowledgment, then he

looked at Monalisa. He wanted to say something to reassure her, but the thought of what might happen had him tongue-tied.

She smiled up at him. "You're going to be just fine."

"I hope you are right."

"If you don't want to do this—"

"I do. I want to be myself again and to fight and for you to be free. None of that can happen without that first step."

She threw her arms around him. "Thank you."

He hugged her back. "You are welcome, *zolotse*." He released her. "Now go, stand somewhere safe. With Pandora and her sisters."

She nodded and moved off to join the witches.

He took a moment to clear his head, the same way he did before entering the ring. Then he went through the monologue he used to pump himself up.

His purpose was conquest. He shook his hands and rolled his shoulders. His purpose was the defeat of his enemy. The outside world fell away. His purpose was the honor of his family. A calm overtook him. The feeling of victory.

Nothing existed in him but purpose. It filled his lungs, pumped through his veins, and colored his vision. His inner beast came to life, and in his mind's eye, he saw his dragon form, wings unfurled and flames billowing from his open jaws.

He lowered his head, dropped his crutch, and limped into the center of the clearing.

Monalisa almost couldn't bear to watch, but she had to know what was happening. She wanted to see for herself that he was going to be okay. Not even dealing with her father made her feel this stressed out. She pressed her hands to her mouth. Her pulse beat in the tips of her fingers, making them tremble along with the rest of her.

She couldn't remember a time she'd been so nervous. She took a few deep breaths, trying to find some kind of calm to get her through.

"He's going to be okay," Pandora whispered.

She nodded, unwilling to speak and break the dead calm that had fallen over those assembled. They all seemed to understand the brink upon which Van stood. Even the wind had died down.

She took her eyes off of him for a moment to look at the faces around her. Most were lined with tension or taut with worry. She imagined that was what she looked like too, and something about all of them feeling the same way allowed her to relax a little. They were in this together. Her and Van and all of them.

It was incredible that they'd all shown up. Really spoke to the strength of the supernatural community in Nocturne Falls. When people showed up to support her father, it was because they were afraid of him or wanted to curry favor. But these people had come because they genuinely cared. Amazing. But she understood. Van was a great guy.

Her gaze returned to the man she was steadily falling for.

He stared down at the ground, hands loose at his sides. Then his eyes closed, and his fingers tightened into fists. His knuckles whitened. The muscles in his jaw twitched. His injured knee bent slightly, and he grimaced. She knew he must be willing the change to happen and was experiencing the first onslaught of pain because of it.

Shimmers of heat rose off him in thin, wobbly lines that rippled the air like a distant heat mirage in the middle of summer, but this was February, and summer was a long way off. Then the snow under his feet melted.

He was clearly struggling against the toil of the effort, but there was no sign of any change. Not yet. She wished there was something she could do. Anything besides stand idly by while the seconds ticked away and the circle of bare earth under his feet expanded.

The cold around her seemed to be lessening.

She took her hands from her face and reached out like she would toward a roaring fire. Van was the reason the temperature had changed. The heat rolling off him wasn't overwhelming, but it was enough to gently warm her bare skin.

She looked toward Jayne, the winter elf who'd offered to help. The woman caught her gaze. She nodded as if sensing Monalisa's request that she do something, but then raised her brows in question.

Monalisa glanced at Pandora for reassurance.

Pandora put her hand on Monalisa's arm and whispered, "No. He needs the heat right now to burn that venom out."

"But…" Monalisa whispered back. Her heart ached. She wanted to help. Wanted someone to help. She hated that he was going through this alone. Because, despite the gathered crowd, he was the only one physically dealing with this. And it was all because of her.

Pandora leaned in. "I know it's hard, but trust me, he's going to be fine."

"I hope you're—"

A loud, guttural bellow rang out across the open space, and Van fell to the ground on all fours. Tiny wisps of smoke rose off his back as his body was racked by a shudder that Monalisa swore she could feel.

A few people gasped. Monalisa grabbed Pandora's hand and squeezed.

Van's whole body tensed. His back arched, and his muscles contracted so sharply that they were visible beneath his coat. More curls of smoke spiraled off him as his next roar of pain ripped across the clearing, shaking the trees. The heat emanating from him caused several people to back up.

Monalisa stepped forward. She glanced at Pandora and Jayne. "Help him, please."

Pandora gave a nod, so Jayne moved toward him, hands raised.

Van's head came back. His eyes gleamed red, and a pattern of scales appeared on his skin. His dragon was struggling to get out. Cords of muscle in his neck tensed. The grass around him, dried out by the intense heat, burst into flames.

He opened his mouth and let out one more deafening roar as a brilliant shower of sparks and smoke erupted off him.

Monalisa threw her hands up against the explosion. Billows of smoke filled the small arena. She coughed and waved it away to no avail. "Van!"

No answer. At first. Then a low rumble greeted her. It came from above. Odd.

As the smoke cleared, she understood why.

"Van," she whispered as she craned her head back. He was still at the center of the clearing. But now, he was a dragon. A rather large one. "You did it."

Several in the crowd retreated a little as a nervous but happy buzz wafted through the space. Monalisa took another step forward, careful to mind the small fires still burning while staring up at the enormous creature before her.

He was breathtakingly beautiful. His coloring

ranged from midnight blue through deep teal to emerald green, all with an iridescent purple sheen. Then the sun broke through the clouds, and his scales glittered like jewels.

He arched and unfurled his wings in what looked like a well-enjoyed stretch. His wing tips almost touched the trees on either side. Then he shook his head and snorted, sending two hot blasts of steam into the air.

"Van?" She wasn't sure how much understanding he had in this form. Most shifters were just as capable, if not more so, in their second forms, but the legendary types might be different.

He tucked his broad, leathery wings down along his spine, then bent his head to look at her, dipping low to meet her eyes. She saw recognition in his gaze. He definitely knew who she was.

"Van, you're so beautiful. And huge." She wanted to touch him, but he *was* a dragon. Maybe touching him wasn't a good idea. She kept her hands to her sides. "Can you understand me?"

He nodded. His head was the size of a Christmas turkey. Bigger, maybe.

"Good, a yes. Are you still in pain?"

This time, he shook his big head.

"Oh, that's excellent news. So the shift did it. The venom is gone."

His mouth curled back, exposing teeth that looked positively Jurassic. She almost sucked in an alarmed breath, but then she realized he was smiling.

She grinned back. "Your smile is a little scary, just so you know."

He snorted, causing her to jump back to avoid the steamy blasts.

"Hey!"

He jerked his head up, then brought it right back down and laid it at her feet in what seemed to be a plea for forgiveness. He looked up at her with wide, sad eyes.

In that moment, he reminded her very much of Grom. She kept that to herself. "It's okay. I know you didn't mean it. At least you put out the last of the fires."

He wiggled his head back and forth, agreeing with her.

His easy manner in this form gave her some confidence. "Can I touch you?"

Another nod.

She stretched out her hand and stroked the scales between his eyes. They were the color of the ocean at the horizon, a deep, unfathomable green, and they had the warm, smooth feel of polished leather. "Wow."

Pandora walked up to them. "I hate to interrupt, but is everything okay, Van? I'm assuming so since you shifted, but figured I should check. Everyone wants to know. And I promised to call Cole and Kaley at home and let them know as soon as you were all right."

Monalisa clenched her hand, still relishing the feel of his scales under her fingertips, and faced Pandora. "He said the pain is gone."

Her eyes widened. "You can hear him? Like in your head, or what?"

"No, he didn't talk like that. I just asked him some yes-or-no questions."

"Oh, right. Cool." She smiled. "Excellent news." Then she twisted to face the crowd and gave a thumbs-up. "Van confirmed it! The shift worked!"

Everyone cheered and clapped. Monalisa joined them, ecstatic for a moment, until she realized what this meant. Van was actually going back into the ring, this time on her behalf. That ramped her nerves back up. Once again, he was going to face a risk because of her. The burden of that weighed on her tremendously.

Something disturbed the air behind her.

She turned. Van (human Van) was standing a few feet away, looking just as he had been before he'd shifted, clothes and all. "You're back."

"I am."

Happy to see his smiling face again, she ran toward him. "Not that you left exactly, but you know what I mean."

"I do." He moved toward her, no limp in sight, and caught her in his arms. "It is so good to be whole again. And free from that poison. Thank you."

She frowned. "Why are you thanking me? You did the hard stuff. And it was Pandora's idea for you to try shifting again."

"Because I would still be sulking and in pain, thinking my life was over, if not for you."

"Glad to hear you enjoyed my interference so much."

He laughed and pressed a kiss to the side of her head. "I did. Now, let's thank everyone and go home. We have a trip to prepare for."

"And a fight," she reminded him. "You need to be as ready for that fight as you can be. If anything happens to you, I won't ever forgive myself."

"Nothing will happen. I am healed. And I will be ready." He released her and took her hand, then he faced Pandora and her sisters. "Thank you so much for urging me to do this." He looked at some of the others. "Thank you all for your support."

The sheriff and a few others nodded.

Van put his free hand over his heart as he spoke to them all. "I am very glad to call this place my home."

"Good to have you back," Nick Hardwin called out.

Van pointed at him as the rest of the crowd began to disperse. "Soon, we will go flying."

"Sounds good," Nick said, grinning. "But don't forget, you owe me tickets to a fight."

Van nodded. "Then get ready to travel, because it's happening in four days."

Monalisa shivered.

Van looked at her. "You all right?"

"I'm fine. It's just the realization that, besides you having to get into the ring again, I'm going to have to face my father."

"Remember, we are a team now. You don't have to do anything alone anymore."

She squeezed his hand. "Thank you. Come on, Grom is probably dancing at the door waiting to go out."

Van's mouth opened. "Grom. Who will watch him while we're gone?"

"What about Bridget? She is sort of his people, after all."

"Hah, very good. I will call her."

By the time they got back to the house, Monalisa had been silent a long while. Van knew it was because she was worried about seeing her father again and dealing with him. He didn't know how to make her believe that everything would be okay, but he felt it in his gut.

He would also do everything in his power to make it true. Power that was fairly substantial, given that he could shift again. Winning the fight would be easy.

Not easy, exactly, but there would be no distractions, and if necessary, he would shift and put Ronan down fast.

He'd never done it before, as a matter of balance and fairness, but this fight wasn't about that. It was about getting Monalisa free.

Maybe if they made a plan, she would feel better. They needed to do it anyway, to be on the same page when they got to Vegas. Her father would have to be dealt with carefully so that they each got the results they wanted.

He resolved that the plan would be the next order of business as soon as they got inside.

They went up the porch steps. He unlocked the door and stood back. Grom came rushing out, as Van expected. He caught the dog in his arms, lifting the squirming, wriggling animal for a bear hug. "Missed us, did you?"

Monalisa laughed and scratched Grom's back. "I think he missed you."

Grom twisted around and licked her on the face, making Van laugh. "See? It was both of us."

"Ew, okay." Still laughing, she wiped at the slobber.

Van put Grom down. The dog took off for the yard, but instead of his usual marathon around the house, he did his business promptly, then jogged up onto the porch and right back inside.

"I guess he's had enough of the snow," Monalisa said.

Van looked out at his property and the blanket of white. "I am not so fond of it either."

"You grew up in Russia. Isn't it all-snow-all-the-time there?"

He laughed. "Yes, there is a lot of snow in certain parts. Especially where I grew up. Maybe that is why I am tired of it."

"Spring will be here soon enough." She leaned into him. "Too bad it's not here now, though. I bet it's beautiful here in the spring and summer. All green and flowery, right?"

"Yes." He nodded. "Very different than what you're used to."

"Very. Everything can get pretty brown in the desert." She sighed. "I hope I'm here in the spring to see it."

He put his arm around her. "You will be, *zolotse*. I promise."

But Monalisa wasn't going to hold him to that promise. That wouldn't be fair, because it wasn't one he could keep. Her father was a stubborn man who only wanted what was best for himself. She doubted bringing Van back for the rematch would be enough to earn her the coin that was rightfully hers, no matter how optimistically she wanted to think. And without that coin, without the freedom that came with it, there was no way she could know where she'd be by spring.

Her father just wasn't the kind of man who kept his word. Sure, there was a first time for everything, but would this be it? She hoped so very much it was.

Van was, so she smiled and nodded. "I'd love to be here for the change of seasons. It would be fun to go on a picnic. You, me, and Grom."

"Then that is what we will do. But right now, we need to make a plan."

"For Vegas, right?"

He nodded. "Also, I could eat. Shifting gives me an appetite. You wanted to go out for dinner, so let's go. We can talk over the meal."

"You have a place in mind?"

"There is a nice bistro in town. It's quiet and romantic. What do you think?"

"I think that would be great." It was what she'd wanted anyway, and now it sounded like a perfect date. What could be better than quiet and romantic? "I'll go change."

"Me too. After I feed Grom."

They went inside, and she headed upstairs to pick through the clothing she'd brought. She'd already worn the fancy dress her mother had slipped into her suitcase, so she didn't want to trot it out again. Plus, that might be too dressy for a bistro dinner. But Van had said quiet and romantic.

She opted for a black skirt, her knee-high black boots, and a marine-blue silk blouse that, with the top two buttons left undone, looked less officey and more professional sexy. Didn't hurt that the color reminded her of Van's gorgeous scales.

A little more makeup, a quick brush of her hair, and she was ready. She went downstairs just as he was walking out of his bedroom.

Except his bedroom was really the one she was leaving. He should have it back now. "You won't have any trouble with the stairs now."

"I will not." He was in charcoal dress pants and a black V-neck sweater that clung to his sculpted chest and arms. It was a good look.

"I can move my stuff into the little bedroom when we get back."

He gave her a curious look. "Why?"

"So you can have your real bedroom back."

He glanced toward the upstairs before answering her. "That room is yours until you have a place of your own. I am fine down here."

"But it's your house."

"Which means it's also my decision. I stay where I am."

She smiled as she walked over to him. "You're very sweet for a guy who makes his living beating the crap out of other guys."

He laughed. "My opponents do not think I'm sweet."

She slipped her arms around his neck, leaned up, and kissed him. Whatever the outcome of the rematch, she doubted she'd be back here any time soon, so she wanted to make as many happy memories with Van as she could. These last few days might be enough to get through a few more years of misery.

He kissed her back, his hands coming to rest on her ribs. Something about him was different. Maybe it was the fact that he was no longer in pain, maybe it was being able to shift again, but he'd changed. He seemed more relaxed, for one thing. His kiss was slow and easy, like they had all the time in the world.

More than anything, she wished that was true. After a few long seconds, she broke the kiss, happy despite what lay ahead.

He held on to her. "You look very nice, by the way."

"Thanks. So do you."

"Ready to go? I called a Ryde before I changed, and he's only one minute away."

"Just need my coat and purse." Both were by the door.

Van helped her into her coat, then slipped into his own. He put his hand on the doorknob, turning to give Grom a little talking-to before they left. "Be a good boy."

Grom whined.

"Okay," Van said. "I will try to bring you a doggy bag."

She giggled. "You can understand what he says that well?"

He opened the door for her. "He is male, and men are simple creatures. Love us, appreciate us, feed us, we are happy."

"Good to know." She patted his chest as she walked past, mostly because she liked touching him. And she could.

A black SUV waited in the driveway. As Van locked the door, she said, "Hey, I thought you were going to drive. Do you not like to? Or are you just used to being driven around? I guess you must get chauffeured everywhere when you're on tour."

"I could have driven. And I do like to drive." He took her hand and looked into her eyes. "But then I would not be able to pay as much attention to you as I would like."

She grinned, unable to stop herself. "Like I said, very sweet."

"And deadly," he reminded her.

"Yes," she said. "Very deadly."

And, she hoped, very much hers.

Besides calling the Ryde, Van had phoned ahead to Café Claude to see if they needed a reservation. They hadn't, but the man who'd answered the phone asked if they were coming in for a special occasion.

Van had told him it was their official first date. Saying those words had felt good. Like he was making a formal proclamation that he intended to woo Monalisa into becoming his woman. It was a serious undertaking, but he knew what that meant. Keeping her happy, providing for her, listening to her, being there for her in whatever way she needed. All things he was more than willing to do. And very happy to do. Because doing them meant sharing his life with her. And that thought never failed to bring him the most surprising joy.

Before her, he'd never really seen his future with anyone in it besides himself. Did that make him selfish? He wasn't sure. He hoped not. Certainly with Monalisa around, he could learn not to be. There was no doubt in his mind that she made him a better man. And he'd definitely never felt this content.

But first of all, he had to help her get her freedom.

There would be no future together, and no real future of any kind for her, until that happened.

The server led them to a nice secluded booth, making Van wonder if that was because of his date comment or just chance. Either way, it was a good table.

Monalisa slid around until she was next to him. He liked that. Liked having her close. Loved it, actually.

Maybe even loved her.

He stared at her with that thought stuttering in his head. It was frightening and wonderful and way too soon. He understood that. Saying such a thing would scare her off, he thought. Yes, he would keep these feelings to himself awhile longer. Give himself a chance to make sure that was what his heart was telling him.

His dragon side already knew. But his dragon side was much more emotionally driven, and given to impulse. Both sides of himself had to be completely sure before he let those words slip from his tongue.

"Can I bring you a bottle of wine?" the server asked.

"Not for me," Van said. He was training now. He had to respect the process, and that meant no alcohol. He looked at Monalisa. "But get whatever you like."

"Are you not drinking because of the fight?"

He nodded.

She turned to answer the server. "No wine for us tonight, thank you."

The server gave them a little bow. "I'll give you a few minutes to look over the menu, then."

Van put his hand on hers. "You can have wine if you want. Get a whole bottle. I don't care. It won't affect me or my training. And money is no issue."

"You're right, money isn't an issue, because this is going on my father's credit card. But hey, we're a team, right? So none for me either. If you're training, I'm training. Or at least abiding by the same sort of guidelines. That's what team members do."

Her fierce insistence was endearing, and he was thrilled that she saw them as a team the way he did. "All right, then. But if you are going to be part of my team, you need an official title."

She leaned back. "I guess you don't need a rehab therapist anymore, which is good. Especially since I'm not one."

They both laughed. He nudged her. "How about manager? I am thinking I will fire my old one anyway. He hasn't been much use to me in a long time, and the League assigned him to me, so what do I care?"

She tilted her head, a seriousness in her gaze. "Is this really going to be your last fight?"

"Yes. I am ready to be done."

"What are you going to do with yourself, then?"

He stared at the flickering candle in the center of the table, hoping the flame would give him an answer. "I am not really sure."

A few moments of silence passed before she spoke. "Why don't you train other fighters? You're so good at what you do."

"But I am no longer a champion. I was defeated."

"You're about to rectify that, but it's also kind of beside the point. You were a champion for years. One loss in how many fights?"

"Twenty-seven in eleven years." It was a career he'd been very proud of. Until this last fight.

"Wow, that's a lot of winning. No wonder my father made so much money off you." She frowned. "Sorry. I really hate to keep mentioning him."

"No, it is good. I need to know more about him. What he's like. How he thinks. What pushes his buttons. Tell me everything." That was the best way to defeat an opponent. Know more about them than they knew about you.

"Well, that's sort of a detailed conversation. Maybe we should figure out what to eat first?"

"Good idea. Then you will tell me."

"I will." She opened her menu. "Everything looks great. Have you eaten here before? What are you getting? You know, I'm actually kind of starving."

He laughed. "I have not eaten here before. I've never been in town longer than three weeks at a time. But I have wanted to. I am probably getting steak."

She slanted her eyes at him. "You do like your red meat."

He shrugged. "Dragon."

"I think I'll get the onion soup and the salad Niçoise."

He shook his head. "You do like the green stuff."

She closed her menu. "It does a body good."

He couldn't argue with that. "If that is why you

look the way you do, don't change a thing. In fact, I will plant a garden."

She snorted with laughter. "A garden. Really. Are dragons known for their agricultural skills?"

"There is a first time for everything."

The server returned then, and they ordered. Van asked for a bottle of sparkling water as well. It seemed like they should have something festive to drink.

With that out of the way, he settled back on the banquette. "All right. Your father. What do I need to know?"

The question flattened her smile, but it was information he had to have. "My father is Padraig Devlin. King of the leprechauns. It's a title he enjoys lording over everyone, family included. Although, I think if he went back to Ireland and tried to assert himself, he'd be drummed out."

"He is not really king, then?"

"No, he is. He's just been in the United States so long that I don't think they'd give him much respect. Especially since he left his home country behind. He put his younger brother in charge in his stead."

"Why did he leave?" Van could understand leaving one's home. Sometimes there were very good reasons. Like life and death.

"He always says that Ireland might be the Emerald Isle, but America is the Land of Green, so I'm sure it had to do with making money. He bought the Shamrock before I was born."

"What else?"

"You already know he's greedy. Ambitious. Willing to use anyone for his own purposes. Including me. Obviously."

Which also made him a horrible father. "What are his weaknesses?"

"He hates feeling like he's being disrespected or not listened to. He hates the thought that people talk behind his back. He's got an enormous ego." She tapped her fingers on the table. "But his biggest weakness is his money, of course."

"He has a hoard also."

"Sort of. I don't know if he has a room like yours, though. He'd never show it to me if he did. My mother may have seen it."

"What kind of supernatural is your mother?"

"A pixie." Monalisa frowned. "She sides with him more and more every year. It's like she's realized there's no point in fighting him."

"I am sorry your life has not gone differently."

She smiled, but it was a little sad. "It got me here, right?"

"True."

The waiter came with their sparkling water and two goblets. He poured for them, then left again.

Van raised his glass. "To us. And to the future."

They drank. He set his glass down. "What else can you tell me about him?"

She thought for a moment. "He's a trickster. Loves to twist words, play pranks, and generally make everyone else the butt of his jokes. You can't trust him."

"Obviously."

"But it's more than what he's done to me over the years." She swirled the liquid in her glass. "He will take advantage of every loophole. You have to be very careful making any kind of deal with him."

Van nodded. "I will be."

She was oddly quiet for a minute. "Can I ask what you have planned? Are you just going to go in and fight and hope for the best? Or are you going to tell him upfront that you're done fighting? He won't like that. You make him a lot of money."

It was his turn to be silent for a moment. "I am not sure yet, but I know this much. Whatever happens, the outcome must be your freedom."

Monalisa felt her pulse trip at Van's words. "That is...beyond kind of you. But he probably won't agree to it. You can try all you want to make him give me a coin, but he won't. And even if, by some strange twist of fate, you could get him to agree, it would be a lie. He'd just go back on his word. He's done it numerous times."

"But would he do that to me if he thought there was a chance of getting me to fight again?"

She squinted at him. "So...you'd lie to him? I'm not opposed to that, but I know how he operates. He'd have you sign a contract locking you in before he did anything himself. Then you'd be stuck fighting *again*."

"I could refuse to fight the rematch."

"You'd be in breach of your contact." She shook her head. "Then you'd be in trouble with the League, and that would be a huge mess. He owns too many people in that organization for you to fight it. No, you can't do that."

He growled softly. "I do not like this man."

"Neither do I, and I'm his daughter."

Van's eyes had the dark smolder going on that she'd come to recognize as him in deep thought. She sipped her sparkling water and let him have some time.

The server arrived with their food, setting it before them with a lovely flourish. It looked delicious, from her soup and salad to Van's steak with fries. She thanked the man, but Van just grunted.

It was sort of cute, his grumpiness. Especially since she knew he wasn't really like that. Much like Grom, his bark was worse than his bite. And it was hard to be cross with him when he was trying to come up with a plan to free her from her father's clutches.

She took a bite of her salad and chewed while she studied the furrow of his brow and his intense gaze. He was putting so much effort into rescuing her. How could she not fall hard for a man like this? Really, it was the sort of thing that made her feel like she was already...in love with him.

She moved her gaze back to her plate. Well, that was silly and overly emotional and probably just a reaction to being around a single, available man for the first time in her life. Because she'd only known him a short while, and real love took a lot longer.

Didn't it?

She honestly didn't know. Were her feelings any less genuine because they'd come on so fast? What did real love look like anyway? It wasn't what her parents had. At best, that was a mutually agreed upon business deal. Sure, they liked each other—there was no other way they could spend that much time together otherwise—but did they love each other?

Monalisa didn't think so. How could anyone love a man like her father when all he loved was himself? And money.

Meanwhile, her mother's great loves seemed to be shopping and vacations with her girlfriends. No, her parents' marriage was based more on a shared appreciation for things rather than love.

Monalisa poked at the bubbly crust of cheese on top of her soup (which smelled and looked divine) and sighed.

Van's head came up, and the hunk of steak on the end of his fork stopped midway to his mouth. "What's wrong?" He groaned, squeezing his eyes shut for a second. "I am ignoring you. I am sorry. This situation with your father—"

"No, it's not that." She smiled and hoped he understood how she felt about him, at least to some degree. "I was just lost in my own thoughts."

"About what?"

She laughed softly and shook her head. "Nothing."

"Tell me." He gave her a mock-serious expression. "We are supposed to be getting to know one another."

She sucked in a breath and dug deep for some courage. "I was just thinking that…" She swallowed.

"I don't think I know what real love is. Or how to recognize it. Or what it feels like. What I mean is, I haven't really had any examples of it, you know?"

He stared back at her, eyes rounded, mouth agape. A little like a deer in headlights. Or a dragon in headlights. If headlights had that effect on dragons. Whatever, he clearly wasn't ready to delve into *that* topic.

She shrugged one shoulder and gave another easy laugh to lighten the mood. "Way too deep for dinner conversation, huh? Sorry, just me musing. As you were."

"Not too deep." He caught her hand as she picked up her fork. "If you have never seen real love, then you must trust your gut to know what it is."

She let go of her fork. "That's hard for me to do. My life has been one disappointment after another. Enough of that and you have a hard time trusting anything."

He twined his fingers with hers. "But you must start somewhere."

She nodded, content to look into his eyes. "I'm just not sure I know how."

His head dipped toward hers, and their mouths met halfway. The kiss was soft and gentle but lingering. To her, he tasted like a future just out of reach, a future she wanted so much she was afraid of how hurt she would be when it vanished. But in that moment, she decided to believe it was a future she could have.

That was trusting in something, wasn't it?

Their mouths parted, but their heads stayed close together.

"You can trust in me," he whispered.

She smiled. "I will try. And you can trust me." She leaned back. "Even though I wasn't very trustworthy when I got here."

"That is all forgotten." He went back to his steak. "Let's eat and enjoy this night."

She picked up her spoon, ready to dig into her soup. "I already am."

But as she was lifting a bite of gooey cheese to her mouth, he didn't seem quite ready to move on to lighter topics. "Can you control any supernatural with your powers?"

She ate the spoonful of cheesy, oniony goodness anyway. She nodded while she chewed.

His expression turned skeptical. "*Any* supernatural?"

"Yep. Or human." She took a drink of her water. "Even you."

"Show me."

She laughed, then realized he was serious. "I don't want to. It's not something I like to demonstrate."

"I understand, but I want to know what you are capable of." A mischievous glint sparkled in his eyes. "Or perhaps it is all just a big bluff."

She knew what he was doing. And it was working. "Fine. Give me one of your fries."

"I will gladly give you one of my fries, but I feel no compulsion to do so."

"That's because I haven't used my gifts yet. I just

wanted to say it in my normal voice first, so you could hear the difference."

"All right. Compel me."

She opened herself up to the power inside her, threading it through her voice. "*Give me a French fry.*"

His expression went slack, and his hand jerked once, like he was fighting the magic, but then he reached down, picked up a fry, and held it out to her. There was a little surprise in his gaze.

"Thank you." She took the fry and released him from her hold.

He slumped back, blinking at her. "That was impressive. You are very powerful."

"It's more of a curse than a gift." She sighed and ate her ill-gotten gain. It was a good fry. "Especially because the downside is that anyone who's under my spell for any length of time begins to lose themselves."

"What does that mean? How do they lose themselves?"

"My magic causes the mind to deteriorate. They'll forget the day, the year, where they live. Their name. Their family. Their purpose." She frowned. "It's what Will-o'-the-Wisps are known for, leading people off into the moors, and then those people are never heard from again. It's because their minds are wiped clean, and they wander until they're lost forever."

She stared at her soup. "It's not a heritage I'm proud of."

"But the future is yours to change."

"True." She ate another spoonful while she thought about that.

They focused on the food for a few more minutes, then he paused again. "Why don't you just use your ability on your father?"

"If only it was that easy. I tried when I was thirteen. I wanted him to buy me a horse. What thirteen-year-old girl doesn't have that dream at some point? Anyway, I was just coming into my powers and really understanding them, so I thought it would be a snap to get exactly what I wanted."

"What happened?"

"The second I walked into his office with the page I'd printed out from the horse auction site, he started laughing and telling me I was wasting my breath. He not-so-politely explained that if I ever thought about using my powers on him again, he'd ground me one month for every word that left my mouth and that I should know my gifts wouldn't work on blood relations." She shifted as the uncomfortable memory played out in her head. "Life was bad enough. I didn't want to be grounded too. I never tried it again."

He shook his head, then straightened. "Enough of this talk. It doesn't make you happy."

"No, it doesn't, but we still need to come up with a plan for Vegas."

"When we arrive and he sees I am there to fight, he should give you the coin."

"And if he doesn't? Which he won't."

"Then I will do the only thing that will make sense to a man like your father." Van's big fist closed around his steak knife. "I will use force."

Beating up the man who controlled the supernatural side of Vegas wasn't ideal. Van understood that. But from everything Monalisa had told him, it seemed like the only way for her to get the coin she needed.

Van was done fighting anyway. The League could fine him or sanction him or ban him, and none of that would matter, because he was done. He'd have to be, because laying hands on Padraig Devlin would destroy Van's reputation and ensure he'd never fight for the League again.

They ate the rest of their meal without another word of the plan or her father. He took that to mean that while she might not like it, she understood they had very few other options.

After dinner, they walked to Main Street, neither of them ready for the night to end. Most of the snow had been cleared from the streets and sidewalks, and despite the cold weather, there were a lot of people out walking and window-shopping.

She linked her arm through his, and they strolled in a comfortable silence, enjoying the evening. Perhaps because they both knew it could be their last. He would buy them next-day tickets to Vegas when they got home, and once they got to Nevada, he would go into full fight-prep mode.

And she would have to confront her father.

So tonight was about forgetting all of that for at least another hour or two. He wished it could be different, but there was no avoiding what lay ahead of them.

Her arm tightened around his. "Do you smell that?"

He inhaled. "Chocolate."

She grinned. "Yes. Where is that coming from?"

"I am not sure, but I have an idea." He tapped the side of his nose. "Let's follow it and see."

The scent led them to Delaney's Delectables. He'd heard a lot about the shop from Pandora, especially since Delaney had made the cake for the housewarming party and everyone in town knew Delaney Ellingham. But he'd yet to step foot inside. Dragons weren't much on sweets.

Based on Monalisa's reaction as they walked inside, Will-o'-the-Wisps clearly felt differently about sugar. She closed her eyes and inhaled, the most rapturous look coming over her face. "Am I dead? Because it smells like I'm in heaven."

"Welcome to Delaney's Delectables." A woman behind the counter smiled at them. "Let me know if I can help you."

Monalisa grinned at Van. "This is another great place to use my father's credit card. What do you want?"

He smiled back. "I do not like sweet things so much. But maybe a coffee."

"Coffee?" She looked aghast. "All this deliciousness and you just want coffee?" She slanted her eyes at him. "You don't like sugar at all?"

He glanced past her at the glass display cases. The things inside were beautiful, little works of decadent art. But none of it appealed to him. Until he spotted a small Lucite tray on one of the top shelves. He brought his gaze up to the woman behind the counter and pointed at the tray. "What are those?"

She glanced down at the tray. "Those are new. They're millionaire truffles."

"Why are they called that?" Monalisa asked.

"Because they're enrobed in single-bean organic Ecuadorian dark chocolate. The inside is a whipped ganache cream flavored with Dom Perignon rosé champagne, and they're hand-decorated with twenty-four-carat gold leaf."

Monalisa's brows went up. "Fancy. Are they a million dollars apiece too?"

The woman laughed. "Not quite. But they are fifty-five dollars a pound."

"How many in a pound?" Van had to know, because they were starting to sound good. At least, the gold leaf part was.

"About six," the woman answered.

Monalisa whipped out her father's credit card. "I'll take the whole tray. And a coffee." She winked at Van. "To start with."

Monalisa knew her father would question her need to spend four hundred and twenty-three dollars at a place called Delaney's Delectables, but she didn't care. She planned on ignoring him. And eating as much of the evidence as possible before they were face-to-face again.

The Ryde driver pulled away as they walked up the steps to Van's house. He shifted the shopping bag from Delaney's to his other hand so he could get the house key out.

"You want me to hold that?"

"I have it." But he gave the bag a sideways look. "That is a lot of chocolate."

"You'd better help me eat some of it."

He made a face as he unlocked the door. "Maybe one of those millionaire truffles, but otherwise, you are on your own."

"Well, I'm going to leave that big box for Norma. She was very nice to me."

He pushed the door open. "She will like that very much."

They went inside. Grom lifted his head from where he'd been sleeping on the big leather sofa, eyed them sleepily, then dropped it down and went back to snoring.

Van shook his head, which she took to mean Grom wasn't really allowed on the couch. "You know, you could give the chocolates to her yourself when you return, Monalisa."

She occupied herself with taking off her coat. "Except we don't know that I will return. In fact, we both know there's a better chance I won't. We've been pretending otherwise all night, and it's been fun, but I've lived this life for thirty years. What are the real chances I'll get free now?"

He started to say something, but frustration made her answer the question for him. "Slim to none. Those are my chances."

He took the bag of chocolates into the kitchen and deposited them on the counter. "I know it must feel that way—"

"Yes, it does. Because it's reality." She smiled at him as best she could. "I appreciate your optimism, I really do, and tonight was wonderful, but I can't keep pretending that we're just jetting off to Vegas for a long weekend getaway."

She turned to look out the window because she couldn't meet him eye to eye right now. If she did, he'd see how much pain she was feeling. "My heart may never recover."

"I am *not* leaving you there."

She glanced back at him. He was standing in the kitchen, coat still on, looking as determined and handsome as she'd ever seen him. "So I come back here until my father summons me? And then what? I suffer until I can't take it anymore? What's the point of that?"

"Maybe he would not call you back."

"He will. He always does." A wave of sadness swept over her. "You don't understand, Van. I'm falling in—"

She clamped her mouth shut. "I should go upstairs and pack."

He was in front of her before she could take another step. "Monalisa."

She shook her head. Her breath was stuck in her throat, and any moment she was going to break into a hot, ugly cry. "I can't do this."

"Please—"

"No." She could barely get the word out.

"I love you."

"I can't stay because—" She jerked her head up to look at him. "What did you say?"

She'd heard him. She just couldn't believe what he'd said. And she really wanted to hear it again.

"I love you." He took her hands in his. "I know it is too soon for these words, but I cannot deny my heart. My dragon side cannot imagine being without you. And my human side agrees."

She stared up at him, on the verge of becoming an emotional mess as she tried to sort her overwhelming feelings into words that would make sense. "Van…"

"I know that you do not feel the same. It is okay, *zolotse*. But I cannot go on without saying what is inside me."

She wished she could say what was inside her, but words eluded her at the moment. Instead, she clasped her hands on his shoulders, leaned up, and kissed him, letting her mouth express what her brain could not.

He scooped her into his arms, kissing her back just as passionately. He pulled back to look into her eyes. "Does that mean you might love me someday too?"

She wrapped her arms around his neck. "You silly Russian. I love you right now."

His smile was enormous. "You do?"

She nodded. "I do."

"This is very good." He kissed her again, just a quick one. "I'm going to buy our tickets."

"That's going to be hard to do with me in your arms."

He laughed and set her down. "If there are seats available, we'll leave tomorrow."

She nodded, feeling the somberness return. "I'll give you my father's credit card to pay for mine."

"No. I will pay for it. You need a clean break from him. It starts now."

She crossed her arms. "Are you bossing me around?"

Crestfallen, he shook his head. "I would not do that."

She grinned and gave him a playful tap on the

arm. "I'm teasing you. And I understand what you're saying, but those tickets are going to be expensive on such short notice. You should let him pay for this one last thing."

"You will fight me on this?"

"I will."

Van frowned. "Fine. But after this, I will take care of things. Until you are on your feet. Deal?"

She wasn't crazy about being indebted to him, even if it was the kindest, most generous thing anyone had ever offered to do for her, but what else could she do? She'd be homeless without his help. "Deal."

"Good."

"But I'm paying you back."

He shrugged. "Okay."

She dug out her father's credit card and turned it over to Van. "I'm going to pack." She headed for the kitchen.

He jerked his thumb in the opposite direction as she walked past. "The bedroom is that way."

"But the chocolate isn't." She took out the box of millionaire truffles and tucked it under her arm. "Don't worry, I'll save you one."

Emails to Pandora and Nick sent, Van now stared at his computer screen. He didn't usually make his own flight arrangements because they were handled by the League's travel department. It wasn't hard, it was just unfamiliar. He sighed. The only flights to Vegas with vacant seats were tonight at eleven, tomorrow at eight, or two days from now on that same eight a.m. flight.

He picked the eleven p.m. flight. The seats were first class, which was all that was available, but also the only category he was interested in. He wasn't built to fly coach. Plus, they could sleep.

He started to book the tickets, then realized he'd better check that he had Monalisa's name right. He called out to her. "Monalisa, I need you in my office, please."

"Coming," she called back.

She walked in a minute later, still carrying the box of truffles and, from the looks of it, doing a pretty good job of making them disappear. "Did you find flights?"

"Yes. Tonight at eleven. Not the best, maybe, but there was not much to choose from."

"It's okay. We have to get there. The sooner the better for you."

"We will have to leave in about an hour. Can you be ready?"

"I'm ready now."

"Good." He liked that. "I need to make sure I have your full name right for the ticket."

"Okay. Monalisa Abigail Devlin." She leaned against the doorframe of his office and popped another ten-dollar truffle into her mouth. "What's yours?"

"Ivan Petrovich Tsvetkov."

She smiled like something was very funny.

"What?"

She sucked the chocolate off the tip of one finger. It was very distracting. "I thought your middle name was 'The Hammer.'"

He watched as her tongue worked on another bit of chocolate at the corner of her mouth. "Those truffles are good?"

"Very." She held the box out, wiggling it back and forth, teasing him. "You want one, Hammer?"

It wasn't the truffles he wanted. "Bring them over."

He spun his desk chair around as she came toward him and pulled her onto his lap so that she was sitting across it.

She let out a little shriek at the sudden movement, then laughed. "You almost made me drop the truffles."

He took the box out of her hands and tossed it onto his desk. "I do not like chocolate anyway."

Then he put his hand on her hip and tugged her closer. "You are all the sweetness I need."

She smiled and cupped his face in her hands. "I'm okay with that. More chocolate for me."

He laughed. "I will set you up with an account at Delaney's if that is what makes you happy."

She shook her head. "You make me happy."

He kissed her, tasting the truffles on her tongue. Maybe chocolate wasn't so bad after all.

A soft moan of pleasure vibrated out of her throat,

sending a thrill through him. He wanted this woman in a way that made him feel desperate and reckless. He knew without a doubt that he was willing to do dangerous things to have her.

He'd never prepared for a fight with so much on the line. It was daunting. But thinking about not having Monalisa in his life caused the fire in him to rage.

He would win. And her father would grant her freedom.

Or some very bad things were going to happen in Vegas.

As they settled into their first-class seats, Monalisa realized she had no idea what Van had done about a place to stay for them. She put her hand on his arm. "Van?"

He turned to look at her. "Yes?"

"Did you book a hotel? I have an apartment at the Shamrock, but I don't think it's the best place for us to go."

He nodded. "It's taken care of."

"For both of us? Or…"

"I have a condo in the Skye Towers. It is my home away from Nocturne Falls. We will stay there."

"Nice. Okay." Skye Towers was one of the swankiest addresses in town. It sat a block off the Strip and was home to a lot of the big entertainers who played the Strip, most of whom were supernaturals. And since the building catered to that crowd, it made sense that he'd have a place there.

"You should try to sleep." He slipped his hand under hers.

"I will." She smiled at him, so happy in the moment despite everything that was going on. "You're a good man."

The side of his mouth came up in a wry smile. "That sounds like a goodbye."

"No, not at all. Just wanted you to know."

"I appreciate it." He pulled her hand to his mouth and kissed it before returning it to the console between them. "Speaking of good men, Nick Hardwin and his girlfriend, Willa Iscove, are coming to the fight. I get ten tickets for each of my fights, and he has been wanting to see one. They will be staying at the condo too. Also, Pandora is coming with them."

"That's great." She thought about that a moment. "I know those Skye Towers units are big, but just how large is your condo?"

"Four bedrooms. Plenty of space."

"Okay, awesome."

Van winked at her, then leaned back and closed his eyes.

She did the math. No doubt Nick and Willa would be in one bedroom, and Pandora in another, so that meant there was still a bedroom for her without crowding Van out of his. That was good. She didn't want to interrupt his training in any way.

She also wasn't ready to bunk with him. Their relationship was way too young for that. Plus, sleeping with a guy she was about to be separated from might kill her. She knew she was emotionally immature, never having had a real relationship before. It was a big factor in how fast she'd fallen for

Van. She was all right with that, but she didn't want to cause herself so much heartbreak that she'd never recover.

Although, being intimate with him was an incredible temptation. What would it be like to be the focus of that man's complete attention?

Parts of her started to warm, and she fidgeted in her seat. That was enough of that line of thinking. She sighed and shook her head, a little embarrassed by how quickly her mind had gone there.

Van opened his eyes. "What is wrong?"

"Nothing, just thinking about…everything. I'm going to try to sleep now." She closed her eyes, hoping she could drift off.

She must have, because the next thing she knew, Van was gently shaking her leg.

"Monalisa, we are landing."

"Hmm?" She yawned and blinked. "Are we there?"

"Almost."

She pushed the button to raise her seat up. "What time is it?"

"It will be close to one in the morning when we land. That is why I thought we should sleep."

"Did you?"

He nodded. "A little."

"I can't believe I slept as much as I did."

"You must have needed it. But you missed the cookies."

"What?" She sat up farther. "There were cookies?"

He laughed. "There was a big snack." He reached

into the seat next to him, pulled out a napkin-wrapped object, and handed it over. "I saved you mine."

"You did?" She took it and opened the wrapping to see a fat cookie stuffed with chocolate chunks. "Oh, you are definitely a keeper."

He grinned. "I don't know how you can eat that after all the chocolate you had at the house."

"It's one of my superpowers." She bit into the cookie. It was delicious. Not as delicious as the remaining chocolates that were packed in her bag, but good. "And I'm really glad I brought all that stuff from Delaney's, because you're going to have a house full of people I can share it with."

"That is true."

The pilot announced the final descent, so they got their seats into position. Van reached over and took her hand. It was a sweet gesture and very much him.

Once they'd deplaned and gotten their bags, all of which Van insisted on carrying, he sent a quick text before they walked outside. She wasn't surprised when an SUV pulled to the curb in front of them and a sharply dressed young man, probably about her age, jumped out and came around to take their bags.

He smiled at Van. "Good flight, sir?"

"It was." Van shook the driver's hand. "Good to see you, Harlan. Everything is all right?"

"Yes, sir, right as rain. Good to have you back."

"Excellent." Van gestured to Monalisa. "Harlan, this is my girlfriend, Monalisa."

He reached out to shake her hand as well. He had

amber-colored eyes and sandy brown hair that made his darkly tanned skin seem to glow. His whole look reminded her of a lion. "Nice to meet you, Monalisa."

"You too, Harlan. Do you always pick Van up from the airport?"

"Whatever he needs," the young man replied.

"Harlan is a member of my training team," Van said to her.

Harlan grinned as he took the bags. "I make sure the fridge is stocked, his errands are run, and he gets to wherever he needs to be whenever he needs to be there."

She looked at Van. "He's your Las Vegas Norma."

Van tipped his head back and forth. "Sort of. Harlan forgot to mention he is also my most frequent sparring partner. I do not think Norma would do that."

Monalisa snorted. "No, I don't think she would."

Harlan put the bags in the back while she and Van climbed into the car. Van sat up front in the passenger's seat.

Harlan took the driver's seat a few moments later. "Straight home?"

"Yes."

Harlan pulled out, and they were on their way. Monalisa sat back to watch the lights go by. She'd flown in and out of this airport many times, but tonight everything looked and felt so different.

"You got my text last night?" Van asked Harlan.

"I did. I'll have the groceries with me when I come over in the morning. Eight a.m. okay?"

"Fine." Van twisted around to look at her. "You can sleep in, though. If you want."

She shrugged. "I'm more used to this time zone than Nocturne Falls. I'll probably be up. In fact, I can make breakfast."

Harlan glanced at her in the rearview mirror. "Ma'am, I usually do that. But you're welcome to if you want."

She laughed. "You really are Van's Vegas Norma. No, go right ahead. I'm happy to let you do your thing. Just don't call me ma'am. I'm pretty sure we're the same age. Monalisa is just fine."

"Very good, Monalisa. I'll be there at eight to make breakfast, and then Ivan and I can head to the gym."

Van leaned over. "She likes vegetables."

"They're on my list," Harlan answered.

She smiled. Van took care of her in a very different way than she was used to. Everything that came from her father felt begrudged. With Van, it was a kindness. She couldn't wait for the day when she was making her own money so she could spoil him back. Although, she might not ever be able to spoil him in the style he was used to.

She turned to watch the lights again, and Van and Harlan started discussing the training regimen for the next day. She finally had to interrupt. "Harlan, I hope you don't mind me asking, but if you're sparring with Van, you must be equipped to handle that kind of punishment. What sort of supernatural are you?" She expected him to say feline shifter.

He smiled, making quick eye contact in the

rearview mirror again. "I'm a ranger-class gargoyle."

"Oh, wow, how cool. You'll have to forgive me. I don't know much about the classes. Where does that put you?"

"Right in the middle. Can't fly, but when I shift, I'm about the size of this vehicle."

"And he is fast," Van added. "The two classes above him can fly, and they're larger, but they do not move with the same speed."

Harlan nodded. "Also, I can take a hit like you wouldn't believe."

Van snorted. "I have had the bleeding knuckles to prove it."

She scooted to the middle to see both of them better. "So Harlan, do you fight for the TFL too?"

"No, ma'am. I mean, Monalisa." He grinned. "I'm a lover, not a fighter."

Van looked at him. "Since when? You have not had a girlfriend since I've known you."

Harlan shook his head. "What about Sasha? And Laurette? And Monica?"

"One date does not a girlfriend make."

Monalisa liked Harlan. She also liked teasing Van. She poked him in the arm. "One date is all we've had."

Harlan let out a sharp, "Hah."

Van turned to look at her again. "What about the housewarming party?"

"That didn't count."

"Lunch at Howler's, then."

"Hmm." She tapped her finger on her chin. "I'll

give you half-a-date credit for that one. But dinner at Café Claude's last night was really the only official date we've had." She actually didn't feel that way, but it was fun to give him the business.

"I see. So I am failing as a boyfriend, then?" His eyes glimmered with happiness, showing her he was in on the joke.

"Oh yes, miserably." She laughed even as she said the words, because it was such a fat lie. He was amazing in every way.

Van nodded like he was taking it all into consideration. "I will strive to do better. Up my game, as the kids say."

She leaned up and kissed him, just a quick one so that Harlan didn't have to endure anything too personal between them. "I can't wait to see what that looks like."

"We're here," Harlan said. "And just in time."

Monalisa ducked to see through the windshield a little better. "Wow, a drive-through lobby? That's fancy."

Harlan nodded. "This place caters to all kinds of supes, and sometimes, the more privacy the better. Although, I think the drive-through is most helpful to the vamps who live here. The desert is a very sunny place."

"Good point." She sat back and grabbed her purse.

Van clapped Harlan on the shoulder. "I'll get the bags. You go home and get some sleep."

"You got it, boss." Harlan looked over his shoulder. "Nice to meet you, Monalisa. See you in the morning."

"See you in the morning. Thank you for driving us." She hopped out as the doorman opened her door.

"Good evening." He smiled.

"Good evening." She looked around. The Skye Towers lobby was exactly what she'd expected. Vegas chic, which meant smoked glass, steel, and sparkly quartz. A dazzling cobalt blue chandelier washed everything in a mellow light.

Van retrieved their bags, then closed the SUV hatch and gave it a tap. Harlan waved through the open window and drove off.

"Help you with those, Mr. Tsvetkov?"

"No, thank you, Roger."

"All right. You have a good night, sir."

Van gave him a nod, then they walked to the elevator banks. Van set the bags down to tap in his floor, and one of the doors opened immediately. He picked up the bags, and they got on, riding up in silence. Despite her nap on the plane, she was still a bit tired.

The elevator stopped, opening onto another smaller lobby. More steel and quartz, this time with cobalt blue accent lighting. There was only one other door.

She pointed at it. "Is that yours?"

He nodded. "Punch 9089 into the keypad by the door."

She went over and did as he asked. A soft hiss came from the door, followed by a sharp snick.

"It's open," he said.

She pushed it wide but looked back at him. "You have the whole floor?"

He nodded. "It's a good place."

She guessed so. Then she walked in, and there was no more guessing.

Van tapped the lighting panel to bring the space to life. He had owned his condo in the Skye Towers for ten years. This was the first time he'd ever wondered if a woman would like what he'd done with the place.

He tried to see it through Monalisa's eyes as she wandered ahead of him.

Maybe it was too masculine. All the grays and browns mixed with chrome and leather did nothing to add a feminine touch. Or too industrial. The concrete countertops and glass wall panels offered no warmth. It was definitely too modern. Where were the soft edges? And the flourishes?

He sighed. At least the suede couches were comfortable. And the artwork, all bought from local galleries, offered some color. And the view was remarkable, especially at night like this, when the city was a jewel box of lights.

But she lived in the Shamrock. She must be used to

a level of luxury that made this place look like a sad hotel.

"Oh, Van."

He braced himself.

She turned, face beaming. "This place is amazing."

"You really think so?"

"Yes. It's so sleek and snazzy. I love it."

He couldn't believe it. "Very good. I am glad."

She walked to the wall of windows that made up one side of the living room. "And this view is just to die for."

Now he was grinning. "It is good. Come. I'll show you the room you can have."

Still carrying the bags, he led her down one of the short halls on the other side of the living room. There were two reasons he wanted her in this room. First, it was the plushest and done with the most color, although only one—blue. But many shades of blue. And secondly, it was the closest to the master bedroom.

And he wanted her close.

He turned the lights on and stood back to let her go in.

"How pretty. This looks like a spa bedroom. If spas had bedrooms." She sat on the bed, bouncing a little. "This is great."

He set her bag down on the chaise in the reading nook and tipped his head to the left side of the bed. "The bathroom's through that door, other side is the closet. If you need anything, just let me know."

She stood and took a few steps toward him. "There is one thing I need."

He rolled his shoulders. "Anything. Just name it. If I don't have it, I'll have Harlan get it in the morning. Or now. I can call him, or—"

She put her finger to his lips. "You have it."

He raised his brows.

She nodded and took her finger away. "Yes."

"What is it?"

"Time."

"You want…time?"

She smiled and slipped her arms around him. "With you. I'm not ready to go to bed yet. I know I should. I know tomorrow begins a very stressful, busy stretch of time for both of us. But I'm just not ready for all of that yet."

"Me either." He leaned his head against hers. "What do you want to do?"

"We can sit on the couch and stare out at the lights, for all I care."

"Okay." He thought for a second. "It's cold outside, but I have a fireplace on the balcony as well as inside. The view from out there is even better, though. You can see the city and the stars."

"That sounds perfect. And I won't be cold if you keep me warm."

"I will not let you be cold." He took her hand, and they walked out to the balcony, which was a huge space that held a large seating area, a dining table and chairs, and an outdoor kitchen. He started a fire with two taps of the remote control, then they settled onto the center of the biggest couch.

He held her wrapped in his arms and allowed his inner furnace to burn a little brighter. "Warm enough?"

She nodded and laid her head on his chest. "Perfect."

They sat there in absolute, comfortable silence for a long time. He ran his hand over her hair, marveling at the silkiness of it.

She splayed her fingers on his chest. "I have to see my father tomorrow."

"I know." He let a few more quiet seconds tick by. "Do you want me to go with you?"

"Yes. But no." She sighed. "I don't want him to know that you and I have become close. He'll use that against me."

"Do you want him to think that I am here because of your power over me?"

She shook her head a little. "I'm not going to ask you to do that."

"I will do anything that will help you earn your freedom." He didn't think he'd ever spoken truer words. "Would that be best for him to think?"

She didn't answer right away, and when she did, there was resignation in her voice. "Yes."

"Then I will do it. I remember what it felt like. I can imitate it again, if need be."

She sat up to look at him. "You won't have to do it much. You might not have to do it at all, really. Would you normally see him before a fight?"

"Yes. At weigh-in and for a few minutes in the dressing room."

She stiffened a little. "Oh."

"Don't worry, *zolotse*, I can handle it."

"I know you can." She put her head back down, and they returned to companionable silence.

Until a new thought crept into his head. "Won't he wonder why you are not staying at the Shamrock?"

"If it comes up, I'll tell him I need to keep you in my sway. It's happened before. He doesn't monitor my every move. At least, I don't think he does. In theory, he shouldn't need to since I'm sort of tied to him anyway." She took a few deep breaths. "Do you not want him to know where I'm really staying?"

"The only thing I want is for you to be safe. You can tell him you're staying here if you want. He will not get farther than the lobby anyway."

"Okay." She yawned and sat up again, this time putting her arms around his shoulders and nuzzling his neck.

The soft caress of her breath on his skin sent shivers of desire through him. He tilted his head to give her more access.

Gentle, feathery kisses below his ear followed, and he moaned in pleasure.

She pulled back, smiling, eyes heavy-lidded. "I do love you, Ivan Tsvetkov. And no matter what happens in these next few days, I want you to know that I have had the time of my life with you. Thank you for everything."

"You are welcome, beautiful Monalisa. Now we should go to bed. To our own beds," he clarified. "Otherwise, your kisses may lead us down a very different path."

She woke bright and early with a heavy mix of emotions on her heart. She'd never been happier in her life. And she'd never dreaded a day more than she did today.

Seeing her father would be, at best, unpleasant. At worst, it could turn into the biggest fight she'd ever had with him.

Either way, today would not be boring.

Since she planned to go by her apartment at the Shamrock before seeing him, she showered, did her hair and makeup, then just threw on jeans and a sweater. She'd change into something dressier before going to his office.

It was seven fifty-eight when she walked into the kitchen. Harlan was already there, scrambling eggs and cooking bacon. And also, apparently, grilling a couple of steaks. She dropped her bag by the door.

He gave her a quick smile. "Morning."

"Morning. Is there coffee?"

"Absolutely." He put down the whisk and took a step toward the sleek machine at the end of the countertop. "What would you like? Cappuccino? Latte?"

"Just plain old cream and sugar, and I'll get it. You've got enough to take care of. Just tell me where the cups are."

"Second cabinet in. Coffee is in the carafe, cream is in the fridge, and sugar is in that dispenser next to the coffeemaker." He went back to whisking.

"Thanks." She got a cup, filled it, doctored it with cream and sugar, then took a seat at the counter. "Is Van up yet?"

"Yep. He's downstairs on the treadmill getting his miles in." Harlan poured the eggs into a pan.

"Downstairs? I bet this place has a killer gym."

"It probably does, but he's literally downstairs. He owns the floor below this one too. Turned it into his personal gym. It's where he trains."

"Oh. How about that?" She sipped her coffee. Van certainly wasn't the kind of guy to let anything stand in his way. She liked that about him so much. And while it was a trait he shared with her father, the way Van did things was night and day compared with Padraig. "I guess those steaks are for him."

Harlan looked up from stirring the eggs. "You want one? I can make another one, no problem."

"No, no. Just curious. The man brings new meaning to the word carnivore, doesn't he?"

"He is a dragon." Harlan shrugged. "And when he's training, he needs the protein more than ever."

"How did you guys meet?"

He got plates out and laughed. "I came to Vegas hoping to work in one of the shows here. I'm an amateur magician. But I'd like to be a professional. I figured I could get my feet wet working on one of the productions, maybe get to know some people, work my way up, that sort of thing."

"Hey, that's cool."

He set the plates down, then with a flourish, flattened his hands, palms down, and crossed them over each other. He next flipped his hands over to show her they were empty. A quick snap of his fingers, a small puff of smoke, and he was holding the forks and knives.

"Wow." She nodded. "I'm impressed."

He chuckled. "Thanks. That's kind of basic, but I've got some much bigger stuff. Anyway, the only job I could get was working as a bouncer at this high-end club called Ultra. Ivan was in one night, saw me deal with a couple of rowdy drunks, and asked me if I'd ever thought about fighting."

"You said that wasn't for you."

"It's not. But I am a gargoyle. Just because I don't want to fight for a living doesn't mean I don't like to mix it up now and then. Sparring with Ivan is a good outlet. And he pays a helluva lot better than being a bouncer."

A door opened and closed somewhere in the apartment.

She nodded. "That's cool."

"What is cool?" Van walked in wearing track pants and a tank top with a towel draped around his neck. He was dripping sweat and looking about as hot as Monalisa had ever seen him.

She turned to face him, crossing her legs as she

took in the view. "Harlan was just telling me how you two met." She drank her coffee, eyeballing him over the rim.

He seemed to notice her close study of him and took a slightly different posture, chest out, hands on hips. Judging from the gleam in his eyes, he enjoyed her ogling him. "You like what you see?"

"I do." She put her cup down. "Very much."

He spread his arms wide. "Maybe you would like a big hug."

She laughed and squealed. "Not until you've showered."

He walked toward her, grinning. "Why not now?"

"Because I am showered." She put her hands up, giggling.

He stopped inches away, put his hands on the counter behind her, and leaned in. "Kiss me, or I will hug you anyway." He waggled his brows. "Then you will need to shower again."

"You drive a hard bargain." She kissed him, tilting forward so that their mouths were all that touched. "How was your workout?"

"Good." He straightened. "Now, I will shower and eat, then the next round begins in an hour. Sparring this time."

"Steaks are almost ready," Harlan said.

"I will shower fast." Van started for his bedroom, then hesitated and turned around to look at her again. "Why is your bag by the door?"

"Because I'm going to swing by my apartment

before I see my father. I need clean clothes. And I need to change into something professional."

Van nodded. "You are sure he will not give you a hard time about staying here?"

"Not if he thinks I need to keep you influenced to ensure you show up for that rematch."

"Okay. Good. Do you need a car?" He shrugged. "I will call you a car. Do not leave until I come back."

"I hadn't planned on it." She smiled as she turned her chair back around. She'd never been wanted the way Van wanted her. Or so well taken care of. It was heady stuff.

"Ready to eat?" Harlan asked.

"Not yet," she said. "I'll wait for Van."

He was back out in a few minutes and joined her at the counter. At her request, Harlan did a few more magic tricks while they ate. It was a lovely morning and one that took her mind off meeting with her father.

But breakfast lasted only so long.

Monalisa changed into trim black leggings, high-heeled black boots and a long, subtly striped maroon cardigan with a matching shell. She packed quickly, ditching her small rolling bag in favor of a larger one and a better selection of clothing.

The driver Van had called for her had insisted on staying until she was ready to return, so she picked up the phone and asked for a bellman to take her bag down to the waiting car.

He got to her apartment in under five minutes, one of the few perks of being Padraig Devlin's daughter. And with that done, there was nothing left to procrastinate on. She picked up her purse, checked that she had her ID badge, and headed for the second floor where her father's office was.

She stepped out of the elevator on the second floor and clipped her badge to her sweater. The security guys waved her through with deferential smiles.

Several other people greeted her as she wound her

way through the labyrinth of offices. Deeper in, she passed the heavily guarded doors that led to the finance offices and the vaults. Besides the guards, the steel doors had biometric locks that required a fingerprint and a retinal scan. And every inch of this floor was videotaped. No one got in or out of here without being recorded.

After seeing Van's hoard, she thought about where her father kept his stash of gold. Behind those doors? That was what she'd long suspected.

She stopped to glance back at the armed guards standing on either side of that entryway. Yes, the casino and the hotel took in tremendous amounts of money, but it would stand to reason that her father would want that same level of security for his personal wealth as well.

Which meant that somewhere behind those doors was the coin she so desperately wanted. Doors that she didn't have the clearance to get through. She never had. Her father had told her numerous times that neither she nor her mother needed to worry themselves with the money end of things.

She snorted softly. He was such a condescending idiot.

That thought fueled the rest of her march to his office.

His administrative assistant, a woman named Seela, gave her a nod. Seela was a banshee, a supernatural whose voice could shatter glass and stop a heart, and she also served as a first line of defense for Padraig. "Hello, Ms. Devlin."

"Hello, Seela. I need to see my father. He's expecting me." He wasn't exactly, but it wasn't too far from the truth.

The woman nodded. "I don't see you on his calendar."

"He asked me to come in when I returned to the city." Monalisa made herself smile pleasantly. "And here I am."

Seela got up from her desk. "I'll just go let him know."

By which Seela meant she'd see if Monalisa was lying.

Monalisa held on to her smile until the woman turned her back, then she pulled out her phone and sent her father a quick text. *Home. Need to talk.*

Seela was gone only a minute or two, and when she returned, she wore a slim, frosty smile. "He'll see you now."

Monalisa's grin was real this time. "I guess I *was* on his calendar." She tucked her clutch under her arm and strode through the tall double doors that led into her father's office.

His office was an enormous space filled with dark walnut furniture, vibrant green malachite stone wall panels, and hand-knotted carpets laid over slate floors. The fixtures were gold-plated, and cut-crystal objects were everywhere. The seat behind his desk was more throne than chair. She'd once heard him boast that decorating his office had cost more than the hotel's presidential suite.

Instead of a view of the gorgeous mountains

beyond the city or the bustling streets below, his privacy-coated windows overlooked the casino floor. And not just any section of the casino, but the high-dollar tables.

He was standing in front of them now, hands clasped behind his back.

She could see his face in the reflection. He was staring down into the pits, watching the whales lose their shirts. Her eyes narrowed. She hoped one of them got lucky and broke the bank.

Her father stayed where he was, not bothering to greet her or even acknowledge her with a look. "I take it you brought the dragon back with you?"

"I did."

His gaze remained on the gamblers below. "And he'll be ready to fight?"

"He will."

"Excellent news."

"I'd like the coin now."

That got him to turn around. "I'm sure you would."

"I did what you asked. The job is done."

His eyes narrowed disapprovingly. "So eager to leave the nest."

"I'm thirty years old. I've been here long enough." She took a breath and reminded herself to keep her voice even and calm. "I'm ready to start my own life. You know that. We've been through this."

He lifted his chin so he could look down his nose at her. "You'll have it. As soon as he steps into the ring."

"The rematch is a done deal."

His lip curled. "When he's in the ring. Ask about it again and I may change my mind."

Anger bubbled up in her. She wanted to scream at him. Tell him what a horrible father he was. That he was the lowest of the low and bog scum and that he deserved every bad thing that came to him.

Instead, she managed a tiny bend of her mouth that hopefully passed for a smile. "I'll see you at the fight, then."

She turned to reach for the door.

"Actually, I'll see you at dinner tonight. Your mother's request."

Monalisa didn't bother turning around to answer. "I can't. I have to stay with the dragon and keep him under my influence. Wouldn't want anything to keep him out of the ring."

"Monalisa—"

She opened the door and walked through it, shutting it firmly behind her.

Van stood on the balcony, letting the sun warm his face. He'd put in three solid hours of training today, which wasn't that much, but for what lay ahead, it was enough.

He'd never shifted in the ring before. Never wanted to. Never had a need. But on Saturday night, for the first time, he would. The days of balance and fairness had ended when Padraig Devlin had forced Monalisa to disrupt the last fight.

This time, Van planned to step into the ring and claim victory as soon as possible. Ronan, even in his manticore form, would be severely outclassed by Van as a dragon. And his fangs would be unable to pierce Van's scales.

Van would win decisively, but regaining the championship title didn't matter. Just Monalisa's freedom.

It bothered him even now that she'd been gone as long as she had. He worried that her father would command her to stay. Or worse. Those dark thoughts caused heat to build in his bones.

Harlan stepped outside. "The doorman called up. You have visitors."

Van whipped around, his mood already cooling. "Monalisa's back?"

"No, the friends you invited. I told the doorman to send them up. That was okay, right?"

Van nodded. "Of course."

"Good." Harlan rubbed the back of his neck. The kid had done well in the ring today. "If you don't need anything else, I'm going to split." He grinned. "I've got a date tonight."

"Have fun."

"Thanks. See you tomorrow, right?"

"Yes, we will probably all go out for breakfast, so you won't have to cook." Van walked inside as the door chime sounded. "Coming."

"I'll get it," Harlan said, jacket in hand. "I'm

headed out anyway." He opened it. "Hello, Ivan's friends, and goodbye, Ivan's friends."

Pandora, Nick, and Willa laughed as they spilled into the apartment. Harlan gave a wave and headed out.

Van met them in the foyer. "I see you all made it. And on the early flight. How was it?"

"So. Early." Pandora gave him a hug. "But you're worth it. Where's Monalisa? Cole and Kaley send their love and best wishes."

"On an errand, but she will be back soon. That is kind of Cole and Kaley. I wish they could have come."

She shrugged. "It's midterm season, and they are both up to their eyeballs in work."

Van shook Nick's hand. "Good to see you."

"You too. Thanks for the tickets. Very generous."

"Yes," Willa said. "That was very kind. I've never been to anything like this before."

Van got the feeling fights weren't her thing, but it was nice that she'd come along with Nick, who was clearly into the whole idea. "This is my last fight, so I am pleased to know I will have friends in the audience."

Pandora nodded. "You definitely will. And hey, I found a book in the attic that might be of some help with Monalisa's situation. Well, Gertrude found it. By which I mean she dropped it on my foot when I was up there giving Kaley a lesson, but anyway, I started reading it on the plane and nothing yet, but who knows?"

Gertrude was the ghost who lived in Pandora and Cole's attic. She was also the former owner of the house and, besides being a witch, also apparently a bit of a hoarder. Van nodded. "Good. We will need all the help we can get."

A new chime sounded, the one that indicated the doorman was calling. Van went to the panel by the door and pressed the button to answer. "Yes?"

"Your guest, Monalisa Devlin, is here."

Van rolled his eyes. Sometimes this building was too strict. But relief flooded him. Monalisa was back. "She is allowed up anytime. No need to call."

"Yes, sir," the doorman responded.

Van opened the door so he could see her when she got off the elevator. He leaned against the doorframe to wait, but looked at his guests. "Are you hungry?"

Nick nodded. "Always."

The women nodded too.

"Then we will go eat lunch when Monalisa is ready. I know a place." He knew many places, actually, and all of them would willingly make room for him and his guests, even without a reservation. It was one of the perks of being a celebrity in this town, at least among the supernatural crowd, but he'd gladly leave it behind for life in Nocturne Falls with the woman who made his world right.

The elevator dinged, and that woman walked out.

She exhaled, then offered him a weak smile. "It's good to be back."

Van went to her side and took her bag, instantly concerned. "Was there trouble? Did he try to stop you?"

"No." She slipped her arms around him and leaned in. "It's just good to be back here with you."

He wrapped his free arm around her. "It is very good to have you back." He kissed the top of her head. "Pandora, Nick, and Willa have arrived. They are hungry, so I thought we would go eat. Okay with you?"

"Okay with me."

Late lunch turned into early dinner, and with all five of them together, they lingered over the meal. It was a chance to eat, drink, and make merry with friends, something Van hadn't done much of in his life.

And every time he looked at Monalisa, she was smiling or laughing, and for that, he was grateful. The presence of Willa and Pandora seemed to lighten her mood significantly. It made him think that her transition to life in Nocturne Falls would be an easy one. That pleased him. Her happiness, after so many years of unhappiness, was important.

After dinner, they went back to Van's and lounged around in the big outdoor area, taking advantage of the stunning view despite the cold. The men gravitated to the balcony railing, and the women settled into the plush seating by the fireplace—and the fire that Van had started for them.

While he and Nick talked about the possibility of taking a quick night flight, the women shared the pictures they'd been taking all night and indulged in the rest of the chocolates from Delaney's.

All of a sudden, Pandora, who'd been taking more

selfies and pictures of the group than anyone else, called out to the men. "Come over here. I need to ask you guys a question."

Nick and Van joined the ladies.

Van stood behind Monalisa, his hands on her shoulders. "What is it?"

She turned her phone around to show them a picture. "Look at the guy in the background having dinner with that gorgeous woman."

Van shook his head. "What about him?"

But Nick looked closer. "Is that Julian Ellingham?"

Pandora nodded. "I think it is. How do you like that? Someone should warn that poor woman she's about to get her heartbroken."

Van squinted. "Let me see the picture again?"

Pandora held it in his direction.

He snorted. "Julian's the one who should be warned. That woman is Desdemona Valentine. She's an entertainer in town and a bit of a man-eater. Literally. She's a vampire. An old one."

Monalisa tipped her head back to look at him. "I love her show. I've seen it three times. But I had no idea she was *actually* a vampire. Makes sense, though, considering some of the stunts in that production." Then her eyes narrowed. "Have you seen her show? It's very sexy."

Van almost smiled at the jealous bite to her words. "I have never seen it."

Monalisa's mouth quirked up. "And yet you know so much about her..."

"She lives in this building. That is how I know her.

That, and her billboards are everywhere in this town. I am more of a Will-o'-the-Wisp man, myself." He bent to give her a quick kiss, then straightened. "I don't want to end the party, but I have to train early, so I am saying good night."

Pandora stood. "That's a good idea. I want to dig into that book Gertrude gave me. And do some shopping tomorrow. That takes energy."

The rest of them agreed, and they all headed for bed. Monalisa walked with Van to their side of the condo. He kissed her good night at her bedroom door, then went to his own room.

He stared out the windows at the city below and thought about the fight to come. Not the one in the ring, but the one with Padraig Devlin.

If getting physical with the man wasn't enough to make him give Monalisa the coin she needed, Van wasn't sure what their next step would be.

The man liked gold. Van had a lot of that. Maybe he could trade his hoard for her freedom. He nodded at that idea.

Better to have the woman who made him feel like the richest man in the world than to be alone with his riches.

Monalisa got up early enough to see Van before he went to get his first round of training in. She wanted to kiss him and tell him she loved him as much as she could before their time ran out. She knew he thought he would be able to convince her father to turn over the coin, but she knew her father better than Van did. And he was a very stubborn man.

With Van off to the gym, she went into the kitchen to get coffee started for their guests. She smiled. *Their* guests. Like this was her home too. But then, in a way it was. At least, until she had no other choice. Van had made it clear he wanted her with him as long as possible.

Willa, Nick, and Pandora wandered out a few minutes after the scent of brewing coffee began filling the space.

Pandora was in her pajamas and robe and clutching a small, leather-bound book with a tattered cover and yellowed pages. Her hair was piled on her head in a messy bun, and her lids were still heavy with sleep. She settled into a chair at the counter and blinked a few times like the morning light was hard on her eyes.

Monalisa started filling mugs with coffee. She set the first one in front of Pandora. "Hard to sleep in a strange bed?"

"No, I slept okay. I was up late reading this book. Lots of interesting stuff, but nothing yet on how to get you free from your father. But I'm not done with it either." She wrapped her hands around the mug and inhaled. "This should do it, though. Cream and sugar?"

"Coming up." Monalisa set both on the counter, then brought coffee to Nick and Willa as well.

"Very kind of you," Willa said. "But you don't have to wait on us."

"I'm happy to." Monalisa filled a cup for herself. "You all came out here to support Van, and I think that's just awesome."

"He's a good guy," Nick said.

"That, he is." She leaned against the counter by the coffeemaker. "And speaking of Van, he left a bunch of menus from local restaurants for you guys to look at. He said they all have great breakfasts, and they're all less than ten minutes away. As soon as he gets back from the gym and showers, we'll head out to eat."

Nick stood. "Why don't you let Willa and I handle breakfast? Unless you guys want to go out because the cupboard is bare."

"No," Monalisa said. "The kitchen is well stocked. But are you sure you want to cook on your little getaway?"

Willa nodded. "We've got this." She patted Nick's arm. "He makes great pancakes. And I can take care of the rest. You go do whatever you want to, and Pandora can read the rest of her book. Breakfast is handled."

Monalisa looked at Pandora and smiled. "What do you think?"

Pandora picked up her book and her coffee and slid out of her seat. "You don't have to tell me twice. I'll be in the living room. The indoor one." She shuffled off, calling over her shoulder, "I want fruit in my pancakes."

Nick looked at Monalisa. "Do you guys have any fruit?"

"There was fruit salad with breakfast yesterday. There should be blueberries or strawberries left in the fridge."

"Perfect," he said.

Van joined them shortly, looking as sweaty as he had the morning before. "What's happening? I smell food. I thought we were going out."

Monalisa smiled at him. "Nope. Willa and Nick are graciously making breakfast for everyone."

"Very nice." He nodded at them. "Thank you."

"No problem, man," Nick answered.

Van used the end of the towel around his neck to wipe the sweat off his face. "I will shower fast."

"You've got a little time," Willa said. "We haven't even cracked an egg yet."

"Okay. But I still need to shower."

Monalisa opened her mouth to agree, but Pandora came running in, looking very much awake.

"You guys!" She shook the little book at them. "I think I found it."

"What?" Van asked.

"How to get Monalisa free." She put the book on the counter and opened it, pointing to a passage. "Right here it says, *A child of a leprechaun will be subject to their father's will until the day they are bequeathed a coin from his pot of gold—*"

"That much I know," Monalisa said.

Pandora lifted a finger. "Wait, there's more. *Or until the father-child bond is broken by another bonding. Only a true bond of the heart has proven worthy of this task, and few are achieved due to the children so often being sequestered in order to make love matches impossible. A false marriage will do neither party any good.*"

Pandora looked up from the book, eyes bright and wide, and stared directly at Van. "You have to marry her."

Then she looked at Monalisa. "But it won't work unless you love him. Do you? I know you guys haven't known each other for very long, but maybe a little?"

Monalisa put her hand to her heart. Could it really be this simple? "I do love him."

"And I her," Van said. "But can it be this easy?"

"You read my mind," Monalisa said.

Pandora's brows shot up. "I don't think falling in love and getting married is easy. That's why it's the only other way to break this bond. And it *has* to be real, or it's not going to work."

"Explains why my father has done his best to keep me away from men all my life."

Willa tipped her head. "But he sent you to Van's house. That was essentially putting you into immediate contact with a man."

"Yes," Monalisa agreed. "But he's always told me how awful the fighters are, always painted this picture of them as angry men just looking for trouble, wanting to control their women and fight at every opportunity. Because of that, I had a pretty strong prejudice against guys like Van."

She looked at him, marveling at how fast he'd changed her mind. "Then I met Van, and he was nothing like that. The exact opposite, really."

Van shrugged. "I am very lovable."

Pandora laughed. "Yeah, you are." She chucked him playfully on the arm. "So? What's the deal?"

Van's gaze settled on Monalisa as his expression turned hopeful. "I will do whatever Monalisa wants to do."

She took a breath. They were all looking at her, all waiting for her answer. She'd never made a decision this big before. Never had the chance, really. Her hands were shaking, and her mouth suddenly went dry. She licked her lips and found her voice as she gazed into the eyes of the man she had no trouble picturing herself with for eternity. "Ivan Tsvetkov, will you marry me?"

"*Da*," he said with a wink. "But not before I shower."

After taking the fastest shower of his life, Van stood in his robe, staring into his closet and trying to decide which suit was nice enough to get married in.

Married.

He grinned, giddy that the answer to Monalisa's problem was such a boon for him. Oh, her father would not like it all, but once it was done, it was done. She would be free of that man and able to live her own life.

With Van.

He thought of a thousand different jewels in his hoard that he wanted to give her, but that couldn't happen until they were back in Nocturne Falls. He had no ring for her. That bothered him. Maybe he would take a trip to a jewelry store before they went to the chapel. They would need rings, after all.

Harlan's voice sounded from the hall. "Ivan, you decent?"

"Yes. Come in."

The gargoyle walked in. "Are you really getting married?"

Van nodded. "As soon as we can."

"Wow." Harlan shook his head. "That's great. I'm really happy for you."

"Then why do you look so miserable?"

He smiled weakly. "You're leaving the business, aren't you?"

"I am. But it is time."

"I'm just..." He sighed. "I'm going to miss working for you. You've been a great boss. And friend. You helped me out when no one else would."

"You could always move to Nocturne Falls."

Harlan's head came up. "You mean you still want me to work for you?"

Van couldn't commit to that yet. "I mean there is life beyond Las Vegas. Nocturne Falls is a good town. With good people. And there is opportunity. Nick, my friend who is here, he is a gargoyle too. He works for the town. Maybe you could do the same thing."

Harlan looked skeptical. "Really?"

"Go talk to him."

Finally, a real smile. "Okay, I will. But don't you want some help?"

Van snorted. "I can pick out my own clothes."

"No, I mean with the wedding stuff. You should really make a reservation at whichever chapel you're going to use. Plus, you need to get your license from the courthouse, and won't you want something afterwards, a dinner or a party or something?"

"I did not think about all that." He gestured toward the front of the condo. "Yes, we want help. Tell Monalisa. Do whatever she wants."

"You got it, boss." He headed out.

Realizing that they might not be getting married as quickly as Van had thought, he threw on a T-shirt and jeans before going back to the kitchen. Delicious smells filled his house, causing his stomach to growl on the way. "I hope we're eating soon."

"We are," Nick answered, looking over his shoulder from his station at the cooktop.

Harlan, Monalisa, and Pandora were at the dining table, phones out. Harlan was making notes on a legal pad.

Monalisa looked up at him. "Hiya, fiancé."

He grinned. "Hiya."

"We're getting hitched at four o'clock this afternoon. Harlan took the first reservation they had. You good with that?"

"I am great with that."

"Good. Also, I want to get a dress." She bit her lip. "Is that silly? I know it doesn't really matter what we wear, but…" She shrugged.

He shook his head, a little overwhelmed by the joy filling him. "This is your wedding—"

"*Our* wedding," she corrected him.

"Our wedding. Nothing you want to do is silly if it makes you happy. And you only get married once, right? So do it the way you want to do it."

"Okay," she said softly. A smile lit her face. "Good."

Pleased that she was pleased, he turned his attention to his sparring partner. "Harlan."

The gargoyle looked up. "Yes?"

"You have my cards. Whatever she wants. Whatever it takes. Make sure the stores know that."

"You got it, boss." Then he got a slightly terrified

look on his face. "Wait. You want me to go dress shopping with them?"

Van rolled his eyes. "No, I want you to call the shops they are going to and tell them to call you when it's time to pay. You will be with me getting a tux. You cannot be best man without one. Because if Monalisa is getting a dress, we are getting tuxes."

A broad grin bent his mouth. "Best man? Thanks, boss, that's awesome. Okay, I can do that." He picked up his phone and got to work.

Van went into the kitchen where Nick and Willa were cooking up a storm. He was happy to see porterhouses on the grill. He glanced at Nick. "Looks good. I guess Harlan told you I like steak when I'm training?"

"Actually, Monalisa did." He flipped a large blueberry pancake from the griddle onto a tall stack. "And I think they're about done."

"Good. I will set the table. One of my few domestic skills." He got plates out of the cabinet.

Willa laughed. "You're about to be a married man, you better learn a few more." She lifted slices of bacon onto a serving platter. "Gotta keep your woman happy."

"Happy wife, happy life," Nick said.

Pandora snorted. "I think you have to have a wife before you can say that, Nick."

"Hey," he responded. "We're getting there."

Van enjoyed the bantering going on. He started laying out plates on the table at the unoccupied end.

Pandora leaned back to see Nick better. "Then put a ring on it, already."

Nick looked over at her, then looked at Willa. "Want to make it a double ceremony?"

Willa dropped the spatula she was holding. "What?"

Right there in the kitchen, Nick got down on one knee. "Willa Iscove, will you marry me right here and now?"

She stared at him, as did the rest of them. "You're crazy."

Nick grinned. "Is that a yes?"

She glanced over her shoulder at Monalisa. "I don't want to take away from your special day."

Monalisa waved the comment away. "You won't be. How can more love make our day less special? Do it."

Van nodded. "I agree."

Willa smiled at Nick. "Then that is a yes."

When the cheering and clapping died down, Van pointed at Harlan. "We need another reservation."

Breakfast went by in a flurry of conversation, passing plates, and delicious food. Harlan was on the phone during part of the meal, securing a second reservation for Nick and Willa. There was an urgency to the meal they all felt, but a buoyancy too. Joy filled the air despite the pressure of all that had to be done.

As soon as they were done eating, they all went to the courthouse to get the licenses. From there, the group split. The women left to buy dresses and get their hair done. Van couldn't imagine how long that might take, and renting tuxes shouldn't be such a big deal, so he, Nick, and Harlan went back to clean up the breakfast mess, then headed out to a formalwear shop that Harlan had already called.

But due to Van's and Nick's size, the tuxes took a lot longer than anticipated. By the time they were done (having dropped a large sum of cash and thoroughly exhausted two hardworking seamstresses), they barely had time to buy some simple wedding bands and get to the chapel.

Harlan dropped Van off at the door, then he and Nick went to park.

Pandora was in the lobby when Van went in. She wore a lavender bridesmaid dress. "Wow, you look great in a tux."

"You look very pretty too." The place was covered in ivy, white roses, and tiny sparkling lights. Off to one side, a tall gold cage housed two fancy white doves. He rubbed his forehead as it all became real. He was about to get married.

She grabbed his arm. "You okay?"

He nodded. "Fine. Just...I am getting married."

She laughed softly. "Yes, you are, but you're going to be great at it."

"Are you sure? I want to be a good husband."

"You will be." Her eyes got a little teary. "You're a great friend and a wonderful person. You're the brother I never had, and I couldn't be happier to have you in my life. I love you, and so does Monalisa. I know that for a fact after spending time with her today. And while I totally approve of her, she's still lucky to have you, and if she ever forgets it, I will be the first to tell her."

He smiled and kissed her on the cheek. "*Kotyonok,* I love you too. Thank you for that."

"You're welcome. Anytime."

Nick and Harlan walked in.

Pandora looked past Van. "All right, the gang's all here, including grooms one and two. Let's make some happily ever afters."

The thudding of Monalisa's heart threatened to drown out all other sound. But nerves were not going to keep her from walking through those chapel doors. Nothing would. And since she had no one to give her away, she'd asked Pandora and Willa to walk with her down the aisle instead of going ahead of her.

They stood beside her now, holding their bouquets of lavender roses and greenery and looking so pretty in their bridesmaid dresses.

She glanced at both of them, taking comfort in these new friendships. Not only was she getting married, but she was going to be part of Willa's wedding right after her own. "It means so much that you're here with me. Thank you."

"I am honored," Willa said.

"Me too." Pandora looked like she was about to weep. "Van is crazy about you, you know."

Monalisa nodded, not wanting to start crying herself. Who knew getting married could make you so emotional? She'd almost shed a few tears at the bridal shop when she'd seen herself in the white gown she now wore. She'd never thought there'd be a dress like this in her life, and yet, here she was, draped in silk. A bride.

"Okay, no crying," Pandora said, laughing. "You're going to make me start too, and I still have Willa and Nick's ceremony to get through. You have everything, right? Your old, new, borrowed, blue?"

Monalisa nodded. Pandora knew all this, but she was clearly trying to help lighten the moment. "For the old, I have this coin Van gave me." She pulled the small gold coin from the sash of her dress, showed it to them, then tucked it away again. "For my new, I have my dress."

"Which is perfect," Pandora added.

"I agree." Monalisa lifted her wrist. "And for borrowed and blue, I have this gorgeous bracelet from Willa."

"Ooh, that is so pretty." Pandora looked at Willa. "What is that?"

"Iolite, topaz, and moonstone." The fae jeweler smiled. "Some of my favorites, which is why I had it with me."

"Good thing." Pandora glanced toward the chapel as the sweet strains of Pachelbel's Canon in D began to play. "That's your cue, Monalisa."

Willa put a gentle hand on Monalisa's shoulder. "Are you ready?"

"Yes," Monalisa said. Pandora's distraction had helped. Monalisa's pulse was almost normal now. It also helped knowing that Van was waiting for her in that chapel. "I absolutely am."

Pandora nodded to the chapel ushers. In one graceful motion, they opened the double doors.

Monalisa drew in a breath when she saw Van. She couldn't imagine a man looking better in a tux than he did right now. So handsome and strong and perfect. And *that* man was about to become her husband. He *wanted* to spend the rest of his life with her. It was almost impossible to comprehend.

He turned, and when he saw her, he swallowed hard. The muscles in his jaw tightened as if he was trying to rein in his emotions. A second later, he smiled and let out a soft, happy laugh as he shook his head like he couldn't believe what he was seeing.

She wanted to remember the look on his face for the rest of her life. She walked slowly toward him, smiling through a thin veil of happy tears, the only veil she wore because she hadn't wanted one between them. Everything about the moment felt wonderful and surreal. Pandora and Willa went off to the left, and Monalisa stepped up onto the small dais to take her place beside Van.

"You look beautiful," he whispered. "So beautiful."

"Thank you." She took a breath, inhaling the comfortable smokiness that wafted off him. It calmed her almost as much as him being at her side. "You're very handsome."

The officiant cleared his throat, beaming an indulgent smile at them. "Are you both ready?"

Van glanced at her, and she nodded. He stared up at the officiant. "We are."

"Then let us begin." The music softened. "Dearly beloved, we are gathered here today to wed this man and this woman in the bond of—"

"Like hell you are."

Monalisa spun around at the same time Van did, her blood cold at the sound of an all-too-familiar voice. "Father. What are you doing here?"

"Stopping this sham." He strode toward them, eyes blazing in anger. The head of his security team, Sean, stayed by the door. "What kind of a trick do you think you're pulling?"

"No trick." Rage and fear stormed inside her, causing her to tremble. "I am marrying the man I love."

"No, you're not." He didn't even look at Van. "You're coming home with me. Where you belong."

Van stepped off the dais and into Padraig's personal space, giving her father no choice but to notice the dragon shifter. "She belongs wherever she wants to belong. And right now, that's with me."

Her father was much shorter than Van and weighed a significant amount less, but that didn't seem to bother him. Of course, her father was used to people doing whatever he told them, regardless of their size. "Get out of my way."

Van crossed his arms. The tuxedo jacket strained against his back and biceps. "*Nyet.*"

Padraig threw his head back and let out a chilling laugh. "Big and dumb. You fighters are all the same, but then, I don't know why I expected different." He tried to wave Van away. "Enough. You've made a valiant effort. Now move."

Van stared the man down. "Get scorched."

Monalisa shook her head. "I'm not going with you."

Padraig glared at her. "I can make you. I will make you. This is your last chance to come under your own power."

"Touch her and I will touch you," Van said. Wisps of smoke curled from the sides of his mouth, and little shimmers of heat wavered off him. "And not gently."

Another short laugh broke from Padraig's throat, this one with a nervous tremor that hadn't been there before. "I don't need to touch her." He reached out his hand toward her. "Let's go, Monalisa."

"No." The back of her head started to ache. She braced herself for it to get worse.

"Bollocks." He rolled his eyes. "What a right mess you've made of everything."

"You made the mess by refusing to give me my freedom."

"You wouldn't know what to do with it. Look at you now, in that silly dress in this tourist trap of a chapel. You couldn't look more desperate if you tried."

A deep, feral rumble vibrated out of Van's chest. His lip curled back. "Apologize."

Padraig snorted, but that was the extent of his answer. "Monalisa, I command you to come home now."

The pain in her head increased. She stepped off the

dais, her arm brushing Van's. She planted herself directly in front of her father in the hopes that she could keep Van from doing something they'd regret later. The last thing she wanted was for her father to have reason to detain Van. "You are a horrible little man. I hate you." The words barely made it out between her clenched teeth.

Her father grabbed her elbow and tried to guide her toward the door. "You'll thank me in the morning when you realize what I've saved you from."

She jerked away from him. "No, I won't. I won't ever thank you for anything. Do you hear me? Because I don't think you do." She pointed at Van. "That man right there loves me more than you ever have and more than you ever will. You're not saving me from anything, you're ruining my life. Again. But that's what you do best, isn't it? Destroy things."

He stared at her, the hard glint in his gaze a sign of his anger. "I destroy things? Girlie, you've forgotten who you are and what you do best."

He looked at Van. "You know that about her, don't you? That's what she does. Destroy people. Lead them to ruin. And you, fool that you are, were about to marry her. Sure, it's all very cute, the dragon saving the princess, but in the cold light of day, regret is all you'd be left with. Come to think of it, maybe it's you that should be thanking me."

She threw her bouquet at her father, clocking him on the side of the head in an explosion of greenery and flower petals. "Don't you dare talk to him that way."

Anger twisted Padraig's face. He brushed a sprig

of baby's breath out of his hair. "You stupid git."

He pulled back to strike her, his hand flying through the air.

Van caught his arm before he made contact.

Padraig snarled. "Let go of me, or I'll—"

"You'll do nothing," Monalisa said.

Sean started forward, but Van shoved Padraig back as he released the man.

He stumbled a few feet but didn't fall. He gestured at his security man. "Sean, grab her."

Sean nodded. "On it, boss."

Monalisa had had enough. More than enough. She was drowning in it. A lifetime of anger and disappointment and frustration welled up in her and spilled into her blood. Her gifts, useless as they were against her father, bubbled over into her voice and came out of her unbidden. "*Leave us alone.*"

Sean's pupils widened. He staggered to a stop.

Then she saw that her father had done the same thing.

A few soft words of Russian hissed out of Van. He nodded at her. "Do that again."

This time, she purposefully channeled her power into her words. "*Back up.*"

Both men retreated. She watched them, mouth open in utter shock. She'd always been able to control Sean, that was no surprise, but her father?

"How is that possible?" Van asked.

She shook her head. "I don't know."

Van came to stand beside her. "Yes, you do. He lied to you. Just like he's always done."

"I've been a fool. I should have known." Her hands tightened into fists.

"You're not a fool. You were just brainwashed by a man who should have been completely trustworthy for you. You are not to blame for this."

"Maybe not." But that didn't do a whole lot to make her feel better about all the years she'd spent trapped that could have been spent living her life her own way. "Time to make up for what I missed out on."

She raised her hand toward her father. *"Padraig Devlin, I command you to give me a coin and grant me my freedom."*

He swayed slightly, the weight of her command clearly bearing down on him. "I...I don't have a coin to give you."

"Liar. That's all you do is lie."

Pandora sidled up next to her. "Maybe he means he doesn't have one on him now."

Okay, she hadn't thought of that.

Pandora nudged her. "Give me that coin in your sash."

Monalisa dug it out and handed it over. Pandora took it and walked toward Padraig. Then she looked back at Monalisa. "Tell him to hold out his hand."

"Open your palm," Monalisa commanded.

He did as she told him.

Pandora placed the coin in his hand, then came back to stand by Monalisa.

"Will that work?" Van asked.

"I have no idea." Monalisa focused on her father

again, but kept the power from her voice so that he could answer with a clear head. "There's a coin in your hand. Who does it belong to?"

He blinked a few times as he looked at it. "Gold," he muttered. His fingers closed around the coin. "Mine." He shoved it into his pocket.

She took a breath and released it with a little prayer that this would do the trick. "All right," she said softly. "Let's try this again."

No fight Van had ever been in compared to this moment. The level of tension running through him made him feel like a cord strung so tightly it was on the verge of snapping. But then, he'd never been in a fight with so much resting on the outcome.

His beautiful Monalisa slipped her hand into his, but her eyes stayed on her father. She raised her hand toward him again. *"Padraig Devlin, I command that you give me a coin and grant me my freedom."*

All eyes were on Padraig as Monalisa's power directed him. "I have...a coin." With the faltering movements of the inebriated, he dug into his pocket and pulled out the coin Pandora had just given him.

He held it up, peering at it.

"Is that yours?" she asked.

He nodded. "Mine."

"And will giving it to me break the bond of power between us?"

Again, he nodded.

She turned her hand over, palm up. "*Give it to me.*"

His gaze shifted to her. He stumbled forward, muscles taut and mouth bent in an ugly sneer. He was fighting it.

Van knew what that felt like, but there was no resisting. Monalisa's gifts were undeniable.

The man reached his hand out, the coin pinched between his fingers. He dropped the coin into her palm.

"*Say the words,*" she commanded.

"I...release...you."

She let out a sob as though she couldn't believe what had happened. Or maybe it was a reaction to suddenly being free. She tucked the coin into the same spot she'd pulled it from.

Van let go of her hand to put his arm around her waist.

She slumped against him. "I think it's done."

"We have to test it."

"You're right. I have to know for sure." She straightened. "Father, you and Sean should leave now."

There was no power in her voice that Van could detect.

Padraig shook himself, rocking his head side to side. He grabbed hold of one of the pews like he needed the support. "What did you do to me, girl?"

"Something I should have done years ago." She lifted her chin. "Now, please, leave. Or I will ask Van and his two gargoyle friends to escort you and Sean out in whatever way they see fit."

"You little—you think threats are going to stop me?" He snapped his fingers and pointed to the spot beside him. "Get over here. Then I'll leave."

She stiffened. Then relaxed with a hearty laugh. "You don't affect me anymore." She looked at Van. "It worked." She grabbed his arm. "It really worked. I'm free."

Pandora and Willa started clapping, while Harlan and Nick both let out loud whoops of celebration.

Van pulled her into his arms and off her feet to whirl her around. "This is very good."

"Monalisa Devlin, you will do as I say—"

"Not anymore I won't!" She tapped Van's shoulder. "Put me down for a second."

He did as she asked, and they both faced her father. She pointed toward the door. "I am no longer yours to control. You gave me a coin and set me free. Your words have no effect on me. None. Do you understand?"

His gaze said he didn't believe her. "Come over here, Monalisa."

"Not a chance." She crossed her arms and shrugged. "See? Nothing. Not even the slightest twinge of a headache."

His mouth fell open.

"That's right. I'm free. And you need to get out. This is your last chance before I set these three on you."

To add menace to her threat, Van called up his dragon, turning his eyes glowing red and letting curls of steam escape his mouth.

Nick and Harlan added a few rumbly growls of their own for good measure.

Padraig's eyes widened, and he backed up. "You stupid girl." He poked a finger in Van's direction. "He still owes me a fight."

Monalisa shook her head. "I don't think so. Not after I tell the League's commissioners what you forced me to do during the last one. And if that's not enough, well, I guess I'll just use my gifts to persuade them otherwise."

Padraig's chest was heaving with anger, but he seemed to be out of words as he backed out of the chapel. Then he found a few. "You will regret this. You both will."

Monalisa smiled. "Not in a million years."

Nick and Harlan went after him and Sean, but stopped in the lobby just outside the doors. After a couple seconds, Nick turned to them and nodded. "They're gone."

"Wow," Pandora said. "That was crazy."

Monalisa took a deep breath. "I'm free. I can't believe it, but I am." She put her hands on Van's chest. "If you hadn't given me that coin…"

"We probably could have scrounged up some change," Pandora said. "But it was good you had that."

Monalisa looked at the witch. "No, regular change wouldn't have worked. The coin had to be gold."

Pandora's brows lifted. "In that case, nicely done, Van."

Nick and Harlan strode back into the chapel. Nick

looked at Van. "So…is this wedding still on?"

Van opened his mouth to answer, then closed it. Monalisa no longer needed to marry him to gain her freedom. "Perhaps Monalisa and I could talk for a moment?"

Nick nodded. "Everyone into the lobby."

They all followed him out, including the officiant, and shut the doors behind them.

He faced her, taking her hands. "I love you, Monalisa. But you no longer need to marry me. That is a good thing."

"It is?" Confusion filled her eyes.

"Yes. Now you can marry me when you want to. When you're ready."

"I'm ready now. I think." She laughed. "Okay, maybe it wouldn't be such a bad thing to get to know each other a little more. I know I love you, but I wouldn't mind getting to know you even better. And taking our time means we could plan something a little more elaborate than a quickie chapel wedding."

"Yes, but…what I mean is, you have never lived on your own. Never experienced life as a completely free person. Move to Nocturne Falls and see what you think about that first." A sadness settled over him at the thought that her new life might not have a place for him. "Give yourself some time to find out what that is like. Maybe you will like that life very much. Maybe so much that you don't want to tie yourself down again."

Her expression turned serious again. "My feelings for you aren't going to change with the passing of time. Except that I'll just love you more. Look, new life, old life, same life, I'm still me."

He smiled a little. "Time will tell."

She smiled a lot. "Yes, it will. You'll see. And don't forget, you're about to embark on a new life too. Life as a retired fighter. You've got to figure out what that means to you. Maybe that will change how you feel."

"Never." He spat the word out like an oath.

"So you're okay retiring without being champion?"

"I am."

"Then let's spend six months being boyfriend and girlfriend. That should be enough for both of us to realize our feelings aren't going to change."

"Six months?" He nodded. He could do that standing on his head. "That is good."

"Then it's a deal. But I do have one stipulation."

"What is that?"

She leaned in and kissed him. "I want the whole enchilada. Dates and a proposal and a ring and a big wedding with all my new friends. The whole relationship experience."

He grinned. "Done."

She straightened his tie. "We should go tell them we're not getting married today."

"We will. Right after this." He pulled her back into his arms and kissed her.

She kissed him back with a new passion, and for the first time since they'd been together, light spilled through him, sending bright tendrils of happiness to curl around his bones.

She leaned into him, sharing herself with him in a way that he realized now she hadn't been able to before. For all her father's talk of destruction, Van understood that Monalisa was a creature of light. There was more for her out there than what Padraig had led her to believe, and Van would happily spend the next six months helping her find her path.

So even if they weren't getting married today, their future lay before them in a clear vision, and Van could see there was nothing in their way.

They walked into the foyer a few minutes later. Van looked at Nick and Willa, who were talking quietly by a large vase of flowers. "The chapel is all yours."

Nick took Willa's hand. "You're not getting married?"

Van turned to Monalisa and smiled. "Not today."

Willa let out a soft sigh. "Neither are we."

The officiant threw up his hands and walked away, causing Pandora to burst out laughing. Harlan shook his head.

"Why?" Monalisa asked. "What happened?"

Willa shrugged. "We got to talking, and we do want to get married, but I want my family to be there and the rest of our friends. So we decided to postpone it until we can plan things out a little more."

"But we are getting married," Nick said. "Soon."

"Then it is settled." Van put his arm around Monalisa and gazed into her beautiful green eyes. "But we look too good to just go home. How about we give you a real taste of freedom? We are in Vegas. At least for a little while longer."

She nodded, grinning. "Let's do it."

"Good." He looked at Harlan. "Chapel bill?"

He held up a slip of paper. "Paid."

"Limo?"

"Outside, boss."

Van took Monalisa's hand. "Now I show you how Russians party."

Freedom was a powerful thing.

One month later and Monalisa couldn't get over how different her life was, or how happy it was possible to be. Smiling was just her everyday thing now.

And Van…Van was…so good.

But he wasn't the only reason she smiled a lot. She had a place of her own. Sort of. It was actually Pandora's house, but Pandora had moved into the big Victorian with Cole and the aura-reading Kaley. (And who could blame Pandora? The house and the man were gorgeous.)

Pandora had told Monalisa not to worry about rent, but Monalisa had insisted. People paid rent. It was what they did. It was what she wanted to do.

Plus, she had a job. Pandora had hired her to work as a receptionist in the real estate office. Monalisa was studying to get her own license so she could sell houses too. It might seem odd to work for your landlord, but she and Pandora (and Willa) had become fast friends.

The rest of that circle, which was mostly Pandora's sisters, Charisma and Marigold, hung out with them too, sometimes, as did Roxy when she wasn't on deadline.

But the best part of all was that four nights a week—because one night was girls' night, one night was book club at the library, and one night was just for herself—she and Van had a date. Dinner out or sometimes in—although in was mostly at his house, because cooking was still a learning process for her— or a movie, or taking Grom to the dog park, or window-shopping on Main Street with a stop for ice cream, or one of a thousand things that there were to do in this town.

She was getting to know Van, getting to know the town, and falling even more in love with both of them.

Tonight was dinner in at Van's, and he'd said he had a surprise for her. When she'd asked him what to wear for that surprise, he'd just said whatever made her feel pretty.

She knew exactly what that was. The week before, she'd used part of her paycheck to do a little shopping and had splurged on a flowy red halter dress. It was still a little cool for a dress like that, but she could already picture herself wearing it this summer. Until then, she could put a cardigan on with it and she'd be fine.

But now, as she walked up the steps of Van's

porch in that dress and cardigan, she wasn't sure it was going to be warm enough after all. March in Nocturne Falls had given them a little hint that spring was coming, but with the sun down, that hint of spring had become a reminder of winter.

She shifted in her high heels and wished she'd worn her coat.

Grom started barking inside the house, and she smiled. No need to knock with that dog around.

Van opened the door. "There you are."

"Here I am. How are you?"

"Good. Better now." He stepped out of the way to let her enter, catching her in his arms as he bumped the door shut with his hip. "You look beautiful. I like this dress."

"Are you sure it's not too much for the surprise?" He was in jeans and a T-shirt, which showed off his body and his ink, so she didn't mind one bit, but it did make her feel like she might have overdressed.

"No. It is perfect." Grom wound around them, pushing against their legs. Van laughed. "You better greet him, or he will only get worse."

She bent and took Grom's big head in her hands. "How are you, Grommy? Did you miss me? I missed you." She kissed the dog's nose and got licked in return. "Oh, good. I've been slobbered."

"Grom, *nyet*."

"It's okay." She straightened and wiped her chin off. "I hope that wasn't the surprise."

Van shook his head. "It is better. I promise." He held up his finger. "Wait right here."

"Okay." She clasped her hands in front of her as he went into the kitchen.

He came back holding a large woven basket by the handles. The lid was closed. "Now we go."

It looked very much like a picnic basket. But it wasn't exactly picnic weather outside. Still, she didn't say anything, deciding to let his plan unfold as he intended.

He opened the door. Grom zipped out, skidding to a halt on the porch. She followed, then gave Van the lead so he could take them to wherever they were going.

That turned out to be down the hill in front of the house and through a line of trees. Not the easiest in heels, but on the other side of those trees, the land opened up and flattened out.

The sky was turning the soft purple of twilight, letting the first bright stars peek through. Even though the air was chilly, the evening was beautiful. "This is really pretty."

"I'm glad you like it." His eyes narrowed. "You are cold."

"A little." She smiled. "I'm sure you can warm me up."

"I can."

Within seconds, the air around her lost its chill and turned almost tropical. She shrugged her cardigan off and held it over her arm. "Now that's more like it."

He smiled and took her hand. "A little farther."

A few more yards and they came to a large blanket

spread out on the ground. Van set the basket down. "Surprise."

"A picnic under the stars." She shook her head in amazement. "You remembered."

"I did. And I would have done it sooner, but there was much to get ready." He opened the basket and took out a bottle of champagne and two glasses, setting them carefully on the blanket.

She wondered what he'd had to get ready. Picnics weren't that complicated, but maybe it was his first one. She dropped her cardigan on the corner of the blanket now that his radiating heat was keeping her warm. "Are we celebrating something?"

"Yes. I got my official release from the League today. Your statement to them did the trick. The rematch has been canceled." His smile widened. "But even better, they have overturned the decision of the last fight. I have been reinstated as champion. My record remains intact."

She shrieked and threw her arms into the air. "That is amazing! I had no idea they would do that."

"Neither did I. And I have you to thank."

"We are definitely drinking that champagne now."

He laughed. "Yes. But first, there is one thing I must do."

"What's that?"

He pulled out a small velvet box, opened it, then got down on one knee. Inside was an enormous, brilliant orange stone surrounded by tiny diamonds. "Monalisa Devlin, will you marry me? Officially?"

334

She gasped even as she smiled, her heart almost bursting with joy. "I will. Yes. Happily."

He stood and took the ring from its case. "I know this is not a diamond, but the color reminds me of you. Bright and fiery. But if you would rather have a diamond, we will get you one of those too."

"No, I love this. It's beautiful. You're right that it's bright. It practically glows." She held out her hand. The stone seemed almost lit from within. "What is it?"

He slipped the gleaming gold ring onto her finger. "It is a fire opal."

She smiled. "Oh, I love that. A fire opal from my dragon. It's perfect." She held out her hand. "Did Willa make this? Is that what you had to get ready?"

He nodded. "I wanted something as special as you are, *zolotse*."

She slipped her arms around him. "You are an amazing man, you know that?"

He shrugged, eyes twinkling. "I know. And smart too."

She laughed and shook her head. "I think you forgot humble."

He grinned. "I have to be smart if I ended up with you."

She leaned into him. "I feel the same way."

"Good." He kissed her, the temperature around them rising a little more as he did. When he finally released her, it felt as though the sun was shining down on them. "I want you always to be happy. Always to know that I love you. Always to feel safe. If there is anything you ever want or need, you tell me."

She tapped her fingers lazily on his chest. "There is one thing…"

"Anything. Tell me."

She glanced down at Grom, sitting patiently by Van's feet. "After we get married, I want a dog of my own."

"I know just the place." Van's arms tightened around her, and he looked down at Grom too. "You hear that? You're getting a baby sister."

Grom barked, making them both laugh.

Van popped the champagne, poured two glasses, and handed one to her. "To us and our future."

She clinked her glass against his. "I can't wait."

They drank, and she turned, leaning her back against his chest. He wrapped one arm around her waist and let out a pleasurable sigh.

"Life is good," she whispered as she gazed up at the twinkling stars.

"*Da*," he said. "And it's going to get even better."

Want to be up to date on all books & release dates by Kristen Painter? Sign-up for my newsletter on my website, www.kristenpainter.com. No spam, just news (sales, freebies, and releases.)

If you loved the book and want to help the series grow, tell a friend about the book and take time to leave a review!

Other Books by Kristen Painter

COZY PARANORMAL MYSTERY:

Miss Frost Solves A Cold Case – A Nocturne Falls Mystery
Miss Frost Ices The Imp – A Nocturne Falls Mystery
Miss Frost Saves The Sandman – A Nocturne Falls Mystery

URBAN FANTASY:

The House of Comarré series:
Forbidden Blood
Blood Rights
Flesh and Blood
Bad Blood
Out For Blood
Last Blood

The Crescent City series:
House of the Rising Sun
City of Eternal Night
Garden of Dreams and Desires

Can't get enough Nocturne Falls?
Try the NOCTURNE FALLS UNIVERSE books.
New stories, new authors, same Nocturne Falls world!
www.http://kristenpainter.com/nocturne-falls-universe/

Nothing is completed without an amazing team.

Many thanks to:

Cover design: Janet Holmes
Interior formatting: Author E.M.S
Editor: Joyce Lamb
Copyedits/proofs: Marlene Engel

About the Author

USA Today Best Selling Author Kristen Painter is a little obsessed with cats, books, chocolate, and shoes. It's a healthy mix. She loves to entertain her readers with interesting twists and unforgettable characters. She currently writes the best-selling paranormal romance series, Nocturne Falls, and award-winning urban fantasy. The former college English teacher can often be found all over social media where she loves to interact with readers:

www.kristenpainter.com

62792642R00193

Made in the USA
Lexington, KY
18 April 2017